DARK INTENT

CAROLYN RIDDER ASPENSON

SEVERN RIVER PUBLISHING

Severn River Publishing
www.SevernRiverBooks.com

This is a work of fiction. Names, characters, businesses, places, events and incidents are either the products of the author's imagination or used in a fictitious manner. Any resemblance to actual persons, living or dead, or actual events is purely coincidental.

ISBN: 978-1-64875-592-7 (Paperback)

ALSO BY CAROLYN RIDDER ASPENSON

The Rachel Ryder Thriller Series

Damaging Secrets

Hunted Girl

Overkill

Countdown

Body Count

Fatal Silence

Deadly Means

Final Fix

Dark Intent

Foul Play

To find out more about Carolyn Ridder Aspenson and her books, visit
severnriverbooks.com

To Jack
Forever and always

breath, but the job had to be completed quickly in case a group of stoned teenagers from town wandered onto the land to party, as they often did. That was the reason for the grave choice. One day, those stoned teens would discover the body. Just not that day.

The shovel plunged into the mound of dirt with a soft thud, lifted and then emptied with a cascade of soil that fell onto the body with a finality that was almost ceremonial.

The body, barely discernible under the accumulating earth, lay motionless, as enigmatic in death as the figure was in their task. Frozen forever with a look of knowing. Knowing they had gotten what they'd deserved.

It was retribution, an action necessary to right the wrongs done unto others.

The killer's eyes gleamed with satisfaction and anticipation as they admired their work. Each shovelful of earth was a step closer to the fulfillment of a plan forty years in the making. In the silence of the night, the killer's thoughts wandered to the victims, to the reasons they had been chosen, and to the message the grave would send.

PROLOGUE

The moon hung heavy in the starlit sky, its silver glow throwing long, stark shadows across the fallow farmland. It was the perfect spot—just far enough not to be seen, but close enough for future discovery.

A solitary figure worked in silence, the rhythmic sound of dirt hitting a shallow grave the only disturbance in the quiet night. The summer air, thick and hot, nearly smothered the gravedigger with a stifling embrace as they labored over the makeshift grave. Sweat beaded and dripped off their brow, darkening the earth at their feet where the light of the full moon could not reach.

The grave hadn't been hurried but had been meant to appear so—edges rough and uneven, as if the very act of digging it was done with a desperate urgency. The figure's hands, gloved to prevent blisters and possible identification, moved with a steady, methodical pace, shoveling soil over what had become the final and lonely resting place of someone who deserved far worse. Someone who deserved public viewing upon death.

There were no words, no muttered curses, no whispered prayers, only the grave and the act itself, each speaking volumes in silence.

Despite the heat, the figure had covered themselves from head to toe, with only the eyes visible and reflecting the moonlight like two pale orbs. The figure stopped often to check their surroundings and catch their

1

If you asked a realtor, they'd sell you Hamby, Georgia, as the kind of place Norman Rockwell might've dreamed up if he'd taken a detour down South —quaint, equestrian, brimming with boutiques that didn't know the meaning of chain store and restaurants where the chefs actually knew your name. They'd wax poetic about the farmer's market, a Saturday morning ritual where the tomatoes taste like tomatoes and the crafts have more hands behind them than a preschool finger-painting class. It was the kind of town where the schools were good, the churches plentiful, and small-town feel wasn't just a phrase—it was the law.

But peel back the postcard, and the Hamby Police Department, my employer, would tell you a different story. Sure, on the surface, it was all apple pies and handshakes, but they knew the shadows between the sunshine, the secrets tucked away in more than a dozen churches, and the whispers behind the friendly good mornings. In Hamby, even the skeletons in the closet had their own closets, and the HPD held the key to more than a few of those doors.

Two weeks of peace and quiet in Hamby, Georgia, was like a unicorn sighting—rare and suspicious. And it wasn't destined to last. In my book, calm always spelled trouble lurking just around the corner. And, trust me, when trouble decided to show up, it wasn't just a knock at the door; it was a full-blown SWAT raid. Just when I start thinking maybe, just maybe, I could take a breather, the universe laughed and dumped a hurricane of chaos right on my head.

There I was, in the heart of the Hamby Police Department's bustling hive, known as the 'pit'. The pit was where the action, or lack thereof, happened. Officers tapped on their laptops, mumbled conversations mingled in the air, and the scent of stale coffee from the pot a shift commander had refused to trash when the chief bought the Keurigs, reminded me of the pit in my last precinct in Chicago.

My partner, Rob Bishop, and I sat at a small table in the center of the room, engaged in the most intense game of tennis ball catch known to law enforcement. The desks around us, overrun with paperwork and coffee stains, stood as silent witnesses.

"You ever think detectives should just be on call, like doctors?" I mused, lobbing the ball a bit too ambitiously in Bishop's direction.

He caught it with the grace of a cat. "We are on call, Rachel. All the time."

"Yeah, but without the whole *sitting around waiting* part." The ball flew back to him. "Imagine that, freedom until the bat-signal shines."

"Keep dreaming," he tossed the ball back, a smirk playing on his lips. "Being the chief's daughter's godmother isn't your golden ticket to the detective's lounge life."

I sent the ball rocketing toward his head, testing those cat-like reflexes. "Guess I'll pass on cozying up to the mayor's wife then."

Bishop caught it effortlessly. "Too bad. Could've been your in."

He knew how much I disliked the mayor but due to an ages-old DUI concerning the mayor's child, he disliked him even more. "Dang, Bishop. You move quick for an old-timer." I grinned.

He responded with a one-finger salute, his version of a warm hug. Bishop had come a long way since his dance with death at the hands of hired out lowlifes. Post-recovery, he had hit the gym harder than a New Year's resolution, trading his beer belly for something resembling abs. I wouldn't say it out loud, but the guy could probably outrun me. His tactical skills were sharper, too, like he was preparing for round two. I hoped there wasn't a round two, but odds were high there would be.

If it weren't for the shiny dome and his fondness for zingers, I'd hardly recognize him. The old Bishop might have vanished, but the new version? He was a force to be reckoned with—balding, shaved head, snark, and all.

As the ball arced back to me, the light glinting off it like a spotlight on our little game of catch, I lobbed a question at him. "You squared away with a gift for Michels and Ash's wedding yet?"

Bishop caught the ball with the same ease he sidestepped department politics. "Gift?" He scoffed, tossing the ball back. "That's Cathy's arena. I steer clear of the girly stuff."

I laughed as I snagged the ball out of the air. "Yeah, well, Kyle dove headfirst into that arena. Didn't come out looking too girly, either."

Cathy and Bishop, they were a pair. You could bet the house on them making it official sooner rather than later, probably right after Michels tied the knot. Keep the celebrations rolling, I figured, and in our line of work, celebrations were important to balance the tragedies.

"What'd he get them?" Bishop was curious now, his throw a little off mark, challenging my reflexes.

"Something off their registry. Kyle said it was a no-brainer. Found their wedding site, clicked the registry link, and bam, gift bought, courtesy of Amazon." I toyed with the ball, feinting a throw.

Bishop caught on, unfazed when I finally pitched it. "Wedding site?"

I laughed. "Yeah, welcome to the twenty-first century, grandpa. It's all online now."

The idea seemed to pain him as much as investigating a cold case. "Sounds like a headache."

"Preaching to the choir," I said, sending the ball back with a little extra zip. "That's why I let Kyle handle it."

I'd never expected to fall in love again after Tommy's murder, but I had, and I was happy. I hadn't given much thought to marrying again, but Kyle had mentioned it a time or two. The idea freaked me out, but it was starting to grow on me. Who knew, maybe Bishop and I could have a double wedding. I smiled at the thought.

"What?" he asked.

"Nothing," I said. No way would I start that conversation. I'd never live it down.

As Bishop lobbed the ball back, his gaze momentarily shifted to the entrance, a habit born from years of expecting the unexpected. I mirrored his action, feeling the weight of the badge hanging from its chain around my neck, and its constant reminder of the thin line we walked between order and chaos. It was then that the dispatcher's voice cut through the hum of activity, snapping us to attention.

"We've got a 10-54 located at 3356 Providence Road. You'll need to enter at the far end of the property near Birmingham Highway. The main entrance is blocked off. Officers already on scene."

"Copy that," Bishop said. He checked his watch as he stood. "Two hours. We have two hours left on shift and now we have a dead body?"

"I think killers do that intentionally."

He laughed. "Damn straight they do."

The moon did its best impression of a spotlight in a noir film, draping a kind of glow over the farmland that made everything look like a scene from a bad horror flick. The air was thick, not just with the smell of crops dying off as summer faded, but with something else—something that made my insides do a slow roll.

We'd been coasting, thinking we had it all under control. But as it turned out, karma had a wicked sense of humor and was the bitch everyone claimed. The only soundtrack to the eerie tableau opening in front of us was the crickets, bravely chirping away as if to say, 'nothing to see here, folks'.

The officers hanging back gave me the first clue. The call wasn't just bad; it was nightmare-level bad.

Trudging over the uneven ground, I braced myself for the worst and flicked on my flashlight. What I saw next would be etched in my mental scrapbook of *things I wish I could unsee* somewhere below watching my husband die from a gunshot to the head. Every detective had those cases that clung to them like a second skin. I had a collection.

And they'd forever haunted me.

The grave was nothing fancy, just a hole in the ground. Some murderers weren't picky about their victim's final resting place. They had other things to worry about. I studied it carefully. The killer had been hurried, not meticulous, and definitely not interested in taking pride in their work. Without making light of a murder, I'd expected something more from the burial site. Though the partial hand sticking out of the dirt stole the show. Missing a couple of fingers, bloodied, and looking like it was reaching for a lifeline that never came. It was a horror movie cliché come to life, but there was nothing cliché about the chill that ran down my spine.

Whatever pile we'd just stepped into was going to get worse before it got better, and the night would drag on like a bad romance novel.

Death had a way of being blunt, and that was about as blunt as it got. The hand, with its slim fingers and a ring that gleamed dully in the flashlight beam, was a silent scream in the darkness. A call for help that never came. I took a second to steady myself while examining the ring. "That's the ring from the photo," I said to Bishop, more to break the silence than anything.

He cleared his throat, a sound always heavy with unspoken words. "I know," he replied, his voice soft and carrying a weight that was all too familiar.

The scene at the Pendley farm was a noir painting come to life, and it was our job to give it the best ending we could.

Three Hamby PD uniforms huddled over the newly unearthed secret. Slick sleeves, as we called patrol officers, thrived during morbid crime scenes. They saw them as a chance to level up within the department, to look good for the next open position. Everyone wanted to be a detective until they became one. Occasionally seeing the horrors was one thing but seeing them on the regular was an entirely different ballgame.

The farmland had once been bigger, but progress, with its insatiable appetite, had gobbled up most of the acreage. In place of rolling fields sat a legion of mini-mansions, each a carbon copy of the other, stark white, black shutters, screaming modernity with a rustic wink.

Word on the street was the developer, a guy with more dollar signs in his eyes than sense, wanted the remaining Pendley land. But the Pendleys wouldn't sell. Apparently, they weren't keen on seeing their legacy turned into more cookie-cutter houses, replicas of suburban utopia.

Meanwhile, for the PD, the Stepford-esque community had its own quirks, thus no one in the department was thrilled about adding more homes. Break-ins happened like the daily mail arrived, and not from any criminal mastermind, but thanks to the local lushes who, after one too many, couldn't tell their own castle from the neighbor's. But the body in the ground wasn't that simple. Nothing about murder ever was.

"Tell us what we've got," Bishop said to one of the officers. We knew what we had. A dead body, one we believed to be a missing woman, but we needed the rest of the story, both from them and the victim herself.

He walked toward us flipping through his small spiral notebook. "We received a call from a Natalie Pendley, the most recent property owner. Her dad transferred the deed to her name about six months ago." He turned toward a woman sitting on the back of an ambulance with a blanket wrapped around her. A German Shepherd dog sat on the ground beside her. "She currently resides in the Pendley home on the opposite side of the property. Said her dog hadn't come when she called, so she checked the dog's GPS tracker, and—"

Bishop interrupted. "The dog has a GPS tracker?"

"Yes, sir. On his collar. They're very common now."

Bishop nudged my arm and whispered, "Maybe you should get one for Louie."

"Shh," I said, though I had to force myself not to smile as I said it. Louie was my pet Beta fish. He wouldn't swim far, and an electric collar might end his life the second it hit the water. "Go on," I said to the officer.

"Yes, ma'am. Like I said, she checked his GPS tracker, got his location, and then drove her four-wheeler here to retrieve him. She found him about 100 feet away from the grave with something in his mouth."

I swallowed back my lunch. "The missing part of the hand."

"Great," Bishop mumbled. His shoulders slumped as he surveyed the crime scene; his gaze lingered on the flurry of activity around him. A heavy sigh escaped his lips, barely audible with all the chaos. He ran a hand through his hair. "We'll be here all night."

"She then went searching and found the grave." He paused, then added, "Chief said we need to dig up the body, but I don't think we'll need to dig too deep." He glanced back at the dirt pile. "She's not too far down."

Nikki, our crime scene tech, and a genius in her own right, had been crouched down to photograph the hand with her back facing us. She stood, pivoted on her heels and offered us a half smile. "Great, you're here. She pointed to the bloodied evidence bag lying behind her. "That's what the dog took. Definitely a finger and thumb, and from the amount of blood, it was removed before she died. We can start digging her out whenever you're ready."

"Wait," Bishop said. "Are you saying the dog ripped off her hand?"

"No, the killer," she said.

Bishop grimaced. "Then the dog just ripped off the finger and thumb. Great."

Nikki laughed. "The finger and thumb were cut off as well. The dog was just the messenger."

I nudged Bishop with my shoulder. "Feel better?"

"Yes."

After confirming the grim find with Nikki, Bishop and I took turns kneeling beside the shallow grave, our knees pressing into the hard, unforgiving earth.

Kneeling beside the lifeless body, the coarse dirt pressing into my pants was a dark reminder of my profession's reality. Each crime scene evoked a storm of emotions I had to suppress—anger at the cruelty, frustration with the slow grind of justice and a deep sorrow for the life stolen and the pain of those left grieving. Rage, helplessness, and mourning drove my determination to seek justice in a world that too often seemed devoid of it.

Bishop's hand was steady as he pointed to various details in the dim light, his fingers almost brushing against the cold skin of the protruding hand. "Look at the positioning," he murmured, his voice barely above a whisper as if afraid to disturb the victim. We moved with practiced coordination, photographing, measuring and cataloging each piece of evidence with meticulous care. Despite the routine, each movement was a physical reminder of the weight of our responsibility.

There was a certain kind of stillness that hung in the air when waiting for the inevitable, the kind that felt like it was holding its breath, waiting for just the right time to exhale. Watching the officers meticulously excavate around a body soon to be sprawled on a tarp was like being in the eye of a storm—eerily calm but charged with an unspoken urgency.

The spotlights, harsh and unforgiving, threw everything into a stark reality none of us liked. It turned the scene into something out of a macabre play, with each detail highlighted in a way that was both fascinating and unsettling. Shadows stretched long and ominous across the ground, creating an intense contrast to the brightly lit area where the officers worked.

We all knew what was coming, had known it the moment we got the call. Unearthing a body, while part of the job, never quite settled into routine. Murder, as common as it had become, still had the power to sucker-punch us every single time. It carried a certain gravity, a solemnity that a detective couldn't shake off no matter how many scenes they'd witnessed.

I felt it standing there. That familiar tug. A smidgeon of professional detachment overwhelmed by a mountain of human reaction to death. In my line of work, it was a dance one learned quickly, a precarious balance on the tightrope strung between empathy and function. I'd balanced that tightrope well most of the time, but I'd hit the ground hard when I'd fallen off.

Despite the harsh glare of the scene lights, a symbolic, yet real darkness pressed in from all sides, a figurative and tangible reminder of the tragedy we were facing.

It was moments like that night, under a shroud of shadows, that hammered home the fragility of life. The thin, almost invisible line between here and not here became painfully evident. As the officers continued their careful work, the gravity of our job, our purpose, settled upon us.

Sweat trickled down my back, the intense heat from the lights amplifying the already oppressive summer humidity. My jeans and Hamby PD polo shirt clung to my skin, but I wasn't nearly as hot as the three officers working to remove the woman's remains.

Sadly, I wasn't the only one tensing my jaw. A collective tension gripped us all as they worked in a sadness-laden silence while their shovels bit into the loose earth of the shallow grave. The dirt, dry and crumbly, created a fine dust that clung to their clothes and skin. Bishop and I watched and listened, holding our breath as the rhythmic sound of metal against soil brought us closer to retrieving the body.

The first glimpse of the woman was a shock despite our preparedness. There, in the dim light, lay the remains of a young woman. A woman we all recognized.

I quickly tapped out a text message to our chief, Jimmy Abernathy. I knew he'd want to be there.

Bishop sighed. "Jesus. What the hell is happening in this town?" He stared at the body with his hands on his hips and dropped his chin toward his chest. "Give the girl some dignity. Get the job done and cover her up, for chrissake."

She no longer cared, but we did. No one deserved to be found partially clothed with their lower half naked and exposed like that.

"Yes, sir," an officer said.

Nikki held out her hand. "I'll do it. I want to take her body temperature before Barron gets here."

"Got it," the officer said. He whistled to another officer behind him. "Grab a blanket, please."

"It's her," I said with a deep exhale.

"I know," Bishop sucked in a breath then added, "but I was hoping it wasn't."

The woman's skin, once fair, would be forever marred by the pallor of her unnatural death. The way her body was positioned, as if thrown without care, spoke of pure evil. The visible markings around her neck were brutal, unyielding lines that stood out starkly against her skin. They told us what we needed to know. Her face was frozen in an expression of fear and pain. The haunting image would linger in our memories and drive us to find her killer.

"Her neck," Bishop said. He ran his hand over his balding head then took a few steps back, turned and dropped a multitude of F-bombs. Bishop had a daughter. She was older than the woman in the ground, but that didn't matter. He saw his own child lying there, strangled to death.

"Please don't move her," I said, though I knew they already knew their jobs. "Dr. Barron is enroute."

A deep, gravelly voice bellowed from behind. "I'm here. I'm here. Don't get your undies all up in a bunch."

A smile almost broke through my grief. Barron, much like Bishop, had a knack for echoing phrases my mother and grandmother would say. Normally, I'd point it out with something snarky and witty. But the timing was all wrong. That's not to say we didn't lean on sarcasm and jokes during tough times. In fact, they were almost as common as the tragedies themselves.

Most cops, especially those who'd been in the game for a while, wielded sarcasm like a shield. It was a coping mechanism, a way to wade through the daily tide of tragedy. When you're face to face with life's darker chapters on a regular basis, a sarcastic quip could be the lifeline that keeps you afloat. Most of the time, anyway.

Barron stood over the grave and blew out a breath. Shaking his head and not bothering to look at us, he asked, "Jennifer Berman?"

"Unofficially, of course," I replied.

Jennifer Berman was last seen two weeks before at the Hamby summer festival. We didn't put much effort into the investigation, not by our choice, but by the mayor's directive, though most departments didn't when a drug addict went missing. More often than not, the addict would show up a few days later, either dead or alive, and since the area's drug use had skyrocketed since the pandemic, like most others, our department lacked the resources to search for every missing person. No one liked it, even the police, but it wasn't something we could control. We'd checked out a few leads, but the investigation hadn't gone anywhere. Unfortunately, that happened more often than not.

"Wonder if her family will still give a rat's ass about her now that she's dead?" Barron crouched down, groaning as his knees creaked, and dug through his medical bag. Bishop and I crouched beside the doctor. "Girl goes missing and her family doesn't even have the decency to report it?"

Barron's face turned deep red. "I don't know what the hell is wrong with people anymore." He glanced over at Nikki who had been watching his every move. "You take her temperature?"

"I did, sir. Thermometer measured at 92.7. Based on that, I'd say she's been deceased approximately six hours."

Nikki and Barron had recently developed a mentor/mentee relationship which had allowed her genius to grow exponentially.

"Excellent," he said. Glancing up at me and Bishop, he added, "I'll do my examination and let you know my initial thoughts." He carefully picked up the butchered hand and studied it.

The chief arrived and asked, "What's Barron say?"

Barron answered for him. "Barron's initial examination says the girl was strangled to death." He nodded to Nikki. "Do we have the finger and thumb?"

She pointed to the evidence bag. "Right there. Removed prior to her death."

"Yes," he said. "This poor woman. From what I understand, she didn't have an easy life."

He hauled himself upright, every inch of the way marked by a groan that echoed the sentiment of the scene. "We'll get the remains over to the morgue while y'all work on finding the psycho that did this to her." After a quick glance at his watch, he added, "Got an eight a.m. tee time," almost to himself. His eyes flickered back to the lifeless form on the ground. "Scratch that. I'll be on this case at first light."

"Dr. Barron," Nikki said. "May I attend?"

"You're always welcome." He turned toward the chief. "If your boss allows."

"Let's get the scene handled and see what time it is," Jimmy said. "I don't want you falling asleep on the job." His frown softened into a smile.

"I'll be fine," she said and got back to work.

Crime scene evidence retrieval was a detailed, stressful job. The team worked together to carefully extract every possible piece of evidence available, from a small clump of dirt to hairs and bugs. It was always a daunting task, but the most important because one small piece collected could be the key to the killer.

We stepped away from the scene and discussed the situation while the men carefully removed the woman's remains from the grave. We all knew it was Jennifer Berman, but until we had confirmation, we chose to call her the victim instead.

An officer rushed over from the grave. "Uh, Chief? We've got a problem."

Jimmy exhaled. "What's wrong?"

2

"We think someone else is buried under her."

"You think?" Jimmy asked.

"You have to see it to understand."

We hurried back to the grave, the air thick with an anticipatory silence that muffled our footsteps. The damp earth released a pungent aroma of decay and wet leaves like it was warning us of what to expect, but I didn't need the warning. I'd learned to expect the worst.

Jimmy's hands clawed at his face, etching lines of disbelief and horror, as curses spilled from him like a torrent of despair.

I groaned. "It's going to be a long night."

Another body had been an exaggeration, but it was clear what remained under our victim had once been one. Remnants of a plastic purse, for starters, and a few things that had all but disintegrated with the passage of time. From the looks of it all, a lot of time.

If rage had a face, it would mirror Barron's—every line and crease etched with a fury that words like *pissed off* could never fully capture. He dropped a string of cuss words connected in ways I'd never considered. I had a new respect for the man. Even while cursing, his hands moved with a surgeon's precision through the dirt, each flick of his wrist uncovering more of the grim scene beneath. I found myself mimicking his movements, kneeling beside him, the earth cool and damp against my knees. My flashlight sliced through the darkness, a lone beacon revealing a tableau so grim, each shadow seemed to recoil at the severity of our find.

He cursed some more, and nothing he said needed a response, but that hadn't stopped the chief from screaming out in frustration. "What the everloving-hell?" Jimmy's verbal angst was less intense than Barron's, but only because he needed to maintain composure around his staff. Barron didn't police his words, nor care who heard them.

Before Jimmy's curse could dissolve into the night, a chill swept over us, unnatural, as if the very earth beneath our feet recoiled at what we were about to uncover. It was a silent warning, a harbinger of the darkness nestled within its embrace.

Jimmy barked out a detailed list of orders for the team, which everyone obliged without a complaint.

"Well," Barron said as he examined the new remains, "obvious as it may seem, this one's not a new victim." He picked carefully through the dirt. "We've got some jewelry and possibly some press on fingernails though I'm not sure. Looks like something plastic as well."

"I think it might have been a purse," I said.

He grunted. "It'd be great if we had some teeth, but we'll have to wait and see if your team finds any."

"At least there's that," Bishop muttered.

Not that the information made things any easier. The fact that one fresh body, for lack of a better term, had been buried on top of another body, or what was left of it, meant things we all dreaded.

"This isn't a coincidence," Bishop said. He rivaled both Jimmy and Barron's frustration. "How the hell long was that body there?"

"From the looks of what's left, a long time," I said.

"This feels familiar," he said, his voice low, threading through the cool night air. "This better not be like the Anderson murders. The way the bodies were...arranged. It's like we're getting a similar message but from another killer."

"Don't even go there," I said. The Anderson murders were twisted attempts at justice from an insane criminal. Too many people had died at his hand, and one of our own had come close.

Nikki's camera clicked and whirred at rapid speed, the flash intermittently slicing through the scene like lightning, leaving long, grotesque shadows across our work area. The sound of the shutter, so sharp and precise in the trauma of the night, was almost invasive, each click a violation of the solemnity that death demanded.

Finally, she said, "I think I've got enough." She looked at Barron. "I'll get down there and dig through it all, but it's going to take a while. We'll have to go at least a few feet down."

"Make sure there's no other remains under it," Jimmy said. He dropped his head and shook it. "Son of a bitch."

Barron cleared his throat. "It'll take a miracle to get an ID, but we'll see what we can do." He examined the necklace carefully. "It's a heart locket." He tried to open it, but it wouldn't budge.

"I'll take care of that back at the department," Nikki said.

Even though the scene was horrific, Nikki was in her element, and she'd do whatever necessary to discover the identity of the necklace's owner.

"Guess you're going to miss more than a tee time," Jimmy said patting Barron on the back.

Barron stared down into the gravel. "I'll miss tee times for a month if that's what it takes to figure out who these remains belong to and who put them in the ground."

"Nikki," Jimmy said. "Your people got this?"

"We do, Chief."

Kyle was home, lounging in our suddenly too-small-for-two townhome when I dragged my tired bones through the door. He popped up like a jack-in-the-box, all concern and muscles, handing me a glass of ice water that looked as inviting as a dive in the Pacific on a hot day. I shrugged off my weapon, feeling the weight of the night lift slightly but not entirely. Finding bodies never left the soul.

"Long night, huh?" He had that tone—part worry, part knowing. Kyle always knew.

"The first of many," I grumbled, working through the ritual of equipment removal and check, each piece a reminder of the tragedy and what would happen over the coming days, maybe even weeks. I flopped onto the couch. It groaned in protest. "Unless you're counting the last million long nights, then it's just another drop in the bucket."

"You found Jennifer Berman, so that's something to be happy about." His voice had that lightness, as if he was trying to pierce the gloom I had dragged in with me. Like Tommy, he usually found a way.

"We did," I conceded, sipping the water and letting its chill run through me. "Though happy is a stretch. Finding her alive would've been the real win." I glanced at him, narrowing my eyes. "Wait. Who blabbed? It's not out yet."

Kyle, Mr. DEA with his shiny new management badge, just shrugged, the hint of a smirk playing on his lips. "Savannah and I share intel about the ones we love."

I smiled. Savannah Abernathy, a force of nature married to Jimmy and my ride-or-die in our crazy world. She had this belief about couples and secrets, mainly, that there shouldn't be any. And in our line of work, that said something. Jimmy could tell her the end of the world was coming, and she'd keep it under wraps until the meteor hit. Unless of course, she talked to Kyle. The two were like teenage girls when it came to secrets.

"What's the next step?" Kyle's voice pulled me back.

"Guess Jimmy didn't spill everything to Savannah then." I leaned back, feeling the couch embrace my tiredness.

Kyle edged closer, his eyebrow arching up. "What happened?"

"There was another body under Berman's," I said, pausing for dramatic effect. "Well, not a body, per se. Just jewelry and stuff. Nikki's still there looking for teeth."

"Ashley's going to quit the DEA and come back to Hamby with those kinds of scenes." He stared, his face a blank canvas. "Damn."

Ashley was our former crime scene tech who Kyle's team had stolen a while back. She and Michels, another Hamby detective, were in the midst of planning their upcoming wedding.

"Pretty much the team's reaction." I took another sip, feeling the weariness of the discovery and wondering if I'd sleep. "The teeth are a long shot.

Whoever was there has been part of the earth longer than they were above it. I'm just crossing fingers we don't unearth a whole graveyard."

Kyle's scruff scratched against his palm as he ran it over his face. "Looks like you've got yourself a double homicide."

"Yeah, but how many years apart?" My eyes flicked to Louie, my Beta fish who knew more about my cases than any therapist ever would. "Did you feed our child?"

"Of course. Four pellets. He's now reigning in his castle." Kyle's smile was gentle, a contrast to the night's darkness.

I stood and stretched. "Shower time."

"I wasn't going to say anything, but..." He covered his nose and winked at me.

I reached out, pinching his triceps.

"Ouch," he winced, pulling away.

"Love's tough sometimes," I said with a wink.

"But worth every minute," he replied, his voice warm and inviting. I knew the tone, and what it meant. "Would you like me to show you?"

"Race you to the shower."

Kyle had done an excellent job of distracting me from the night's events, but as he lay snoring beside me, the echoes of the day's grim discoveries still bounced around in my head. After thirty minutes, I climbed out of bed and headed for the kitchen. No need to keep us both up, and I was hungry anyway.

As I sat on the couch with heated leftovers in my hand, my phone pinged with a message. It wasn't a number I recognized.

How's the hunt, Detective Ryder? Not losing sleep, I hope.

Chills raced down my spine. It wasn't some wrong number. The message was too personal, too targeted. I typed a quick response, demanding to know who it was, but the message failed to deliver. No surprise there.

I sent Bishop a screenshot of the text. He responded immediately with a screenshot of the same question posed to him.

Another ping almost immediately. That time, a photo. It was of me, taken from a distance, earlier that day at the crime scene. I sent it to Bishop. He returned one of himself.

My heart hammered against my ribs. It was no joke. The killer was watching us, playing a twisted game. I hurried to the garage and called Bishop.

"The killer was at the scene. We need to go there, now."

"They're not there anymore," he said. "Think about it."

He was right. "How did they know? We kept it out of the news."

"It was the hand," he said. "Whoever buried her kept the hand out on purpose, to be found, and somehow, they found out when the dog found it."

Another message beeped in while talking to Bishop. "I got another one." I read it to him. *Nice place you've got. Would be a shame if something happened to it.*

I took off through the garage, grabbed my nearest nine-millimeter, and raced toward my stairs saying, "Call it in," to Bishop, and then shoved the phone into my sweatshirt pocket.

"Kyle," I said, shaking him awake. "Get up. Someone's at the house."

He flew out of bed, grabbed his pants from the chair beside the dresser and jumped into them. He removed his weapon from his nightstand without saying a word. He didn't ask for an explanation, nothing.

The sirens blaring down our street slowed my heartbeat. Five minutes later, the entire area was filled with Hamby officers.

Lieutenant Grant arrived shortly after and took charge of the search.

"There's a trail three rows down," I said.

"Rach," Kyle whispered, "let him do his job."

"Thank you, Agent Olsen," Grant said. He looked at me. "Detective, we've got this. I promise you we'll check everywhere in the surrounding area, but not having a description of the suspect makes it hard. I wouldn't expect miracles."

He coordinated officers around our property and returned to say, "We'll sweep the area. If someone's been watching, we'll do our best to find them."

Bishop arrived. "I didn't get that text. The killer must have been here when he sent them."

He, Kyle, and I gathered in my living room. "Hold on," I said. The blue and red lights spinning outside would tick off even my nicest neighbors. I jogged outside and asked them to shut them off.

We discussed the text messages and photos, piecing together the chilling realization that whoever killed the woman had been watching us the whole time.

"The killer's intentionally playing mind games," Bishop said, his voice low. "To mess with our heads, trying to rattle us. Don't let it work."

Kyle nodded. "They know about the crime scene and know where you live. This isn't just about evasion. They want to play a game."

"They left the hand visible for a reason. You're right," I said to Kyle. "It's all part of their sick game."

We dove deeper into the discussion, analyzing possible motives, methods, and the unsettling fact that the killer was brazen enough to track us. It was another level of sick we hadn't expected.

"Looks like the killer wants to play a game of cat and mouse," Bishop said.

I smirked. "Then let's go catch us a mouse."

3

The prior night's events played on repeat in my mind, and I'd spent most of the night processing everything while working to keep my emotions in check. I awoke to the gritty remnants of a sleepless night clinging to my eyelids, the world around me dulled as if viewed through a fogged lens. The craving for caffeine pulsed through me, an intense ache that promised only a semblance of alertness if met, but it was better than nothing. I stopped at Dunkin' and ordered enough coffee and donuts for the entire team. Bishop had been on a clean eating kick since his near death beating last year, but he always snagged a Boston Crème. Some habits never changed.

He and Jimmy were already in the investigation room when I arrived. I set everything on the table, then excused myself to get my laptop from my cubicle.

"I already got it," Bishop said as I walked out the door.

I flipped around and said, "Oh, thanks."

"You okay?" he asked.

I raised an eyebrow. "You think a psycho killer stalking and taunting us is going to scare me? I'm revved up and ready to kick ass."

His eyebrows shot up. "Okay, then."

"I read last night's report," Jimmy said. "I'll put Levy and Michels on this. Take the heat off you two."

Bishop slammed a hand on the table. "Like hell you will. This nut job is coming after us. We need to fight fire with fire."

I looked at Jimmy. "I'm with him."

I was oddly calm. Was it shock or was the anger simmering to a boil? Sometimes it was better for me to separate myself from the events, to step back and be present to keep myself in check. So, I did. I focused on the room instead of the situation. I'd have to focus on that soon enough.

The overhead lights blazed with an intensity that pierced directly through my skull, igniting a throbbing headache that pulsed in time with my heartbeat. The stark fluorescence washed over everything, creating long, harsh shadows that mirrored the jagged edges of our tension. The room was charged with tension, the air heavy with the weight of unspoken concerns and the metallic tang of determination. The large oval table, a cold island of metal in a sea of uncertainty, stood ready to anchor us through the storm of the investigation. My eyes wandered to the white dry-erase boards lining one wall scrawled with a labyrinth of notes and diagrams. They were the silent proof of the long hours we had already poured into our previous investigations and the hope for the ones we'd met the previous night. On the opposite wall, a projection screen hung dormant, awaiting its call to duty for briefings or to display crucial inputs from Bubba or Nikki.

Against the far wall, our excuse for a coffee station loomed like an old friend none of us were sure we could trust. Like those whiteboards, it was our silent nod to the overtime hours staring down at us. The smell of fresh Joe, thanks to the seven Dunkin' cups I'd lugged in, and the sugary perfume of a dozen and a half donuts sitting pretty in an open box gave the place hope, though I didn't feel like I had any. Right then and there, that caffeine and sugar hit felt less like breakfast and more like the necessary juice it was for the detective marathon we were gearing up to sprint. Same day, different investigation, one pumped up to max volume.

A lone phone placed centrally on the table beeped. "Chief, the mayor's on line one."

"I'll take it in my office," he said. He stood, grabbed a Dunkin' cup, and then hurried out.

I slid into a chair with all the give of a concrete slab and winced as it jabbed my spine. The investigation room was a mishmash of cold practicality and half-hearted opposites of cozy, a perfect mirror for the grind of our gig—hard, unyielding, and only a shade shy of soul-sucking unless we netted the bad guy.

Bishop eyed me. "You sure you're okay?"

"I have to be. I can't function out of fear, and I'm really working to keep my emotions in check on this."

"Then I won't ask you again."

"Appreciate that, partner." I fished out my notepad and pencil, drumming the eraser on the table like a jazz beat. "I'm trying to noodle out how two dead bodies end up in the same dirt nap, especially when one's old enough to be your sister."

"And is it really one killer or is there something we don't know yet," he added.

"There's a lot of somethings we don't know yet."

Nikki walked in and stood against the door frame. "I'm exhausted, but I do have something." She surveyed the room. "Is everyone late?"

"It appears so," Bishop said, "but don't let that stop you."

She eyed him suspiciously. "Y'all okay?"

"We'll fill you in when everyone's here," he said. "What do you have?"

"Okay. First, we found teeth. Thank God. I've got photos for everyone, and my team is ready to search missing persons if need be." She took a breath then added, "Oh, and dust. It's only a small amount, and I doubt it'll ID the vic, but we can get an estimate of how long the body's been there from it and hope for a match for the teeth."

"That will help," I said. "You're amazing as usual."

Her cheeks turned a light pink. "Thanks." She eyed the coffee. "Is there one for me?"

"There is. All black, so add what you need."

"Black's great." She grabbed a cup, then walked over to the Keurig and stuck a dark roast pod into the top.

"Uh?" Bishop asked. The corners of his mouth curved upward. "Is the cup not full?"

"Absolutely, but I'm seriously under-caffeinated. Forgot to hook up my espresso IV before I left home, and I haven't been back since last night. At this point, I might just stick a straw into that old fashioned drip coffee pot in the kitchen and call it a day."

Poor Nikki, she worked harder than any of us. Thank God she was younger and could handle it. I hadn't noticed she looked tired until she had made that extra shot. "You need some sleep."

"I'll sleep when I'm dead." She blinked. "Oh, that's not what I meant."

"We get it," Bishop said. He smirked my direction. "And Ryder would have said it intentionally."

"As a coping mechanism," I said, defending myself. All cops joked at tragedy. It was the only way to stay sane. Bishop knew that. He just liked to give me a hard time.

Levy walked in. She gave me a knowing look and mouthed, "You okay?"

I nodded.

The briefing room felt like a pressure cooker when the rest of the team, sans Michels, showed up.

Jimmy strode in last, his face etched with the night's worries, looking like he'd been hit by a convoy on Interstate 85. "Ryder," he said, "You're up."

Great. It was my turn to be the bearer of not-so-great news. Standing at the head of the room, the weight of the case bore down on me, the atmosphere thick enough to cut with a knife. Those damn fluorescent lights above flickered like a morse code for headaches, each pulse a throb in my temples. The night had been rough for all of us, but we all knew it was just going to get worse.

Jimmy stood against the wall, his arms crossed, looking as though he'd crashed and burned on that interstate. Bubba, our tech guru, sat hunched over his laptop, his fingers a blur across the keyboard. The guy was a wizard, pulling digital rabbits out of hats—necessary moves I couldn't even fathom. Detective Levy sat across from my seat, her face a display of impending doom.

"Where's Michels?" I asked Levy.

"Running late, I guess."

"Okay, we'll update him when he arrives." I launched into the summary of the previous night's escapades, leaving events after arriving home for later, and trying to keep it concise yet detailed. "All right, as you all know, we received a call late last night of a body buried on the Pendley farm. Upon arriving at the scene, we confirmed there was a body buried in a makeshift grave. The victim was strangled and left naked from the waist down. Obviously a woman, most likely in her late twenties, with long brown hair and brown eyes. Her face showed signs of meth abuse, including hollowed cheeks, scarring and new sores. Her teeth were rotting, and the top front four are missing. We have unofficially identified the victim as Jennifer Berman."

The room was silent, the gravity of the situation hitting everyone like a brick. I imagined the gears turning in their minds, piecing together the horror of the scene.

"How was she killed?" Levy asked.

"Someone slit her jugular," Bishop said. "Not sure yet why the pants were missing."

"Jesus," she said. "So, we've likely got a sex crime."

Michels barged in and froze when he saw the looks on our faces. "Sorry." He appeared flustered and annoyed.

"Everything okay?" Jimmy asked.

"Some asshole ran me off the road on the way here. I pursued but lost them before I could get a tag number."

I glanced at Bishop. He nodded once. He wasn't aware of what had happened, but he would be soon enough.

"Did you call it in?" Levy asked.

"Yeah, but there was too much traffic to see where the vehicle went." He sat beside Levy, his partner. "Sorry to interrupt."

"No problem," I said, and then asked Levy, "Everything okay with you this morning?"

"Perfect," she said.

I caught Michels up on the conversation.

He made the same assumption Levy had. "Sex crime?"

"We don't know yet," I said. "Barron didn't confirm. You know how he is.

He prefers to leave those findings to the morgue to give the victims privacy. He's promised to do the autopsy this morning."

"Have her parents been notified?" Levy asked. "Not that they deserve to know."

Jennifer Berman's parents hadn't reported her missing. Old enough to be on her own, but still hanging around the area, Berman had been missing for four days before a friend reported it.

"We're not releasing the identity to the public until it's official. Bishop and I are meeting the family at the morgue in two hours," I said, glancing at my partner, who nodded solemnly. "But of course, there's more fun stuff," I added, pausing for a moment to gather my thoughts. "There was another body beneath hers." I eyed Nikki.

"What the hell?" Levy asked.

"Nikki can tell you more about that."

"There wasn't much to find from that victim," she said. "It's been there too long, though we don't know how long, but," she said, "we did find a few things."

"Clothing?" Bubba asked.

"Jewelry," Bishop said.

Nikki eyed Bubba. "Yes. As for clothing, remnants, but not much, mostly just strings, though we did get a piece of plastic I believe was a purse." She paused, letting the information sink in. "And a heart locket necklace, but as I told Bishop and Ryder earlier, we have a set of teeth."

"Teeth?" Jimmy asked.

Seeing the confused look on her colleague's face, Nikki paused to elaborate. "Bone decomposition varies based on environmental conditions— moisture, pH of the soil, presence of microorganisms, all play a role. In this case, most of the skeletal remains have degraded to the point of turning to dust, which isn't uncommon for a burial in acidic soil. Teeth and jawbones are denser and more resilient than other bones. They can withstand conditions that cause the rest of a skeleton to decompose more completely. That's why we can still find them when other bones have already deteriorated."

Both could be crucial evidence, but it was the luck of the draw depending on when the body was left there, and if we could find a match on any missing persons data.

"I managed to open the locket found on the necklace," she said, "but the picture inside was too deteriorated to identify. Aside from those, I found what I believe to be bone dust in the dirt. It's a long shot, but we're testing it. Don't get your hopes up though; the chances of it leading to anything are slim."

"We need a win from one of those, and our best bet is the teeth," I said.

Everyone absorbed the information, though no one looked happy about it.

Nikki continued, "As I mentioned before, there were also bits of material, likely from clothing. Just tiny strands, and some long, blond hair strands too."

It was those small, seemingly insignificant details that often cracked a case wide open, so I understood the excitement in Nikki's voice.

"What's the next step?" Levy asked. She'd directed her comment to Jimmy.

"After Rachel and I arrived home," Bishop said, "we received text messages we assume are from the killer and are treating them as such."

We showed them the messages and told them about the search around my place.

"Hell." Michels's eyes widened. "You think the person who ran me off the road is the killer?"

"It's possible," I said.

"Until we know otherwise, let's assume it was," Bishop said.

"We all need to be careful and keep an eye out for unusual situations," I said.

"I just spoke to the mayor," Jimmy said. "The discovery of the remains from a previous victim lit a fire under his ass, and that fire got bigger when I told him about the text messages. He wants us full throttle on this thing, so it's all hands on deck. I don't care how you do it, just figure it out, and keep me updated." He looked at Bishop and then me. "Bishop and Ryder are lead." He then looked directly at me. "Leave the emotions at home." He gave us all a nod and walked out of the room.

I'd already done that.

"Let's get to work," Bishop said. "Ryder and I will head to the morgue for the ID with the parents. Bubba, can you run through NCIC for previous missing persons, I don't know, from 1970 and up? Check for anyone with dental records we can compare to. Bonus points if it's a blond."

The National Crime Information Center database, a computerized index of criminal justice information run by the FBI, contained information about crimes and criminals, including data on missing persons, and while it was an excellent resource, I hated that the FBI controlled it. Most police departments despised giving the FBI any credit, and vice versa. But as a tool, it was golden.

"Also pull ones with mention or photo of a heart locket necklace and plastic purse or bag," I said.

"I'm on it," Bubba said. He closed his laptop, gathered the rest of his things and rushed out.

"Nikki's coming with us," I told Bishop. "She wants to be a part of the autopsy."

"I'll drive myself," she said. "I won't stay long. We've got too much going on here. I just want to see what Dr. Barron can find right away."

"Better her than me," Michels said.

"What about us?" Levy asked.

"Catch up on the file from the night. Jimmy made sure everyone wrote a report. Then go through Jennifer Berman's file. See what you think. We'll discuss when we get back."

"Got it," Levy replied.

"Was it a burner phone that texted you?" I asked.

"Probably," Bishop said.

"Had to be," I said. "But my text wouldn't go through, so it's probably disconnected.

The Bermans were waiting when we arrived. Identifications used to be made in the refrigerator room, as Barron called it, but he'd fought for, and won, a small viewing room. It wasn't much bigger than a small walk-in closet, which was the point. Barron didn't want the deceased's families to view bodies under stark lighting and see the surgical equipment that would be used to take the body of their loved one apart the minute they left.

Mrs. Berman wiped her swollen, red eyes with a tissue. I already knew it was Jennifer Berman in that grave, but looking at her mother confirmed it. They shared the same eyes, eyebrows, and lips, though the victim's were less pronounced from drug use. Mr. Berman, a tall, thin man with olive skin, stood stoically beside his wife, his lips flattened into a thin, straight line. He stared at the wall behind us as we talked, his jaw clenched, and the cords of his neck hard. Some men played tough before seeing the body. Those were the ones that usually lost it during the identification process. Other men lost it beforehand, and then were oddly calm and accepting when making the actual ID. Mr. Berman played tough.

After Bishop introduced us, Mr. Berman shifted on his feet, a sign of restless, nervous energy. "Can we move this along? My wife is a wreck, and I don't want her here any longer than she has to be." His voice was tight, strained with barely contained emotion.

Bishop nodded, his movements slow and deliberate. "After you." He gently opened the door a few inches, the creak of the hinges loud in the tense silence.

The parents stood on the left side of the gurney, and Barron stood on the right. We stood behind the parents, ready to handle whatever necessary. Barron had placed a rounded cover over everything but her head so the parents wouldn't see her bottom half. Not everyone needed to see or know all the things. They'd already be haunted with what they did know for the rest of their lives already.

Mr. Berman wrapped his arm around his wife, a protective gesture that showed his love for her. He then nodded to Barron. "We're ready."

"Okay then," Barron said softly, his voice steady. He always gave the final warning. Knowing it was going to happen was one thing, but most people needed that last statement to push themselves to look.

Mrs. Berman gasped. Her hand flew to her mouth at the sight of her daughter. She buried her face into the side of her husband as her body trembled with suppressed sobs.

Mr. Berman cleared his throat. "That's her," he whispered, his voice barely audible.

We escorted them outside as quickly as possible.

Outside the room, Mrs. Berman cried, her body wracked with grief. Mr.

Berman remained stoic. "What happens now?" he asked, his voice hollow and reserved as if he'd mastered controlling his emotions.

"An autopsy will be performed," I said, my voice soft yet firm. "We've already begun investigating. If you'd like, we can find a room and share what we know so far."

"No," he said, shaking his head adamantly. "My wife can't handle that, and it doesn't matter. We lost our daughter six years ago." He pointed to the viewing room, his hand trembling slightly. "What's in there is just the shell." He looked at Bishop and then me. "Thank you." He escorted his wife down the hall while Bishop and I stared after them, a heavy silence falling between us.

"Wow," Bishop said once they were out of earshot, his voice low and reflective. "I'd say that was brutal, and it is to a certain degree, but he's right. Drugs took their daughter long before someone murdered her."

"I know. It's the biggest tragedy of drug abuse," I said. "I'd like to stick around for the beginning of the autopsy. You good with that?"

Bishop wasn't a fan, but who was? "Not too long. I'd like to get moving on this ASAP," he replied.

"Ditto."

I'd lost count of the number of autopsies I'd been to. The ritual was always the same, but it still managed to leave its mark each time. Bishop and I slipped into scrubs over our regular gear and shrouded our shoes in those bootie things that looked more at home on a surgeon's head. We weren't planning to get hands-on with the corpse, but in our line of work, you geared up for the unexpected. Naturally, latex gloves were part of the ensemble.

Nikki was already kitted out when we got there. Despite the morbid task at hand, she practically danced on the balls of her feet, buzzing to soak up whatever knowledge our cadaver had to offer. I admired her thirst for learning, no matter how macabre or tough the lesson.

"As always, we'll start with a thorough visual examination of the body's exterior," Barron said, his voice resonating in the sterile room.

He spoke into the small microphone clipped to his white coat, noting the name of the victim, the general condition of the body, and other important information like weight, height, eye and hair color, ethnicity, sex, and age.

The body was then fully undressed for a closer examination of the skin to look for gunpowder residue, flakes of skin or paint, injuries, scars, tattoos, or any identifying marks. I cringed and swallowed back bile when seeing the remains and the drawn, placid skin. I never lost my lunch in an autopsy, but there was a first time for everything, and seeing that young girl like that pushed my limits. The rest of the process could take up to four hours, if not longer, and neither Bishop nor I wanted to or had the time to stick around.

Barron agreed to let us take the teeth to the forensic odontologist, so we grabbed them and left.

Walking to Bishop's vehicle, he asked, "Who slices a neck like that?"

"Someone that hates her," I said.

He clicked the key fob to unlock the door. "She went missing from Logan Park. It borders Alpharetta. In fact, the APD handled the investigation initially because that's where she was reported missing. Her murder could have happened anywhere."

"Thank God she wasn't eaten by pigs," I said.

"Why do you aways bring pigs eating humans into the picture?"

"I have a sick mind."

"Now," he said, "that much I know."

4

Bishop steered us through a Starbucks drive-thru, ordering black coffees like we were in some kind of caffeine emergency. Which we were. We always were. While we waited, I caught sight of yet another strip mall mushrooming across the street. "What, they're handing out strip malls with Happy Meals now?"

"Not according to Copeland Construction, apparently. They're all over the area."

"Steve Copeland, right?"

"Knew him in high school Steve got away with most of the crap he did back then. When it caught up with him, he did a little time in juvie, but his daddy sprung him early."

"Nice." I asked with a smile, "So, you hung out with him?"

"Uh, no." He took the coffees and thanked the barista. "He was a few years older than me, and we weren't part of the same crowd. If I remember right, he got a job in construction after high school, and I guess he grew up."

"Thanks," I said as he handed me my coffee. "Looks like he's doing well now."

"He is."

I stared into the cup and thought about the findings from the night before. "It's amazing to me that teeth don't decompose for years, yet a cavity can burn a hole in one in a matter of hours."

He eyed me suspiciously. "Got a tooth ache?"

I shook my head. "Don't jinx me. I hate going to the dentist. My point is they could have been down there for a long, long time. Fifty years even."

"Which means we could have a senior citizen killer or a copycat."

I exhaled. "I'll take senior citizen killer for 500, Alex. One that is updated on technology."

Bishop agreed. "But we can't rule out the copycat."

"You think a copycat killed Berman, waited for the hand to be discovered, then hung out while we processed the scene?"

"And came by your place last night."

The light was a stubborn red, holding us hostage in our unmarked cruiser. Bishop drummed his fingers, a sure sign of his impatience brewing like a storm.

"We're almost back," I said. "Take a chill pill."

He narrowed his eyes at me. "A chill pill?"

"Yeah. It's 80s speak, right? Thought it might take the scowl off your face."

"I never said 'take a chill pill.'"

"I see my effort was futile."

Suddenly, a sleek, black luxury car swerved out in front of us, slicing through our waiting game and turned left.

"What the hell?" I blurted, my eyes wide.

Bishop's jaw clenched. He white-knuckled the steering wheel and yelled, "You don't own the road, buddy."

"I'm sure that helped," I said calmly. The car's taillights flared a mocking red as it gunned down the street, disappearing into traffic. I craned my neck, trying to catch a glimpse of a license plate, but it was no good.

Bishop shrugged, his eyes still on the spot where the car vanished. "Maybe he's late for work."

"Or maybe it's our mouse." I pointed the direction the vehicle went. "Turn." I quickly got on the radio and called the vehicle in.

Bishop yanked the wheel and cut off traffic to follow the vehicle, but it was too late. Too much traffic and time had passed, and we'd lost him. I canceled the call.

"Why'd you cancel it?" he asked.

"What kind of vehicle was it?"

"A black luxury one."

"This is Hamby. Everybody and their mother owns a black luxury vehicle in this town."

He exhaled. "If it's our guy, then he's smarter than we think. He's managed to find addresses and phone numbers."

"Right," I said. "And he's hitting us all, so that means Levy's next." I tapped out a text to her and let her know to be on the lookout. I continued our previous conversation. "How does a copycat work in this situation? Is the copycat related to the first? Did they give a death bed confession with the longitude and latitude for the location of the remains? The second killer couldn't have picked the exact same spot by coincidence."

He pulled into the back lot of the department where the city vehicles parked. We climbed out of the vehicle and headed inside.

"There's no such thing as coincidence," he said.

I agreed. "Therein lies our problem."

He opened the door and stared at me with his head tilted to the side. "You really are okay with this, aren't you?"

"I thought we'd cleared that up already?"

"I've been your partner long enough to know you've got a bomb brewing inside you right now."

"It's contained for now. I promise."

He nodded. "Five minutes in the investigation room?"

"That works."

Jimmy stopped us near our cubicles. "Any more messages?"

"Nope," I said.

"We did nearly get hit by a black luxury vehicle," Bishop said.

"Did you get a look at the driver?"

"No," I said. "Tinted windows of course. We called it in but canceled the call. The driver was gone by the time we made the turn."

"You're being watched. Pay attention." He cleared his throat. "How'd they handle it? The parents."

"Wife was a wreck," I said. "Father tried his best to hide his emotions, but he was pretty upset."

Bishop added, "He said they'd lost their daughter a long time ago."

Jimmy nodded. "If I ever catch my kids doing drugs..." He didn't bother finishing that sentence.

Jimmy and Savannah had two children, Carter, just born a few months before, and Scarlet, who was old enough to talk more than not. The kid didn't walk. She sprinted. As a semi-frequent runner who believed herself to be in reasonably good health, catching my goddaughter was always a challenge. She had a knack for dodging and hiding in small spaces.

Jimmy would easily protect them with his life. We all would.

"Any word on the teeth?" Bishop asked.

"Not that I'm aware of," Jimmy said. His cell phone rang. He glanced at the screen and said, "I need to take this. Keep me updated."

"Will do," we said in unison.

∿

"No match yet," Michels said, referring to the teeth. He leaned forward, his brow furrowing as he sifted through the papers in front of him, the dim light on his face exaggerated the fine lines forming around his eyes. "The number of missing women in Georgia alone since 1970 is incredible."

"Nationally, the numbers are almost evenly split between men and women," Bubba said. He twisted a pen between his fingers, his expression thoughtful, eyes squinting slightly as if pondering the statistics. "Here in Georgia missing women top men by about six percent."

"Which means we've got a large database to go through," Levy said. She tapped her fingers rhythmically on the table, her gaze fixed on the whiteboards as if visualizing the data.

"I've run a check based on keywords," Bubba said. He stopped twirling his pen and began drumming his fingers on the table, something he did when his high energy took over. "Teeth, necklace, plastic purse or bag, and heart-shaped locket, but they may be noted differently, so we're working on other keywords."

"And quickly scanning them," Levy said, her voice was steady.

"What about blond-haired women around Jennifer Berman's age?" I asked. I fiddled with the phone cord in the middle of the table, winding and unwinding it around my finger, my impatience growing as quickly as Bubba's.

"Oh, yeah," Bubba said. "I did that, too. Blond is a common keyword, so it'll take a while to pull the report." He looked into his laptop, his fingers pounding on the keyboard like a pianist composing a new piece while we continued talking.

"We can focus on Georgia only," Michels said. He leaned back in his chair, crossing his arms, a gesture that hinted at his desire to narrow the search.

"Not yet," Bishop said. He stroked his chin thoughtfully, eyes narrowed as he considered the broader implications. "We don't know what kind of killer we have on our hands just yet."

"One that likes to text," I mumbled. "But Bishop's right. Better not to limit ourselves."

I stopped playing with the phone cord and began tapping a pen against my notebook, a rhythmic sound that filled the brief silence as I thought of why a killer would come out of hiding after God only knew how many years, kill again, and then taunt the department. Were they trying to get caught?

"That's not what I wanted to hear," Michels said, his shoulders slumping slightly in resignation, "but I get it."

Levy stood and poured herself another coffee. Her cell phone beeped. She removed it from her pocket, glanced down at the screen, and smiled, a rare moment of warmth in the otherwise tense room. Then she quickly looked at me, and her cheeks turned red. I held back a smile.

Last fall, my previous partner from Chicago, Tony Garcia, assisted us in an investigation, one I struggle to talk about because it is too personal. Levy and Garcia hit it off, and what I pegged as a fleeting fling turned out to be a long-distance dance. Levy always feels awkward talking about it, but I'm happy for them.

Bubba smacked his hand on the table and jumped out of his seat. "I think I've got something." His sudden movement caused everyone to start, their attention snapping to him as the room filled with a new, urgent energy. He called Jimmy and asked him to come to the investigation room.

Bubba barely got a chance to speak before the crackle of our radio interrupted him. A female voice cut through the noise. "All units, we have a 211 in progress, First National Bank two blocks from HPD. Repeat. All units, 211 in progress. First National Bank two blocks from HPD." After a small pause, she added. "Hostage situation. No audible alarm used."

"Is it our killer?" Bubba asked.

"Too easy," Michels said.

Jimmy replied to dispatch. "No sirens. Park away from the bank, approach on foot. Wait for orders."

The radio burst into responses. Jimmy made eye contact with Bishop. "Go. All of you."

He added on the radio, "Detectives TOA three minutes. Follow their lead." To us, he said, "Get the earpieces. Go!"

Adrenaline instantly replaced my fatigue. I tugged my hair from its clip as we hurried to the equipment room. Levy tossed us each an earpiece.

"Working," each of us said after checking them for power.

"Levy and Ryder," Jimmy said, "Get inside. Two women look less conspicuous." He ran toward the radio room.

Bishop and Michels slipped on their Kevlar vests. "Put yours on," Bishop said to me.

"It won't fit under my jacket without being noticeable."

"Mine either," Levy said.

He swore under his breath.

"There's an employee entrance in the back," I said. "Try to get in that way." I removed my extra gun from my bag and tucked it into the back of my pants. "I'll see if I can get the code."

Levy said, "We'll try to defuse the situation."

We exploded from the precinct, the world outside hitting me like a slap of humid air. My legs pumped, every stride eating up the distance to the bank. Each tick of the clock screamed in my head, a reminder of what could happen.

Hamby PD had rolled out the welcome mat with cruisers ghosting the perimeter of the area. The bank reared up in front of us, all glass and steel, its windows like dark mirrors, reflecting nothing but the tense tableau of cops on the edge.

My mind raced, scenarios playing out like a deck of cards being shuffled. What were we running to? Hostages? A heist gone sideways? My gut churned with the possibilities.

Was it our killer? Was the robbery a final blow-out? A way for the killer to clear a room permanently and sidestep jail? Was it a show with a murderous ending? My heart beat like a drum in my ears. The uncertainty, the fear of what we'd find, the knowledge that every action we took could mean life or death, all familiar, but never easy.

I glimpsed movement inside as we neared the bank. Shadows against the light. My hand instinctively went to my sidearm. Training and instinct melded into a sharp point of focus because the people inside depended on us. We were the thin line between chaos and order.

"Positions," Bishop hissed, and like a well-oiled machine, the slick sleeves fanned out. Each of them knew the drill, the dance of adrenaline and caution. My breaths came short and fast. It wasn't just a building we were approaching; it was a powder keg, and we were the ones walking towards it with open flames.

I thought of the people inside, their morning turned nightmare. Ordinary lives thrust into extraordinary terror. One wrong move, one misjudgment by us, and lives could end up shattered beyond repair.

We made it to the front of the building. "No casualties," Bishop said. "Use the damn earpiece, Ryder." He and Michels sprinted to the back of the bank, providing information to the other officers via his radio.

Levy and I caught our breath. "You ready?" she asked.

I detailed out the plan. "I'll go first. You catch the door behind me. I'll head toward the perp's right. You go left."

"Let's go," she said.

I pushed through the bank's doors, the cool, air-conditioned atmosphere smacking me with a bolt of energy. Levy stuck her hand out and caught the door behind me, then carefully closed it after spotting the suspect.

The scene inside kicked my pulse into high gear. A man, visibly desperate, held a gun to a trembling bank teller's head with his back facing the door. "I said give me the money!"

"I can't," the woman said. "I can't open the drawer without using the computer."

I counted ten hostages, most huddled in corners, their faces etched with fear. Levy darted left while I moved right. I crouched down next to two women and provided Bishop with the details.

"Do not approach," he said. "Is there an employee near you?" he asked.

I noticed the woman next to me wearing a name tag. "Do you work here?" I whispered.

She nodded, tears sliding down her cheeks.

"The building is surrounded. What's the code to the back entrance?"

"Donuts."

I repeated the code to Bishop.

The perp heard me and flipped around, still holding the gun to the woman's head. The fear in her eyes cut me like a knife. He positioned her in front of him and slightly to the side. "I told you to shut up! Who else works here?" he said.

When no one answered, he jabbed the weapon into the side of the woman's head.

"I do," Levy said. She moved away from the two men huddled behind a small couch. "But it's my day off."

"Why the hell do I care if it's your day off. Get the drawers open!"

"I can't do it without using the computer," she said, mimicking the teller's words.

"Who the fuck can open the damn drawers?" Sweat poured from his temples. His hands shook. Angry criminals handled intense robberies differently than desperate ones. Our guy was desperate. I'd take angry over desperate any day of the week. Desperate meant the unknown, but angry usually followed a path.

There was no way the guy was our mouse.

"The drawers need to be opened with the computer," I said as I stood and moved into his line of sight. "There's no other way to unlock them."

The gunman shouted incoherently, his demands muddled by panic and probably fear. I locked eyes with Levy from across the room. A silent conversation passed between us. We had to act fast.

"Shit," he said, quickly wiping the sweat sliding into his eyes. He glared at Levy and then me. "I don't care how you do it, just open the fucking drawers or she dies!"

My heart pounded, my training the only thing keeping my movements calm and measured. The woman held hostage cried softly, her eyes wide with terror.

I carefully and slowly walked toward the counter, allowing time for Bishop and Michels to get inside. It didn't take long. In a flurry of motion, they burst through a door from the back of the bank, catching the gunman off guard. As he turned toward them, he dropped his hand holding the gun to his side.

Michels dove toward him and smacked the gun out of his hand with a fluid movement I'd never seen. The gunman dropped his grip on the woman. She ran screaming to the other side of the counter. Michels tackled the gunman from behind, knocking him to the ground. Bishop, his gun aimed at the man, kicked his gun away. Levy rushed over and kicked it even further.

The people on the other side of the counter cheered.

"Open the damn drawers," the man cried. Michels cuffed him, then told him to stay on his stomach and shut up.

We spent two hours interviewing the bank robber. He wasn't attached to the murders. He was desperate like I'd thought, needing money for his daughter's medical bills.

5

"Caroline Turner," Bubba said. "We have a match." He glanced at each of us. "Unless you have to work the robbery?"

"We already interviewed him," Bishop said. "Not involved."

Jimmy responded. "I've got someone handling the rest of it."

"The paperwork on that's going to suck," Levy said.

"Right," Michels said. "I almost feel bad for the guy. Did you hear him? He needs money for his daughter's cancer treatment."

"I feel bad, but all he's done is make his situation worse," I said.

"There's other ways to go about finding it," Jimmy said.

"Tell that to a desperate man and see what he says," Bishop said. He tapped his pencil on the table. "Back to the teeth."

"It's a tentative match," Bubba said. "We'll need our forensic odontologist to compare the teeth to the x-rays and make sure, but it looks like it."

Jimmy stood behind Bubba with his eyes fixed on the computer screen. The year 1984 glowed against the dark background. A deep furrowed eleven formed between his brows as he processed the information. His lips tightened into a thin line as he leaned in closer. "She went missing in '84?" He straightened up, running a hand through his hair, his gaze still locked on the screen. "Two murders forty years apart?" He shook his head. "This'll make the nightly news shows, damn it."

"I knew her," Bishop said. "Not well, but I knew her."

"Her face pops up every few years," Jimmy said, "but never like this. I don't know the details, but I know her disappearance shook the town." He mumbled something else about the nightly news. Jimmy hated when our department made the news.

Bishop nodded. "She'd had a rough life. I remember my mom telling me about her mother dropping her and her brother off at the neighbor's and not coming back for almost a month. I think I was around five or six when that happened." He licked his lips and then blew out a breath. "Her father was a long-haul truck driver and wasn't around much. They were put into foster care, but the mother returned and got them back. That didn't work out well for Caroline, and she ended up hitting drugs pretty hard during high school. She was about what, twenty-two when she went missing? I think a friend reported it, but I can't remember."

"Where was she last seen?" I asked.

"If I remember correctly, the Alpharetta Summer Festival," Bishop replied.

"Which is now the Hamby festival," Jimmy added.

"We have a pattern," Michels said.

"We had a pattern when the second body was buried on top of the first," I said.

"But we still can't say whether it's the same person committing the murders," Levy said.

Jimmy pointed to me and Bishop. "Get those photos and the teeth to our forensic odontologist. Let's see if we can secure that match."

Stu Webster, our forensic odontologist on contract, had an office in Alpharetta, just off old Milton Parkway. Bishop drove, as usual. He's always said I drive like a person from Chicago, which was true, because that's where I learned to drive and spent most of my life.

He slowed as he passed a brick oven pizza restaurant. "I could eat. What about you?"

"I'm not very hungry. Can we wait until after we talk to Webster? I'd like to see what his timeframe is with these."

"If my stomach growls while we're there, I'm saying it's yours."

"I can live with that."

The second we stepped into Stu's dental office, that too-clean, antiseptic smell slammed into me, followed by the faint whiff of mint toothpaste. I shuddered. The air was as crisp and unwelcoming as the clinic itself and sent chills running down my spine.

I hate going to the dentist. I'd take a trip to the gynecologist and all their mad scientist tools over having my teeth cleaned any day. The drone of a dental drill buzzed somewhere in the background, a sound that always set my teeth on edge—pun intended. Just the thought of someone prodding around in my mouth with sharp instruments made my skin crawl. But duty called, even if it meant stepping into my personal house of horrors.

The waiting room was crammed with people from all walks of life who'd parked themselves on blue chairs that looked comfortable but probably weren't. They were a mixed bunch—some leafing through magazines that probably chronicled events from a decade before, others lost in their phones, escaping reality one scroll at a time. There was a kid zone too, where a few young ones busied themselves with toys. Clearly, they had no clue what was coming.

Despite the crowd, the room had a kind of hushed calmness to it, punctuated by subdued chatter and the occasional burst of child's laughter. It was funny how a place like that could churn up memories and fears, reminding you that sometimes the monsters from your childhood—like the dreaded dental chair—never really left.

I quickly analyzed each patient for issues, and noted one, a man sitting near the entrance, who appeared impatient and agitated. Agitation was desperation's first cousin and often caused people to make stupid decisions.

Bishop and I made our way to the reception desk where a young woman with a bright smile greeted us. "Detectives, how can I help you today?" she asked, her voice cheerful. Her eyes narrowed as she whispered. "Is it about that missing girl? I read about her on social media."

"We've got some teeth for Stu," I said, returning her initial smile and ignoring her question. "Is he available?"

"Oh, right." She tapped on her computer keyboard, her eyes scanning the screen. "Just give me one minute."

We stepped aside, waiting near a large potted plant that, out of several placed around the room, was the only living thing thriving under the fluorescent lights.

Just then, a dental assistant wearing light blue scrubs and her hair in a ponytail, emerged from behind a door. "You can come back now," she said, gesturing for us to follow her.

I didn't budge.

"Ryder," Bishop whispered. "He's not going to touch your teeth." A smile crossed his lips.

As we moved towards the door, the man sitting near the entrance stood abruptly. He looked to be in his forties, wearing work clothes that looked like he'd come straight from a construction site. His face was flushed with anger. Oh, how quickly his emotions fired up.

"I've been here for over an hour!" he exclaimed, his voice rising with each word. "I'm losing money sitting here, missing work! There are people here who've been waiting longer than me, and you're letting them go in together? What kind of place is this?"

The frustration in his voice echoed off the walls, causing several heads to turn in our direction. The tension in the room thickened, the previously calm atmosphere now charged with unease.

Bishop stepped slightly closer to me. We let the man vent, understanding his frustration, but hoping he would calm himself. The other patients watched, some with sympathy for the man, others with curiosity about the unfolding drama.

The guy was in full rant mode, his voice climbing octaves I didn't think possible for a man his size. It was like a bad toothache, incessant and grating, and equally as annoying. Finally, when he took a breather—probably for oxygen more than anything—I saw my chance. I delved into my jacket pocket and pulled out my badge, the metallic clink sounding unusually loud in the tense room. I flashed it at him, the badge catching the fluorescent light. "Sir," I said, injecting all the calm authority I could muster, "we're here on official business. Now, you can zip it, or you can cool your heels in a jail cell for disturbing the peace."

The transformation was something to see. His eyes bulged, almost comically, as they latched onto the badge. The anger in his face quickly crumbled, replaced by a dawning comprehension. You could've heard a pin drop in the room; every pair of eyes was glued on us, the drama unfolding more gripping than any daytime soap.

His shoulders sagged, the fight going out of him like air from a balloon. He looked around, maybe only just realizing he'd become the center of attention—and not in a good way. Mumbling something that sounded like an apology, he slunk back to his seat and clammed up.

I smiled. Sometimes, just the sight of a badge was enough to remind people that there were lines they shouldn't cross. And in a dental office, of all places, I was grateful for that small mercy.

Bishop and I followed the dental assistant through the door. The corridor was completely different from the waiting area—all white, almost sterile looking and quieter, the sound of our footsteps on the linoleum floor the only noise. I swallowed, the copious amounts of coffee I'd drank that day bubbling up my throat. I told myself to chill out. I wasn't there as a patient.

My cell phone vibrated on my side. I hit the button to send the call to voicemail.

Stu Webster walked into the room and smiled. "Detectives." He fiddled with something in his pocket, pulled out a piece of paper, crumbled it into a ball, and tossed it into the garbage can on the side of the small dental equipment stand. He smiled at me. "I assume you're not here for dental work, so what's up?"

"Nothing personal, but I hate the dentist."

"None taken. You told me that the last time you were here."

Bishop rolled his eyes. "Sorry, Stu. She's been shaking in her shoes since we pulled into your parking lot."

"You would too if some moron pulled three of your teeth with no Novocaine."

"Let it go," Bishop said.

"I was five! It's imprinted on my brain."

Stu's laugh brought us back to reality. I handed over the evidence bag containing the teeth and the X-rays. As he carefully laid them out on the tray beside him, I admired the meticulous way he worked, his movements precise and measured. "We're hoping to get a match."

"Alright, let's see what we've got here." Stu said as he adjusted the light over the tray. "As you probably know, the first step is to compare these teeth with the X-rays. We're looking for unique identifiers—root patterns, tooth positions, and any dental work."

"How can you tell the difference between the work on one person's tooth and another's?" I asked. "Wouldn't the differences of say, a cavity in a bicuspid be hard to determine?"

"The opposite, actually." He picked up a dental tool and gently probed the set of teeth. "See here?" He pointed with the tool. "The way this molar is filled, the material used, its shape—all these are clues."

Bishop, oddly intrigued with the process, leaned in closer. "What kind of material is that?"

He glanced up, "Composite resin. Quite common. But it's not just the material. It's also how it's applied. Each dentist has a slightly different technique. Like a fingerprint, if you will. They're all unique and easily matched because of it."

He placed the X-ray against a light board. "Now, if we examine the X-ray, we can match this filling with the shadow here." He traced the outline with his finger. "Moving on to the alignment and bite. These aspects are crucial." He switched the X-ray to a different view. "See how the teeth fit together? The gaps are clear as are the particular bite patterns."

I asked, "Can the alignment change over time, say, if this person was missing for a while?"

"Absolutely," he said. "Teeth will shift, especially if there are gaps. But the fundamental alignment provides a reliable comparison."

He carefully manipulated the set of teeth as he spoke, comparing them to various angles of the X-rays. "Look here," he said, pointing to a specific area on the X-ray, "you can see the unique way this canine has worn down. It matches perfectly with our specimen."

Bishop, who had been scribbling notes, looked up. "That's excellent news. What about age estimation? Can you tell how old this person was?"

Stu nodded, "I can get close. That's part of the analysis. By examining the wear and development of the teeth, I can estimate the age range. In this case, the degree of wear and certain developmental markers suggest a woman in their low to mid-twenties."

"That matches our other victim," Bishop said.

As he spoke, Stu periodically glanced at a large anatomy chart of teeth and jaws on the wall while he spoke, as if mentally cross-referencing. "Another key aspect is evaluating the bone structures," Stu continued, shifting the X-ray to show a wider view of the jaw. "We look at the jawbone density, the positioning of the sinuses, and any irregularities. All these can help confirm an identity."

As he explained, his assistant entered the room quietly and handed him another set of tools. Stu thanked her without looking up, his focus unbroken.

"Do you ever consult with other specialists?" Bishop asked.

"In complex cases, yes," Stu replied. "This one is cut and dried. But when necessary, an orthodontist or an endodontist can offer additional insights, especially when dealing with unusual dental work or alignments. I'm not sure that will be necessary in this case because the fundamental alignment provides a reliable comparison."

"Good to know," I said.

He manipulated the set of teeth, comparing them to the x-rays. "Look here," he pointed to the X-ray, "the unique wear on this canine—it matches perfectly with our specimen."

"That's obvious," I said after studying the x-ray. "I don't think we'll need another opinion."

"The teeth are excellent identifiers." He turned his attention back to the evidence. "Now, let me document these findings." He began to meticulously record every observation. His handwriting was small and precise, something I envied.

"And if this goes to trial?" I asked, thinking ahead.

"If needed, I'll provide expert testimony," he said. "I'll detail my findings and the methods used to reach my conclusions."

As we wrapped up, Stu handed us his preliminary report. "I'll need a bit more time for the final analysis, but from what I see, the teeth match the X-rays. I'll confirm with a detailed report." He smiled at me. "When are you planning to schedule your free consultation with me?"

Bishop walked out laughing.

Outside he said, "I guess we're heading back in time for this one."

"Maybe our killer traveled forward in time," I said. "Do you have a time machine?"

"I think I can get us a DeLorean."

I smiled, understanding the reference to the 80s movie, *Back to the Future*. "With a flux capacitor?"

He smiled too. "Is there any other way?"

6

Levy and Michels had been going through the case files for Caroline Turner's disappearance. They had laid the papers on the conference table in the investigation room. All four of them.

Levy's expression didn't make me feel warm and fuzzy. "This is pathetic and sad," she said, her voice echoing slightly in the sparsely furnished room. "A girl goes missing and the police write her off as another runaway."

"It's not uncommon," Bishop replied, leaning back in his chair, the leather creaking under his weight. "Caroline Turner's family had their own struggles. Like I said, father was a long-haul trucker. Oh, I just remembered. Rumor was he had a secret family in another state." He sipped his coffee and winced.

I knew why. Police departments were stuck under some kind of java hex. Even the coffee from our Keurig, which should technically be foolproof, had the unmistakable flavor of ground dirt. It was an unwritten rule that any coffee brewed within the walls of a precinct lost its soul on the way to the cup.

"That's even worse," she said, her frown deepening. "Maybe she found out, and he killed her?"

"For the love of all things holy, what sane man wants two families?" Michels asked, tossing a pen up and down in his hand. "And don't get me started on having two wives. I'm not even married yet, but I already know Ashley's all the woman I can handle."

Levy laughed, a genuine, hearty sound she'd been doing more lately. Because of Garcia, maybe?

"I think Ashley's the one doing the handling in your relationship," she said.

Bishop's lips curled into a smile, his eyes twinkling with humor. "Might as well learn that lesson now," he said to Michels. "You may wear the pants in the family, but it's Ashley who controls the zipper."

Lauren and I exchanged glances, our eyes wide with amusement, and then burst into laughter, the sound filling the room and breaking the overall tension.

"Bishop is one hundred percent right on that one," I said, wiping a tear of laughter from my eye. "Any man with a little relationship experience under his belt will say the same thing."

Michels squinted at Bishop. "What do you mean control the—" His jaw dropped, realization dawning. "Oh, *that* zipper."

"Wow," Levy said. "Boy's got a lot to learn."

"Nothing like jumping straight into the fire. Bishop," I said, changing the subject. "Can you tell us all you know about Caroline Turner?"

"And it'd be great if you could figure out a connection to Jennifer Berman," Levy said.

"I'll work on that." He leaned back in his chair and stretched, his arms reaching toward the ceiling, joints popping. He'd taken off his blazer, and I noticed his sleeves tightening around his muscular biceps. "Everything I can say about Caroline is through the eyes of a kid."

"We'll take whatever eyes we can get," Levy said. She leaned forward, rested her elbows on the table, and fixed her gaze on Bishop.

"Caroline Turner's family lived off Wills, across the street from the Castleberry's original farmland. It's all homes now, but back then the Turners lived," he paused, thinking, "about three houses from Atlanta Highway. The place was a dump. I don't think the dad ever did anything around the place when he was home except, from what I'd heard, beat his family. A few times, when my mom and I drove by there, she got angry because Caroline's little brother was playing outside naked."

I raised an eyebrow. "Naked? How old was he?"

"Young enough that my mother said he was still in diapers, so only the good Lord knew where he'd left his mark."

I chuckled at the image. "Are those your words or hers?"

He dipped his chin and looked up toward his eyebrows in my direction. "Hers. She also said someday someone was going to do unto that family the way the Turners had done unto them. I don't know what she meant specifically, but apparently, they'd had some trouble with others." His face slacked, a shadow passed over it, and then he finally smiled. "She lived by the fear of God and believed in an eye for an eye."

"She sounds scary," Michels said, his voice apprehensive.

"You have no idea." Bishop cleared his throat. "Caroline was a senior when I was a freshman. She wasn't always a bad kid, not that I remember anyway, but she had a drug problem, and hung around with the burnouts, so she had a reputation she'd earned."

"The burnouts?" Michels asked, his tone laced with curiosity. "That's so vintage."

Levy rolled her eyes. "You're over twenty-five, so you're an antique."

"Was the reputation warranted?" I asked, ignoring their comedic jabs at each other. "Was she what you would have called a floozy?"

"We didn't use that word," he said, a hint of defensiveness in his tone. "You know how it goes. Guys like to talk, and at that age they like to exaggerate, so I can't say whether the stuff about her was true or not. Not the floozy kind of stuff, anyway." He accentuated floozy with sarcasm when he said it. "She got busted for a break-in with Steve Copeland and a few others and wound up in juvie for six months. Based on her homelife, that was probably a vacation."

"Steve Copeland? The builder we talked about earlier?" I asked, connecting the dots.

He nodded. "I think I mentioned he spent some time in juvie. It was for the same break-in. Two others, John Pendley and Jeff Habersham went too. The only one who had his time reduced was Copeland."

"Why?" Levy asked, her brow furrowing. "What made him special?"

"He was the mayor's son," Bishop said.

The dots began to draw a picture in my mind.

She dipped her chin slightly, pointed her finger at him, and said, "Gotcha."

"If I remember correctly, he was going out with Turner when they broke into that house."

"Going out?" Michels shook his head. "The way y'all spoke back then is sad."

"LOL," I said with a big dose of snark. "Says the generation that speaks in acronyms."

"STHU," he said, smirking. "That's the best I could come up with under pressure."

I laughed. "That's pathetic."

We all stared at Bishop. "What?" he asked. "You think I don't know what it means? Shut the hell up. I'm not that old." He sipped his cold coffee and grimaced slightly at the taste again. "She went missing a few years later. I think they had broken up, but I can't say for sure if they were officially together before juvie."

"Do you know anyone else she dated?" I asked.

He shook his head. "I didn't pay much attention to her."

"I wonder why no one questioned Copeland after her disappearance?" Levy asked, her voice filled with frustration. "He's not even mentioned in the notes."

"Small-town politics were intense. You didn't question the mayor's family about anything, and I don't think they were together when she disappeared."

"You still don't question the mayor's family," Michels added.

"I'm an example of that," Bishop said.

He'd had a run in with the mayor's son long before the current mayor took office. Gave the kid a well-deserved DUI, and the mayor hadn't forgotten about it.

"Then how did he get busted for the break-in?" I asked, my curiosity piqued.

"Because the owner came home while they were in the house. He tackled Copeland. The rest ran, but Copeland gave them up. At least that was the rumor."

"And Turner still dated him?" Levy asked, disbelief coloring her tone. "Not at all dysfunctional."

"She watched her father abuse her mother, and he abused her too, both sexually and physically. She probably saw Copeland as leveling up."

"He seems to have turned out okay," Michels said, his tone light and almost cheery. "He's built half of Hamby and Alpharetta."

"And Cumming," Levy added.

"Construction's done well for him," Bishop said, a note of resignation in his voice. "Whether he deserves it or not. Regardless, I think it's worth talking to him. See what he remembers."

"What about the house they robbed? Who was the owner?"

"Ben Pyott. He died about two years after the break-in. Got drunk and plowed into a telephone pole. Died instantly."

"Ouch," Michels said, wincing.

"Think it could be related?" Levy asked, her detective instincts kicking in.

"No," Bishop shrugged. "Don't see how he's connected."

"We should check it out anyway," Levy suggested.

"We'll do so if necessary," I said. "But let's stay focused on what we've got now."

"It sounds like Turner and our recent victim have some things in common," Levy said, her voice taking on a determined edge. She opened a file and slid it into the middle of the table, the action purposeful. "Berman spent time in juvie in high school. Based on what I can tell, she was either new to the drug game or hadn't been caught yet. Initially, she went into drug counseling , but that didn't work, so the judge dropped her in juvie for six months."

"Probably trying to scare her straight," Michels said, leaning back in his chair, arms crossed over his chest.

"I'm not sure that works in juvie," I said, my tone skeptical. "But stick her in a real prison for a few days, and she might have come around."

"That's harsh," Bishop said, his eyebrows raised in mild surprise.

I was shocked I could still surprise him after so many years as his partner. I held out my palms. "I think that's what a kid on the wrong path needs."

"It might have been worth a shot," Levy said, her voice contemplative. "Looks like she got worse after juvie. Several arrests for soliciting, public intoxication, and theft. But there's nothing to connect her to Caroline Turner."

"I wouldn't think there would be," Bishop said, his expression thoughtful. "Other than the fact that one is buried on top of the other."

"It's not a coincidence," Michels said, conviction in his voice. "The trick is finding out why they're together."

"It could be something as simple as their appearance," I said. "Our killer might hate blonds, but it could be anything."

He flicked his head toward me. "Power, love, money. Pick one, right?"

"Right," I said.

"Okay," Bishop said, standing up. "You two work the Berman murder for now, and we'll work Turner's. We'll stay in contact and get Bubba and Nikki looking for anything that could remotely connect the two."

"Ah, man," Michels said, disappointment evident in his voice. "I was hoping to take a little trip to your glory days."

"There wasn't much glory back then," Bishop said, a hint of sadness in his tone. "I played football, studied, and worked on a few farms. That's about it."

"That blows," Michels said, laughing.

Levy moved the conversation forward before Michels could share his own walk down memory lane. "We'll talk with Berman's family. See if we can get any friends' names, figure out who we can talk to next."

They both stood. "We're on it."

Bishop and I decided to hit up Steve Copeland. He was the most convenient place to start. He was already connected to Caroline Turner, and if we could link him to Jennifer Berman, we'd be one step closer to our killer.

Alpharetta's downtown had done a full one-eighty. The streets that used to be a parade of worn-out shops were transformed thanks to the economic boom from a few years back. The old guard buildings, which had their own rustic charm, were bulldozed to make way for shiny new multi-use structures. Retail and eateries on the ground floor, a mix of offices, apartments, and condos stacked above—a vertical jigsaw puzzle of modern living. I hadn't seen so many rooftop bars crowded together since my last trip to Nashville.

Even in the broad daylight of early afternoon, the place was abuzz. The whole setup was like a magnet for foot traffic. They'd made the area a walker's paradise, and the locals from the condos just behind Main Street and other visitors were all in on it. They'd amble to the microbreweries, hit the coffee shops, or browse the stores. The vibe was lively, a far cry from the sleepy downtown I remembered when I'd first moved to Hamby.

"Downtown's really come alive in the past few years," I remarked, watching people meander down the sidewalks. "And it looks like Copeland Construction's behind a lot of it."

Bishop nodded, his eyes on the road. "Copeland's got his hand in almost every new project. Says a lot about the influence he wields in this town."

The growth was evident everywhere. We passed Lapeer, a fine dining spot known for its exquisite steaks and seafood. Just down the street was Smokejack, a mainstay of historic downtown Alpharetta, famous for its outstanding barbecue and particularly its chicken wings. "I could go for wings. Kyle and I went there a few weeks ago. To die for."

"They're fantastic," Bishop said. "We all should go once this case is resolved."

I was thinking about lunch, but that was fine, too. At some point, I'd have to try some of the other places. "This area makes me hungry. Every time I come here, there's something new," I said, peering out at the newest additions to the small skyline. "Copeland's not struggling. He'll probably hate us for snooping around his past."

"Not our problem," he said.

"Nope. I consider it a joy."

"Of course, you do."

Passing a Mexican place, I suddenly wanted tacos. "I'm starving."

"What else is new?" he asked, smiling.

"It's amazing how food can bring a place to life," I mused.

"True," Bishop agreed. "And a killer can walk around without anyone knowing."

"Thanks for ruining my appetite."

"I'm always here to help."

We finally pulled up in front of a massive building that bore the logo of Copeland Construction. It was an imposing structure, its modern design meant to show off the company's success and influence.

Bishop parked his department vehicle. "Let's see what we can find out," he said. "Maybe Copeland knows something we don't."

"One can hope."

7

"He's in a meeting," the receptionist said. "His schedule is booked solid today, but I can have his assistant contact you for an appointment."

I dug my badge from my jacket pocket. "It's police business. Would you let him know we're here, please?"

She blinked. "Oh, yes." She pivoted her chair to the left and hurried through the glass door.

Bishop gently tapped my shoulder with his. "Nice move. He'll be running like a scalded dog to talk to us now."

I raised my eyebrow. "A what now?"

He rolled his eyes, his frustration with my lack of knowledge regarding catchy phrases always annoyed him. "It's a Southernism."

"Do southerners normally scald their dogs?"

"Why do I even try with you?"

"Try what? To convert me to being a southerner?" I mimicked Savannah. "Honey, I'm a Chicago girl through and through. Don't try to fix what ain't broken."

A grin forced its way onto his lips even though I knew he didn't want it to.

The receptionist returned. "He'll see you now."

We followed her through the glass door and down a long, bright white hall lined with glass office doors, to the end, where two more large, glass doors opened to a stately office and the man of the hour, leaning against the door frame.

Copeland was a sight, no two ways about it. The guy towered over six feet, shoulders broad like the horizon, and arms that looked like they could bench press a small car. His waist, though, was trim, even more proof of some serious gym hours. Obviously, the man was no stranger to a workout routine.

His head was shaved clean, probably a tactical move to outmaneuver the faint horseshoe pattern of hair trying to stake its claim. But honestly, it worked for him. The bald look gave him a certain edge, a rugged charm. I've never been one to fuss over a receding hairline. Tommy had once told me he'd rather go full Vin Diesel than play the losing game with his hair. It was a pride thing for some guys. Copeland, though, he wore it like a badge of honor, part of his imposing, yet appealing package.

"Detectives," he said, "please, have a seat." He motioned for us to sit at a small, round table near his wall-length window. The view was from the back side of the building, a small park in the middle of a grouping of condos. I suspected he planned it that way. "What can I do for you today? I hope none of my project managers have created an issue or that any of my projects have caused a ruckus in Hamby."

"Not to our knowledge," Bishop said. "Mr. Copeland, I know we've met, but it's been a while. My name is—"

Copeland cut him off. "Rob Bishop." He smiled at me. "And you're Rachel Ryder. I'd be a fool not to recognize the two most prominent detectives in Fulton County."

I threw up a little in my mouth. Could he suck up any more than that? Geez.

"Thank you," Bishop said. "This should be on the news soon, but we ask that you keep it quiet until then."

No need, I thought. It had already hit the internet. That piqued Copeland's interest. He angled his head to the side and said, "Of course. This area, Hamby in particular as that's the part of town I grew up in, is very dear to me. If there is anything I can do to help with any recent investigation, I'm happy to. I have to say though, I can't think of anything I might have knowledge of." He hitched his thumb toward his desk, his gaze drifting momentarily to a photo on it. "I spend a lot of time behind that thing or in meetings."

"This isn't just a current investigation," I said. "We've discovered the remains of someone who went missing in 1984." I paused for effect, just because I could, and because the guy's personality in general rubbed me the wrong way. "Caroline Turner." I watched him closely, looking for any flicker of recognition or guilt.

"Caroline Turner?" He blinked, his facade momentarily slipping. "Caroline Turner." He leaned back in his chair and stared at the door behind us, his face losing some of its color. "I haven't heard that name in years."

"Well, you're likely to once word gets out about finding her remains," I said. "It's already on the internet."

He furrowed his brow. "I thought she ran away?"

"It would appear not," I said. "Though we can't be certain of her situation. Unfortunately, at that time, the police wrote her off as a runaway due to her life situation. Which is what we're here about."

"Her life situation? Gosh," he said, acting like he'd have to dig into the bowels of his mind to figure out what I was talking about. "Oh, you mean the unfortunate incident she dragged me and my friends into that caused most of the town to lose their minds?"

Did he seriously just throw a decades-past abuse victim, long since deceased, straight under the bus? Well, congratulations to him for earning yet another illustrious tick on my *Certified A-hole* tally chart. His good looks meant nothing. "You're saying it was Caroline Turner's idea to break into Ben Pyott's home?"

He sighed as if he felt bad for telling us, but I didn't believe that. "Yes, though I hate to speak ill of the dead. She claimed Mr. Pyott had money in an unlocked safe, and she wanted to get her hands on it. She asked us to participate. I did so under, shall we say, duress, but I also won't deny I wasn't the most ethical teenager back then."

"Did you find the money?" I asked.

"We did not. We weren't there long enough, and based on what my father told me later, Mr. Pyott didn't have a safe in the first place. Poor Caroline. She had a terrible addiction, and looking back, I think her brain was playing tricks on her."

"Perhaps she was trying to escape the physical and sexual abuse inflicted on her by her father," I said rather curtly. "Most people who suffer traumatic events find ways to deal with their emotions, and that's often escaping through drugs." I suspected he already knew that, but so, what? I knew I didn't like the pompous ass, and I wanted him to know it as well.

His casual expression flicked ever so slightly to annoyance, but he caught it quickly. Just not quick enough for me not to notice. "I never knew any of that," he said.

He was lying. Bishop didn't run in their circle, and according to him, it was fairly common knowledge. He knew.

"Didn't you date Miss Turner?" Bishop asked.

"Briefly, yes. It was a mistake, and I realized that quickly."

"Was this before or after juvie?" I asked.

He narrowed his eyes at me and then sighed. He must have thought his sighs made him look empathic, but it was quite the opposite. "Both, but I don't count the time in detention since we weren't able to see each other, and after my release we only dated until I could tell her it was over." After a moment's pause, he added. "As I said, she was a troubled young girl. We came from different worlds, and though I did like her in the beginning, I learned she wasn't a positive influence in my life."

I glanced at Bishop. Was he believing anything the guy said?

"Mr. Copeland," he said. "Were you two dating again when she went missing?"

Nice move. Asking the same question in multiple ways was a sure-fire way to get the truth out of someone, especially a liar.

He rubbed his chin. "As I said, we broke up shortly after getting out of juvie. We reunited a few times, but it was more of a convenience than anything else." He cleared his throat. "By the time she disappeared, we'd been long over, though, and I don't want to sound pompous—"

Too late.

"But she'd tried multiple times to get back together over the time between juvie and her disappearance. I was young, and I hate to say it, but when she disappeared, I was relieved. I never even considered something may have happened to her. I just assumed she ran away because she'd been upset at me for continually turning her away. Now, obviously, I know otherwise."

She'd gone missing at twenty-two. They'd broken up long before that, yet he thought she harbored feelings for him the whole time? Not egotistical at all. "How old were you when you entered juvie?" I asked.

"I was a senior, so seventeen."

"And Caroline?" Bishop asked.

"I think she was fifteen, maybe sixteen?" He scratched his chin. "I can't remember. I think she was two years younger than me, maybe?"

"I believe only one," Bishop said. He knew, but Copeland acted like he didn't know much about his ex-girlfriend.

"Had she mentioned anything about anyone in her life?" Bishop asked. "People bullying her? Maybe problems with an employee at work?"

He chuckled. "Caroline couldn't keep a job, but no, I don't recall her mentioning anything about bullying. Of course, this was the 80s, and back then, the boys liked to brag about things concerning girls, if you will. There was talk, but I can't say whether any of it was true, or if it bothered her. Our relationship was more casual than deep conversations or telling secrets."

"Meaning you liked to get high together, and what? Have sex?" I asked.

He grimaced. "Something like that." He scanned his large office. "Obviously, my time in the juvenile justice system straightened me up. After high school, I got a job in construction, and here I am today."

"Can you recall any of Miss Turner's friends?" Bishop asked.

He looked up at the ceiling. "I don't think by definition she had many friends, at least not close ones, but I do recall her friend running around the festival looking for her the night she went missing. Remember, this was a few years after high school, so I can't say who she hung around with outside of the festival really." He tapped his pencil on the table. "I went out with her a few times, Chrissy something or another. I can't remember her last name." A smile stretched across his face. "I ran into her a few weeks ago. She appears to be doing well, and I have to say, based on our experience together, I was surprised. She's married now, but strangely, I can't remember her married name either."

I jotted it down. "Anyone else?"

"I think John Pendley and Jeff Habersham are still around. I don't run in their circles, but I think they got their acts together as well."

"We're planning to look into them," Bishop said.

"Mr. Copeland, can you think of anyone who might have had cause to abduct and murder Miss Turner, or know of any situation she may have been involved in that lead to her death?"

His eyes pivoted from side to side, and then he shook his head. "Not that I can recall. It was almost forty years ago, and like I said, my relationship with Caroline was casual, and I'll be honest, I've put a lot of that behind me. It's not who I am anymore."

I dropped my bomb. "What's your relationship to Jennifer Berman?"

He blinked. "I'm not familiar with that name."

"Kevin and Jeannette Berman?" I asked. "Maybe you did some work for them in the past?"

"I only deal in commercial real estate, Detective." He licked his lips. "Who are these people, and why are you asking me about them?"

"Jennifer Berman is another missing girl whose remains we recently found, and Jeannette and Kevin are her parents."

He steeled his eyes at me. "Are you implying I have something to do with these murders?"

Bishop replied. "We're investigating, and that requires learning if people involved with one victim knew the other."

"I've never heard of a Jennifer Berman," he said.

Bishop gave me his *don't push it* look, so I zipped my lips.

We thanked Copeland for his time. He said he would help in any way possible, and then we left.

Outside, I said, "That guy's lying like a dog on a rug."

Bishop stared at me, a hint of a smile tugging at the corner of his mouth as he opened his vehicle's door. "You used that for me, didn't you?"

"Absolutely." I let out a dry chuckle. "But I meant it."

"You think he's our mouse?"

"It's too soon to tell," I said.

"What about Jennifer Berman? Think he knows her?"

He hadn't given any signs that he did, but that could have been rehearsed. "I think we need to keep our eye on him."

"Ditto," he said.

As we drove past the taco place, I rolled down the window, half-expecting the aroma of food to waft in, but all I smelled was exhaust fumes from the busy street. My appetite vanished.

Bishop's eyes were fixed on the road, but I could tell his mind was elsewhere. "He and I don't see things the same. I think he's forgotten I went to school with him."

I raised my eyebrows. "What do you see differently?"

Bishop's grip tightened on the steering wheel, his jaw set in a firm line. "I agree with you. I think he's lying about his relationship with Caroline. There's something off. He knew more than he let on, especially about her home life. How could he not? It was something everyone talked about at the time. And the break-in at Pyott's? It's too convenient that he blames a dead girl who can't defend herself."

I nodded. "And his reaction when we mentioned her name. He was too composed at first, but there were micro-expressions of fear." I watched a couple walk into a small café. "That ex he mentioned? Chrissy? She might give us more insight into Caroline's life back then."

"Along with John Pendley and Jeff Habersham," Bishop added. "They were part of his circle."

We drove in silence for a few moments, each lost in thought.

"You know," I finally said, "there's one more thing bothering me."

"What's that?"

"The way he talked about his juvenile record and how he's a changed man. It felt rehearsed, like he's used it too many times as a shield."

Bishop nodded. "Given his past, he might have needed to. Seems like he's a key piece in this puzzle, whether he likes it or not."

"Or he's the missing piece," I said. "Either way, we're going to find out."

8

Jimmy stood in front of the conference table in the investigation room. "Give me something good. The mayor's on my ass, and I don't want to have to bring back a public relations person." He dropped his head and shook it. "Someone already let the cat out of the bag. It's all over the internet and the media is already breathing down my neck."

"It's been up since this morning," I said. "Receptionist at Stu's told us."

"Damn internet will be the death of humanity," he said under his breath.

"It's already working hard on that," Michels said.

"Please don't get another PR person," I begged. He'd tried that a while back, and though she wasn't too bad overall, none of us liked the concept, and after several debates over a beer or many, he'd acquiesced to our request to be our own public relations team.

"You two," he pointed to Levy and Michels, "are handling the Jennifer Berman investigation, correct?"

"For the time being," Levy said. "We interviewed her parents. They don't know a thing about her recent life. They disconnected from her six years ago, as I think we all know, but they did give us some names of friends from her life before drugs, and we've got her juvie officer's name, so we're going to talk to her."

"We have that for Caroline Turner as well, though the woman is sixty-seven and retired," Bishop said.

"What else did you find out about Turner?" Jimmy asked.

"That Steve Copeland is a piece of work," I blurted out.

"You talked to him?" he asked.

Bishop shot me his, *I'll handle this* look. "We did. He acknowledged he and Turner were in a relationship, but he claimed it was over before he ended it, and long before she went missing. He was surprised to hear we've found her remains. Claimed he believed she'd run away."

"Claimed being the operative word," I interjected while Bishop took a breath.

"He gave us a few names of friends, but he said something that we found interesting."

"Which is?" Jimmy asked.

"He said the break-in was her idea. That Ben Pyott was rumored to have an unlocked safe full of cash. I don't recall hearing that, so I can't say if it's true."

Bubba said, "I'll pull the case files. I'm sure there's something in them."

"Put a pin in that for now," Jimmy said. "If we need it, we know where to look."

"Yes, sir."

"Any obvious connection to Jennifer Berman?" Jimmy asked us.

"He says he's never heard of her," I said.

"What about his father?" Levy asked. "The former mayor?"

"Deceased," Bishop said. "Last year. Cancer."

"Really?" I asked. "He was going to be my next interview."

"Don't you read the paper?" Michels asked. "He was a Hamby mayor. Got a front page write up."

"I try to stay clear of all things political," I said.

"Not a bad idea," Levy said.

"Especially in this town," I added. "I thought Chicago was bad, but man, small town politics are brutal."

"Which is why I need something for the mayor. He feels this investigation is a personal affront to his position since there's the potential of a former mayor's son, not to mention a prominent figure in the community, under our radar."

"It's not about the mayor," I said. I'd wanted to say it internally, but my big mouth decided otherwise.

Jimmy raised his eyebrows as if he'd expected something like that from me. Because he did. "I'll prepare a statement for the media."

"Can you keep Copeland out of it for now?" Bishop asked. "We don't want him thinking he's on our radar." He narrowed his eyes at me when he said that.

"What?" I asked with feigned innocence. "I behaved."

His eye roll and head shake said otherwise.

"We need to speak to the juvie officer today," Levy said. "Maybe we can get something on Turner from their records?"

"Not without holding a gun to their heads," Michels said. "All that's sealed. We'll need a warrant."

Levy tipped her head back and groaned. "Thanks for the education, professor." She turned to me. "See what I have to deal with all day?"

I smiled. "Could be worse."

"How?"

"He could be Rachel," Bishop said.

My jaw dropped. "Hey, now."

Bishop chuckled.

"I'll call Judge Nowak," I said. "How about Levy and I handle juvie," I said to Bishop, "and you and Michels start talking to people who might have known the victims?"

"Sounds good. I'm sure I can recall a name or two from back in the day."

"I'm in," Michels said. "I could stand to be around some testosterone for a while.

Bubba laughed.

Michel's face reddened. "I didn't mean I'm lacking—"

"Yada, yada, yada," I said as I left the investigation room with Levy on my tail. Once out of ear shot, I said, "You give him a lot of grief."

"I know. I should probably lighten up, but he keeps throwing me softballs, and my mouth responds before my brain has a chance to stop it."

I knew that issue all too well. "All it says to me is you two genuinely care for each other."

"He's my partner," she said walking through the door to the pit where all the department's officers worked. "He knows more about me than my friends. Of course, I care for him. I just don't want him to know."

I laughed. "You must not have many friends."

"Ouch."

"Kidding, but I'm telling him what you said."

"Dear God, please don't. His ego's already inflated because he snagged Ashley. The boy got lucky with that one."

"Damn straight he did."

"I think it's great you've got such a good relationship with Judge Nowak," Levy said.

I need an in like that."

"I know how to work a sports fan."

She laughed. "Among other things."

"He's a good man. I'm sure you could establish a relationship with him too, but you'd have to denounce your loyalty to all teams associated with Pennsylvania."

"For the Cubs?" She blanched. "Never going to happen."

"Then you're out of luck."

She gazed at the building ahead. "I never liked these places," Levy said as we pulled into the restricted lot of the Fulton County Juvenile Justice Department. Though part of the county court system, they'd kept it separate due to the nature of the kids, and the privacy their cases legally required.

"They're imperfect ways to reform, but they're the best we have."

She resigned herself to that truth with a sigh. "I wanted to help kids, but the emotional drain would have exhausted me."

"Doesn't your job emotionally drain you now?"

"Yes, but I was young and naïve then. I thought I could change the world, and then I saw all those kids and what they went through, and I just couldn't face it. So, instead, I decided to change the world by taking down the people who set their lives on those paths."

"How's that working out for you?" I asked as we walked toward the building.

"I'm older, but apparently, still naïve."

I laughed. "Right there with you."

"We can only do what we can do," she said.

"And sometimes it's enough," I added.

The juvenile center loomed over us like a big, grumpy grandpa, all concrete and glass, trying hard to look tough with its barred windows and that fence circling it like a silver necklace on a bouncer. It was supposed to be about hope and fresh starts, but standing there, it felt more like it was flipping everyone who entered the bird.

It had rained on the drive, and it made the dirty sidewalks look worse. Outside, the place had a lingering scent of 'you're not in Kansas anymore, Toto.' It was like a throwback to Chicago, where Mother Nature and concrete were in a boxing match, and Mother Nature wasn't winning the heavyweight title. Fulton County had ballooned up faster than a kid with a pack of bubble gum, trying to keep up with the crowd of people moving in.

The heavy glass doors moaned as we pushed them open. Inside, the place was buzzing with the kind of sounds no one wanted to hear—stern voices, teenage cries, and the uneasy shuffle of teenagers who looked like they'd rather be anywhere but there holding onto their parents like life rafts.

I glanced up at the fluorescent lights that threw down light that made everything look like a hospital waiting room. The place bled teenaged angst.

"Looks like they hired the same decorator as Alcatraz," Levy quipped, her eyes taking in the decor.

I snorted. "Yeah, if Alcatraz was into minimalist chic and the scent of despair."

She grinned. "Maybe they'll start a new trend. Bureaucratic brutalism meets Eau de Desperation."

I laughed. "Catchy. They should put that on the brochures."

"God," Levy said, her tone turning serious. Her gaze lingering on the young faces milling around the juvenile court. She leaned against a wall, a contemplative look on her face. "Look at them. Maybe I made the wrong career choice after all? I should have stayed in the juvie system."

"You're helping them still," I reassured her, offering a small, encouraging smile.

I saw the gatekeeper before we met him. "Look at this guy," I said. "He looks rode hard and put away wet."

"That's how I'd look, and that's part of the reason I chose police work instead."

I turned and gave her a onceover. "It worked," I said, lightening the heaviness I felt coming off her. "You chose well."

We met the gatekeeper at the security desk, badges in hand like a couple of secret agents. Upon closer inspection, he was middle-aged, with a mustache groomed to perfection, giving off a vibe that said, 'I've seen it all, and then some, so don't mess with me'. He peered at our badges, his eyes playing hide-and-seek behind his glasses, then gave us the nod toward the metal detector.

"Empty your pockets, please. One at a time," he droned, sounding like he'd rather be watching paint dry. He peeked up from his clipboard. "Any weapons?" The question was routine.

"No, sir," I replied, patting my jacket like I was burping a baby. "Our weapons are napping in the car. This is a no-toy zone."

When it didn't even garner a smile, we strolled through the metal detector.

"Nice guy," Levy said.

"The best."

Badges back in hand and visitor stickers slapped on our jackets like gold stars in kindergarten, we stepped into a different world. The sound of keyboards tap-dancing intermingled with hushed chit-chat in front of and behind closed doors filled the air and were occasionally spiced up by the sound of a file folder clapping shut or a drawer slamming shut.

But the real soundtrack? Kids. Their gripes and groans bounced off the walls and echoed throughout the place.

Levy and I walked down a hallway that looked like a museum of bulletin boards—legal stuff, 'don't do drugs' posters, and more motivational quotes than a self-help book. The carpet, which probably started life as a nice, respectable blue, had walked itself into a tired gray.

"Feels like high school with more rules and less fun," Levy murmured, eyeing a particularly enthusiastic poster about choices.

I snickered. "Yeah, but high school already had a dress code like ankle monitors and despair."

She laughed. "Right. I always wanted to go to a school where 'don't get arrested' was the top lesson of the day."

"You came from Philly. Wasn't that a given?"

"In an all-girls Catholic school? Hell, no."

"Got it. The nuns put the fear of God and algebra in me, too."

"I keep imaging Caroline and Jennifer in this place. They must have been so scared. How awful." Levy said softly. She tucked a strand of hair behind her ear. It was a small gesture, but it betrayed her concern. Levy had a heart bigger than most, and though she worked hard to hide it, she couldn't always.

Around a corner was a set of double doors with frosted glass windows partially obscuring the activity inside. The sign next to it read *Juvenile Correctional Services*. Pushing the door open, we prepared to present our warrant.

Things got real in there. The space existed somewhere between a school and a detention center. The walls were decorated with artwork—some pieces vibrant and hopeful, others dark and troubled, all crafted by the young inhabitants of the juvenile system. The room was segmented into cubicles and small offices, each a nucleus of activity with correctional officers and social workers engaging with their young charges.

An older, worn looking woman greeted us and examined our visitor tags. "Who're you here for?"

"Officer Daniels," Levy said.

"Got your ID?" She was a chatty one, for sure.

Though we didn't need to, we showed her our badges.

"Over there," she said. She pointed to the far side of the room at a middle-aged woman wearing a professional looking business suit standing in front of a coffee station I assumed had horrible coffee like ours. Her stern demeanor was softened by the genuine concern in her eyes. When she greeted us, her handshake was solid and reassuring.

Daniels' stern demeanor softened slightly as she extended a hand in greeting. "Detectives Ryder and Levy, thank you for coming. Please, follow me to my office," she said, guiding us through a labyrinth of desks and industrious professionals.

We passed a group of teenagers on the way. Their conversations paused, their eyes flicking toward us with something close to fear or suspicion over what I assumed was what our badges represented.

Stepping into Officer Daniels' office was like walking into a masterclass on 'How to Be Tidy 101.' The place was so neat and organized it made me respect her on the spot—and yeah, okay, I felt a little envious too. I was all for keeping things in order, always trying to up my organization game, but Daniels was next level.

Her desk was a picture of precision, not a paper out of place. I figured with the whirlwind that must be her job, being a neat-freak nirvana was her way of balancing the scales. Like me, chaos was probably her constant companion, and her shrine to orderliness was her way of taming the beast.

Levy leaned in, whispering, "Think she'd notice if I straightened that pen just a smidge?"

I elbowed her gently. "Don't you dare. That pen is probably aligned with the magnetic poles or something."

She chuckled softly, eyeing the room with awe.

"Bet she alphabetizes her cereal boxes," I muttered under my breath.

Levy's grin widened. "And color-codes her socks."

We shared a quiet laugh, appreciating the zen-like state of Officer Daniels' domain, where chaos came to die, and organization reigned supreme.

Officer Daniels, sitting straight-backed behind her desk, gestured toward the chairs across from her. "Please, have a seat." She busied herself briefly with some papers, aligning them with a precision that reflected her orderly nature, before her eyes lifted to meet ours with an attentive gaze.

I handed her the two warrants. She took them with a practiced hand, her eyes scanning the documents thoroughly, then handed them back with a nod of acknowledgment. "Thank you for calling in advance. I was able to pull files on Caroline Turner, but as I'm sure you know, her counselor has retired."

Levy, sitting up a bit straighter, said, "Yes, ma'am."

Officer Daniels' expression softened. A touch of sadness filled her eyes. "I was sad to hear about Jen. She worked so hard to clean up her act. I hate how things ended so tragically for her."

Levy nodded solemnly. "Us as well," she said. She leaned forward and spoke with a tone that sounded earnest. "Before we start, we'd like to remind you that this is an ongoing investigation, one we have yet to share details of with the press, and we ask that you respect that."

"Of course," she responded, her face setting into a mask of professionalism. "In my line of work, privacy is the name of the game. I can tell you what I know about Jen and her situation based on facts. If you want opinions, I'll give those as well, but only if you ask."

I nodded, crossing my legs and folding my hands in my lap, mirroring her composed posture. "Understood. Can you tell us how she was initially brought into the system?"

Officer Daniels chair creaked slightly as she leaned back. Her eyes seemed to look past us, focusing on a distant memory. "As I'm sure you know, Jen came from a wealthy family. If I've learned anything in this position, it's that money doesn't equate to love or attention, and Jen was deprived of both." She paused, taking a deep breath. "Her parents had separated multiple times, and, unfortunately, that took its toll on her mother, who suffers from a drinking problem." She exhaled slowly. "I do have additional opinions on that if you'd like them."

"Please share," Levy said. She opened her notebook, her pen hovering above the page in readiness.

Officer Daniels continued, "I suspect there is a drug addiction as well, albeit a well-hidden one. Mr. Berman is a hard worker, and he had been gone for most of Jen's childhood. Traveling overseas, spending months at a time in places in opposite time zones. Maintaining his familial relationships must have been complicated, and Mrs. Berman once told me it was nearly impossible to be both a mother and a father to Jen." She paused, a look of contemplation crossing her face. "She said she spent much of her time feeling like a failure."

Levy nodded as she scribbled notes. "Which caused her to distance herself from her child," she suggested.

Officer Daniels inclined her head in agreement. "I assume, yes. Jen began changing in eighth grade. She'd gone from a good student in middle school, a B average, to struggling as a freshman. She dropped out of clubs and began associating herself with the wrong kids."

"Did she ever say why?" I asked, leaning in slightly, my interest piqued by the unfolding story.

"She said it was hard to be everything to everyone, in her own words of course, so she just decided to stop trying." She opened a binder and read from the thickly bound pages. "'Why should I try to be something for them when they don't pay attention? I just want to be me, and this is who I am.' She was referring to her parents, though she also mentioned her former best friends."

"And her first brush with the law?" I asked.

Officer Daniels leaned forward, her elbows resting on the desk and her fingers interlaced. "There were only two, one a failure to meet with me. The first was a theft issue with a group of teens at the old bowling alley arcade in Roswell. The one that used to be at the intersection of Highway Nine and Holcomb Bridge Road."

"We know that one," Levy interjected, her tone confident despite the fact that she didn't actually know; the place had shut down just six months after I'd moved to town, and quite a while before she'd arrived.

Daniels nodded, a faint line of disapproval creasing her forehead. "It had become a place for troublemakers," she remarked. "And unfortunately, Jen was involved in attempting to steal from the cash registers in the arcade section." She paused, her eyes briefly flickering with a touch of sadness. "The judge gave her probation, but said if she came back to his court, or didn't show up for her probation meetings, he'd place her in detention."

"How long was it until she came back?" I asked, my pen moving in tandem with Levy's, capturing every detail.

"Three months." Daniels sighed, looking down at her hands before meeting our gaze again. "We met once a week after the judge's warning, usually here at the office for the first two months, but she missed three of the four appointments in the last month." Her eyes clouded. "When she was arrested again, she said she couldn't get here, that her mother was too stoned to drive." Shaking her head, she continued, "Of course, I called the house multiple times, and their cell phones, but no one ever answered or returned my calls. I had to contact the judge when she didn't show up for the last appointment, and she was arrested." She looked away briefly, her gaze distant as she recalled the events.

Turning back to us, her face was etched with a deep solemnity. "She was so angry. She refused to hold herself accountable for any of it." Daniels paused, her voice dropping a note. "She'd changed so much in that short time. When tested, we found meth in her system." She took a slow, deliberate breath. "It was so sad. That, and the second arrest, is what got her into the system."

Officer Daniels went on to detail out the rest of her information on Jen Berman, and though she couldn't provide us with a list of kids she associated with during her time at juvie, we knew most would be in the file. She did suggest we talk with her former best friend, Rebecca Hahn, who would likely be able to provide them.

She gave less detail about Caroline Turner, saying she saw nothing of substance in either file to connect the women, but she did give us copies of each binder based on the requirements of the warrant. "Remember, Detectives, these kids are more than just cases. They're lives in the making. Sometimes, what they need most is someone to believe in their potential for change, and unfortunately, neither Caroline Turner nor Jen Berman had people like that in their lives."

Her words lingered with us as Levy and I exited the juvenile court building. We walked in silence for a few moments, digesting the gravity of what we had just heard.

"That's depressing," Levy finally said, exhaling deeply as we stepped outside.

"Makes me appreciate my own screwed up family," I said.

"Amen."

9

Levy and I sat in the cozy living room of Cheryl Jacobs, the retired juvenile officer who handled Caroline Turner's cases. At sixty-seven, Cheryl's eyes looked more resigned than tired, but it could have been because she didn't want to talk about Caroline.

"Thank you for agreeing to speak with us, Ms. Jacobs," I began as we settled into the comfortable, slightly worn sofa.

Cheryl nodded, her brows furrowed. "When I heard it was about Caroline Turner, I knew I had to help. Such a tragic story. I remember it well, even after all these years."

Levy handed over a photo of Caroline from the file. Cheryl took it gently, her fingers trembling slightly as if the weight of memories was tangible. "Poor girl," she murmured. She examined the photo closely, a faint frown creasing her forehead. "It's been so long. May I ask how she was found?"

"Unfortunately, we can't provide the details of our investigation at this time," Levy said, her tone apologetic as she shook her head slightly to emphasize the restriction.

"But it was so long ago. You're certain it's her?"

"We are," I said.

"We understand this is difficult," Levy said gently. "Anything you can tell us about Caroline and her situation could be crucial to finding her killer."

Cheryl leaned back in her reclining chair as a heavy sigh escaped her lips. Her gaze drifted to a corner of the room. "Caroline's story was a tough one from the start. Her family was so troubled. Do you know anything about them?"

"A little," I said, sipping the cup of delicious coffee she'd offered when we arrived. "But please talk as if we know nothing."

She nodded. "Of course. She was a damaged, damaged child. When she came into the system, she said she believed her father had another family in South Carolina. She believed he spent more time with them. She eventually discovered this and confronted him. She went downhill from there, and several years later, she went missing."

Levy leaned forward, her tone probing. "Do you think her father was involved?"

Cheryl looked out her window and spoke. "It was long after she and I were involved, but when I heard about her disappearance, I did have my suspicions. The man had a temper, and Caroline was afraid of him. But the police," she paused and glanced at us with unease written on her face, "I understand they didn't dig deeper. They could have come to me like you have. With her background and her family's instability, they wrote her off as a runaway."

"Was she afraid of her father?" I asked.

"She hinted once that she thought he might do something rash if she pushed him, but she was scared for her brother, though she swore she wasn't afraid for herself. She wanted to protect him, and though she never said it, I believe she had a plan if he ever did try something to keep her quiet. When I heard the news, I assumed that plan had backfired."

Levy took notes diligently.

The conversation continued, with Cheryl recounting the complexities of Caroline's life and the system's failures, her hands occasionally gesturing to emphasize a point, her face a canvas of emotions—from sadness to frustration to regret. Her voice, though occasionally trembling with emotion, remained firm. I wasn't sure I could do that in her position.

Cheryl's eyes moistened, her voice breaking slightly as she expressed her wish to have done more. It was evident that the case, even after years, still deeply affected her.

"And Steve Copeland? Can you tell us more about his impact on Caroline?" I asked.

"Oh, Steve Copeland." Cheryl's voice hardened. "I see his signs all over the place." The cords of her neck stiffened. "I don't care what kind of man he is now, I don't like him. Once a bad seed, always a bad seed. Caroline got mixed up with him and a couple of other boys. They broke into a home, but only Steve was caught initially. He gave up the others, and honestly, I know it was the right thing to do, but it still bothered me. He blamed her, and she insisted it wasn't her idea." She stared at her hands twisted together and resting on her lap. "I can't remember their names. I never trusted Steve, not then, not now. And those buildings he constructs these days? I wouldn't set foot in them." Her disdain for Copeland was evident. "If I remember correctly, he claimed Caroline told him about some safe that had thousands of dollars in it, but there was no way she would know that. Yes, her mother cleaned homes, but she never cleaned that man's home. I can't remember his name either. Sorry, that happens as you get older."

She continued, "Caroline was a good kid deep down, just lost and looking for something to hold on to. Her home life was a mess. Her dad's abuse, especially the sexual abuse, it was too much for her, and the neglect outside of that was heartbreaking. She and her little brother suffered a lot."

"She was sexually abused?" I asked.

"Unfortunately, yes. We did get her to a doctor for an exam, and the poor girl was pregnant. She insisted it was Steve Copeland's child, but there was no way to know."

"Did she ever tell him?" I asked.

"I don't know, but she miscarried, and she never came back from that emotionally."

"Did you think it was Steve's?" Levy asked.

"I didn't know who it belonged to, and it wasn't my place to guess, but she was insistent it was. She and Steve came from entirely different worlds, and that poor girl, she loved him. She thought he could be her redemption, but it's my belief he was part of her downfall, or his family's position in society was, that is."

"Did they stay together during her time in juvie?"

"According to her, yes, but there was no way for them to maintain contact. The system didn't allow that, and to the best of my knowledge, it still doesn't. Besides, Sonny Copeland despised her, and he did everything in his power to keep them apart. Once Steve was released from juvie, early, I might add, it wasn't long before they broke up."

"Do you think he was upset about the breakup?"

"According to Caroline, yes. She wholly believed they loved each other." She eyed the binder Levy had set on the coffee table. "If you read through that you'll find love letters he wrote to her while she was in juvie. He gave them to her when she was released. I asked for copies because I felt they might be important for later, but later never came for the poor girl."

I felt a wave of sadness for Caroline, a girl caught in a life far too harsh for someone so young. "And her mother?" I inquired. "How was she?"

"Unstable, always struggling. Between the abuse and poverty, she was barely holding on. Caroline often acted more like the parent in that house, especially since her mother drank so much. I think all that stress on Caroline is what drove her to become the child she was."

Levy and I exchanged a look. It was a story we had seen too often.

"Her disappearance broke my heart. She'd tried to get her life together. We kept in touch after she turned eighteen. She'd been in and out of trouble. Her friends had tried to help, even offering her a place to stay, but most of them weren't much better off than her. Nothing seemed to work, and I don't think she ever truly got over Copeland. The last time I saw her was about six months before she disappeared. She was at an A&W in Roswell, higher than a kite. I tried to help her, but she told me I was part of the reason she'd become what she had. I've never forgotten that. It broke my heart." Her voice trailed off, and she stared out the window, lost in memories. It was clear that even after all these years, the case still haunted her.

After a moment, she turned back to us, her eyes moist. "I just wish I could've done more for her. For all of them. You try to make a difference, but sometimes it feels like you're just a drop in the ocean."

We talked for a while longer, gathering as much information as we could. Cheryl held onto the photo of Caroline a moment longer before handing it back as we stood to leave.

"Find out the truth," she said, her voice firm despite the tears in her eyes. "She deserves that much."

Though both juvenile officers couldn't discuss the legal situations of other youth, the warrant gave us what we needed in the form of Caroline and Jennifer's files. Levy and I each took a victim and created a list of friends and acquaintances in the investigation room.

Levy's fingers tapped rhythmically against the tabletop, her eyes scanning the contents of Jennifer's files. I leaned back in my chair, stretching my neck as I scrawled down the last name in Caroline Turner's case file. "Tina," I said. "That name keeps coming up."

"In a good way or no?" Levy asked.

"Like the two were friends, but I think something happened. Caroline stopped talking about her, and when asked, she said she wouldn't talk about her anymore."

"What's her last name?" she asked.

"Nothing in the file."

"I hate that."

"You and me both."

"What time is it?" Levy asked, her voice raspy. She brushed a strand of hair behind her ear as she waited for my response.

I checked my watch. "Time for food, if that's what you're wondering."

"Good." She leaned and stretched toward the left side of the table and expertly dragged her phone closer with the tip of her pen. "DoorDash?"

"Oh, Mexican's always good," I said, rubbing my chin thoughtfully.

"I'm not getting Mexican if we're ordering for my partner. I'm strong, but not that strong." She scrolled through her phone looking for alternatives.

We opted for Atlanta Bread Company instead. I quickly texted the team and got their orders, then repeated them to Levy as she typed them into the app.

"Okay," I said after she had finished. "How many names do you have?"

"Five," Levy replied, tapping her pen against the table. "But since her file is fairly recent, I think we'll be able to add to that quickly."

"I have four not including Copeland and the two involved in the break in."

At that moment, Bishop, Michels, and Bubba walked in. Bishop, with his usual casual demeanor, pulled out a chair and sat beside me. Michels took a stance by the door, crossing his arms as he listened in. Bubba, meanwhile, hovered near the edge of the table, then sat, his attention darting between each speaker.

"Everything good?" I asked. "No mouse feces?"

He laughed in a *that would be funny in any other situation* way. "No. How'd it go for you all? Any revelations?"

"I realized I don't have the right to complain about my family," I said.

"Ditto," Levy said.

"There's always someone worse off than you," Bishop said. "It's not easy to remember that in the heat of the moment, but it's the truth."

We discussed what we'd learned about Jennifer Berman first.

"Her first arrest was for theft at the bowling and arcade in Roswell," I said. "A few months later, she missed a probation appointment, and was arrested for shoplifting from Target. The amount was high enough the manager called it in. Testing showed meth in her system. Wound up with six months in juvie."

"That's not a lot," Michels said. "Though, I'm sure it's a matter of perspective." He finally took a seat at the table and opened his copy of our small file on the investigations.

"I'll get copies of the victims' files," I said. I hit the speaker phone and asked for help from the administrative team. A minute or two later, a young woman I'd not met tapped on the door. I handed her the files, told her what we needed, and thanked her.

"Right," Levy said as I spoke with the young woman. "The story's like the rest of them. Family problems. Abusive situation, mother suffering from addiction issues. The poor kid ended up parenting her brother, and she must have broken under the pressure of it all. She started changing in eighth grade."

"Want me to check to see if it's the same principal as when she was there?" Bubba asked. "Or if he or she is still in the system?"

"That would be great," I said. "Can you check the high school as well? Maybe we can get the office to give us her schedule to talk with her teachers from then?"

Bubba eyed me curiously, a brow raised and a slight tilt to his head. "Is that in the warrant?"

"So little faith," I kidded. "Of course it is."

He smiled. "I had no doubt. Just confirming. I'll get the list, and I'll do one for Caroline Turner as well. That work?"

"Yes, please," Bishop and I said collectively.

"We were able to talk with Jeff Habersham and John Pendley," Bishop said.

Michels straightened in his seat. "Talk about enlightening. Pendley's not a fan of Habersham or Copeland, but of the two, he really despises Copeland."

"Interesting," Levy said. "He say that or just come off that way?"

"Both," Michels said. "Pendley works for a roofing company. Project manager. Ran into some tough times after his time in juvie. At twenty he ended up doing a year for theft. When he got out, he tried to rekindle his relationship with Copeland, but Copeland told him, as Pendley put it, to f-off."

Bishop adjusted his jacket, then finally stood and removed it while adding, "He said he'd moved on from his loser friends and had a new life. Copeland was already with the construction company, and I suspect his father had put the fear of God in him."

"Pendley tried to get a job with the same construction company," Michels said. "They interviewed him and were fine with his felony. Even hired him, but on his first day they told him it wasn't going to work out before he even left the front office."

"He thinks Copeland or his father had something to do with it," Bishop added.

"The company still around?" Levy asked.

The food arrived, so I passed it out while they spoke.

Michels shook his head. "Got eaten up by another company apparently."

"Did he say anything about Turner?" I asked. I bit into my club sandwich. The soft, sourdough bread melted like butter in my mouth.

"Said she was a trainwreck, and she and Copeland were attached at the hip," Michels said. He unwrapped his sandwich and examined it while continuing. "I asked if he thought that was Turner's doing, but nope. He said Copeland was just as attached to her as she was to him. He claimed they'd talked about getting married. Even joked about being the next Bonnie and Clyde."

"Hmm," I said. "That's not how Copeland explained things." I popped a blueberry into my mouth.

"According to both men," Bishop said, "Copeland didn't get along with his father. His father wanted him to represent the mayoral family like they were the perfect family, and Steve's goal was to do the complete opposite."

"That changed," I said.

"It had to. Copeland was arrested again after juvie, right before he got the job at the construction company, so he was almost twenty."

"So, it had been a while," Levy said. She sipped her iced tea and then chomped on a potato chip.

"Right," Bishop said. He used the plastic utensils to cut up his salad. "But it was kept on the downlow. He'd stolen a car. The chief called his dad the minute they brought him in. Sonny worked out something with the vehicle owner, and Copeland never did time."

"Were Habersham and Pendley with him when it happened?" I asked.

"No. He acted on his own," Michels said.

Levy swallowed a bite of her sandwich and said, "Worked hard to ruin his dad's career, didn't he?"

"Not after that," Michels said. "Something must have happened with that to scare him straight, but we don't know what."

"Was he still with Turner after that?" she asked.

"According to Pendley, they broke up then. He dated someone named Chrissy, but that didn't last long."

"They think he ended up back with Turner, but neither are sure if they were together when she went missing."

"Weren't we told they broke up right after juvie?" I asked.

"Time's relative to everyone when it's memories," Bishop said.

"According to him," I said, "she kept trying to get back together, so, that was what, four years between when they went to juvie and her disappearance? That's a lot of time to consider relative to memory."

"Sounds like he's downplaying their relationship," Levy said. "Or the others are lying."

"I think Copeland's downplaying it. He's in the public eye. He's got a reputation to maintain," Bishop said.

"Right," I said. "Copeland's a bigwig in the area. His past could come back to haunt him." I took a sip of my Diet Coke. "Especially if it's wrapped around a murder investigation."

"And Habersham?" Levy asked. "Does he like Copeland?"

"Doesn't seem to care one way or another," Bishop said. "He straightened up after juvie. Owns a repair shop in Cumming now. Lives there as well. Didn't have anything bad to say about either of them, and has no idea what happened between Copeland and Turner after the break in."

"Sounds like he's moved on," I said.

"Pendley has as well," Bishop said. "He might be bitter about Copeland, but he didn't strike me as the guy who holds a grudge."

"Agree," Michels said. "He appeared genuine when he said he doesn't wish ill upon the guy, but if he died, he wouldn't go to the viewing."

"That's specific," Bubba said.

"Guy like Pendley is pretty specific about things in general," Bishop said.

"What about Berman?" I asked.

"Neither have any known connection," Michels said.

"I've got the lists," Bubba said.

The guy was a technological genius, we all knew it, but the speed at which he worked still shocked me. "Can you compare it to recent employee lists?" I asked.

"Already done." He jabbed a key on his laptop and the room's printer came to life. "I created a list of staff for the middle school and high school for each victim, then I created a list of the current staff within the county. None of the names from Caroline Turner's schools are on the current list, but I didn't think they would be." He glanced up from his laptop. "Wouldn't most of them be dead by now?"

"How old do you think they are?" Bishop asked. His cheeks had reddened a bit. "This wasn't a hundred years ago, Bubba."

Bubba blushed then shook his head. His eyes widened. "I wasn't saying that." He licked his lips. "I meant—"

Bishop chuckled. "Don't sweat it. Us old people can't handle that kind of stress. We might collapse and die." He exhaled when Bubba's eyes enlarged even more. "I'm kidding."

Bubba's expression relaxed. He hopped from his seat, grabbed the papers, and handed them out. Meanwhile, the woman who'd left with the files returned and handed them out to everyone, then placed the two copies I'd given her in the middle of the desk. They would stay with the rest of the investigation files.

"What about the Chrissy person?" I asked. "Did you talk to her?"

"Bubba ran the name Chrissy and the age range through the system and found several possibilities. One of them is from Alpharetta, the part that's now Hamby. She's now Christina Carter, but our records show she lives in Alpharetta still, and she's Bishop's age. She had a previous name of Christina Canfield."

"Canfield," Bishop said. "That's right. She's the one he's talking about. She was in my class. I remember her dating Copeland but don't recall the details."

"We need to talk with Rebecca Hahn as well," I said. "She was a friend of Berman."

The room went silent for a moment. I crumbled my sandwich wrapper into a ball. "Can you check for her address, too?"

He tapped some more. "She goes to North Georgia. It's her last semester. I'll see if I can get an address."

"We'll take them," Bishop said. He directed his comments to Levy and Michels. "You two start looking into the other names on the lists."

"On it," Michels said.

"Got an address for Rebecca," Bubba said.

10

I flicked open the traffic app as I hopped into Bishop's vehicle. "Looks like 400's jammed up by the mall."

"We'll shoot down nine then," Bishop said. "It's usually clear sailing past Cumming."

The sun was playing it cool, just west of dead center in the sky, as we rolled towards Dahlonega and the University of North Georgia.

Located in Dahlonega's rolling hills, the campus was the big shot in town, a mash-up of new-age and old-world structures cozying up to Mother Nature. It was also a military school for the US Army. Word was it had an excellent nursing school which created a picture-perfect future of a military officer and his nurse wife traveling around the world. Not that that was anyone's plan, but it sounded like a good one.

Bishop threaded the needle on those twisty roads, all business, his eyed glued to the road as we talked about the cases.

"But the million-dollar question," I tossed out, eyes drinking in the farmland still safe from guys like Copeland, "Is how. How is Copeland connected? Maybe this Carter chick was green over Turner? She dated the guy. Maybe she wanted him back?"

"It's possible." He cut a glance my way. "You like the guy less and less, don't you?"

"He just gets under my skin," I grumbled, clearing the cobwebs from my throat.

"His talent for stretching the truth, maybe?" Bishop cracked a grin.

"That, and he struts around like he's king of the hill. Must be tough, walking around with that invisible stick up his butt."

He nodded. "I'd imagine it's a pain."

"I might be barking up the wrong tree—"

"Never."

"Cut it out," I shot back, letting his ribbing slide, "but I've got a feeling about Copeland. Not saying he's our main man, but he's mixed up in this mess. Somehow, he's the connection."

"We just have to figure out how."

"I agree," he said as he pulled into the parking lot of Rebecca Hahn's apartment complex.

The complex was a modern, three-story structure with a neat, landscaped front and a gated entrance. Bishop pulled up to the gate and rolled down his window to access the intercom system.

"Here goes," he murmured, pressing the call button on the video screen.

A crackling voice responded almost immediately and a robust woman sitting in an office appeared on the screen. "Front desk, how can I help you?"

He held up his badge, and his voice was steady, professional. "Ma'am, this is Detective Rob Bishop with the Hamby Police Department. I'm with my partner, Detective Ryder. We're here to interview a resident named Rebecca Hahn." He checked the address. "She's in building 3600 unit 24."

"One moment, please." There was a brief pause, then a buzz as the gate unlocked. Bishop drove through, parking in a visitor's spot in front of the building.

Like most gated apartment communities, the buildings lacked security. We walked up the outdoor steps and down the hall with apartment doors on each side, checking the numbers. Twenty-four was the last one on the left near the second set of external stairs. Bishop knocked firmly.

A moment later, the door swung open, revealing a young woman with a messy bun and glasses perched on her nose. "Yes?" She eyed us with caution, then wrapped her arms around her sides. "I'm good with Jesus if that's why you're here."

"That's good to know," I muttered.

Bishop spoke before I had a chance to continue. Guy liked to ruin my fun. "Hi." He showed her his badge. "I'm Detective Bishop and," he pivoted toward me. "This is my partner, Detective Ryder. We're looking for Rebecca Hahn. Is she home?"

"Rebecca? She doesn't live here anymore." She angled her head to the side appearing slightly confused. "I'm her former roommate, Julie Hansen."

"Did she move recently?" I asked.

She nodded. "She got married a month ago. Her last name is McVoy now. She's still on the lease, if that's what this is about."

"It's not," I said. "We need to speak with her about something else."

"Do you happen to know where she is?" Bishop asked, glancing at me briefly.

Julie shrugged. "Not sure, but she's got an exam coming up, so you could check the library. If she's there, she could be there all night."

"Thanks, Julie," I said, stepping back. "Do you have her new address?"

"I don't know it, but I know it's in Dawsonville near the outlet mall."

"Great," I said. "We'll check the library."

"Oh, she's at the nursing library," she said. "Not the regular one. It's in the nursing education building. It's the Health and Natural Sciences building by title." She rubbed the sides of her arms. "Is she in some kind of trouble, or something?"

"We're looking for information on a friend of hers," Bishop said.

"Are you from Hamby?" I asked.

She nodded. "Who's the friend? I might know her."

"Jennifer Berman."

Her eyes widened. "She's dead. It's all over social media."

"Yes, ma'am," Bishop said.

"You don't think Becca's involved, do you?"

"We're just talking to people who knew the victim," I said.

"I knew her. We used to be friends. She had a lot of family issues. She changed a lot in middle school, so our friendship kind of dropped off. I didn't really talk to her in high school, let alone college. Which I don't think she went to, obviously."

"Obviously?" I asked. "What makes you say it that way?"

"I'm not even sure she graduated from high school. She got in with the wrong crowd. Ended up in juvenile detention for a while, and honestly, I don't think I saw her at school after that." She glanced behind us. "I think that was our sophomore year?"

"Yes," I said. "Can you remember any of Jennifer's friends before she went to detention?"

"I mean, I can't remember their names, but I have my yearbook. I can look at it if you'd like."

"That would be great," Bishop said.

She invited us in. "It's in my room. Have a seat," she said, pointing to the couch. "I'll be right back."

"Who brings their high school yearbook to college at twenty-two?" I whispered when she was out of sight.

"Julie," Bishop said.

She returned with a large black yearbook in her hand. "Becca and I were just looking at this the other day." She set it on the coffee table in front of what looked to be a brand-new leather couch. I would have traded my old one for it in a heartbeat.

I jotted down names as she flipped through the pages. "I think that's it," she finally said. "Though I can't say who she was friends with recently, those are some of the people in her crowd during high school."

"Thank you," Bishop said.

"Sure." She closed the book. "Do you have any idea who killed her?"

"We're not at liberty to discuss an active investigation," I said.

"Oh, right," she said. She gave us the location of the nursing building.

"Julie," I asked as we left. "Would you mind if we borrow your year-book? I'll make sure it's returned soon."

She handed it to me. "Sure. I'm not sure why I have it here anyway."

"Thank you," I said. I handed her my card. "Please call me if you remember anything else. May I have your cell please?"

"Sure," she said.

The nursing building hit us with a vibe I could almost grab, buzzing with the laser-focus of students camped out at tables, buried in a world of medical know-how I'd never understand. The place was airy, light pouring through the main wall's three-story windows, walls decked out in feel-good posters about caring and kindness, a modern-day attempt to end the Nurse Rached's of the world.

Bishop let out a 'wow', his eyes roving over the future Florence Nightingales. "This brain trust here could probably make a dent in our nursing crisis."

I fished out the clip from my hair, working the strands into a tighter, more disciplined bun before clipping it back in place. "Probably need more than this crew, but it's a start." My eyes took a little tour of the room, jumping from one youthful face to another. "Why do all these college types look like they're stamped from the same mold? Hair in clips, wearing sweats, drinking Starbucks."

"Have you looked at yourself lately?"

I glanced down at my Silver brand jeans. "I don't wear sweats to work."

He let out a laugh. His gaze, sharp as ever, met mine. With a casual shrug and that familiar half-smile, he said, "Same song, different verse in college. In my time, it was all about the big hair and neon nightmares. Different era, same tune."

"Gnarly, dude." I laughed at my pitiful attempt at 80s slang.

"I'm not even going to tell you how bad that was."

"You don't have to. I knew the second it sailed off my lips."

He surveyed the large space. "I don't see her."

"I don't think this is the library." I nodded towards a woman sitting alone, focused intently on a laptop screen. We walked to her. "Excuse me," I began, my voice polite but firm. "Can you tell us how to get to the library?"

The woman looked up, her expression shifting from concentration to mild surprise. "Oh, you mean the resource center? It's not really a library."

"Would that be what a non-nursing student would call it?"

"No. They'd call it a resource center. Most majors have one in their building." She smiled. "But non-students like you probably would. It's on the third floor." She closed her laptop. It clicked softly as it locked into place. "Take the elevator up, then it's the third door on your left."

"Thank you," I said, offering her a small smile.

The hum of the lounge area faded into the background near the elevator. Inside, Bishop said, "I'm surprised there aren't more men in nursing school."

"I've seen a lot of male nurses."

"I guess I'd expect them to be hanging out here. The women make a decent sized dating pool."

"You're such a pig," I said smiling.

"Hey, if I'd gone to a school with a large female population in a centralized location, I would have hung out there all the time."

"They're called sororities. Maybe no one ever invited you to one?"

"Good point."

The nursing resource center had the same feel as the law library tucked away in the University of Chicago's law school. Civilians were a no-go there, but cops had the all-clear, and we'd take advantage of it.

I'd burned the midnight oil in places like that more times than I could count, diving into case files, hunting for that golden ticket to lock up the bad guys. Once, the idea of law school had danced in my head. Tommy was all for it, said I'd be a total badass in the courtroom—and he wasn't wrong. But my true calling was out there on the streets, in the thick of it, chasing down the scum, not cooped up in some courtroom, sweating it out with a bunch of suits. If I wanted to feel the heat, I could take a stroll to the clink.

"I could have been a lawyer," I said.

"I pity the fool who might've gone up against you."

"Wow," I said. "That was bad."

"That was Mr. T."

"Is that the big guy with the jewelry? I think I saw him in a car commercial or something."

He turned to me and said, "Shut up," with a grin, then walked deeper into the place.

"What?" I asked hurrying behind him.

He ignored me.

Three women sat at an oblong table, heads down in over-sized books. I pointed to Rebecca McVoy at the far end. "That's her."

We approached her quietly. "Mrs. McVoy?" Bishop asked in a quiet voice. He moved his sports coat slightly to show his badge. "May we have a moment in the hall, please?"

Her eyes widened. "Is everything okay? Is it Tyler? Is he okay?"

"Is Tyler your husband?" I asked.

She nodded. Her eyes brimmed with unshed tears, mirroring the deep well of worry that had quickly engulfed her face. "What's happened?"

"We're not here about him," I said. "But we'd appreciate talking in the hall, so we don't disturb the other students."

"Oh, sure." She followed us out.

"We're here about Jennifer Berman," Bishop said.

Her face softened. "I heard the police found her body."

"Unfortunately, we did."

"I haven't talked to her in years."

"Maybe not," I said. "But we were hoping you could tell us about her from when you knew her. We understand she'd changed, but what you know could help with our investigation."

"She definitely changed. She was my best friend in elementary and middle school. We hung out all the time." Her voice drifted off for a moment. "Her parents were tough on her. They had this image, you know? They acted like the perfect family, but her dad was a real jerk. He used to beat her and her mother. He probably still beats her mom. I wouldn't put it past him murdering her."

"Did she tell you this?" I asked.

"She didn't have to. I was there when he smacked Mrs. Berman once. I think we were in sixth grade? I'm not sure. They were fighting. Mrs. Berman sent us to the basement. I'm sure she knew what was coming. We went, but we snuck outside and hid on the deck and watched. Jenny said it happened all the time, and that one day, she'd stop him." She sighed. "I guess she never did because things got worse. Her mother drank a lot. We could smell the alcohol on her."

"When did you notice changes in Jennifer?" I asked.

"Really, they were happening all along. I just didn't think about it. We'd done a few things together. Stupid stuff. Snuck her mom's whiskey. When she switched to vodka, we snuck that too. Filled the bottle with water, but if she figured it out, Jenny never got in trouble. I spent the night there a lot. Things were rough, but her dad was mostly cool when I was there, and they left us alone. We got high a few times." She blushed. "Am I going to get in trouble for this?"

"We're just interested in your relationship," Bishop said. He acted as though he could charge her for something, which made me want to laugh.

"It was always weed. You know, a blunt or two. I think I realized she'd changed when she had coke. That was eighth grade."

"Did she have any boyfriends or boys she liked?"

"When I was her friend? Sure. Boys were all we cared about. We both crushed on Dylan Harris. He was kind of a bad boy, but he was cute back then. He was in our class, and we used to follow him around all the time. He used to stand outside the side entrance of the middle school and vape. We thought it was so cool that he wasn't afraid of getting in trouble. I think she liked that about him. He didn't care about the rules. Jenny was always afraid. She always seemed attracted to the bad guys."

"Did either of you ever date him?" Bishop asked.

"I didn't. I realized in eighth grade he wasn't my type."

"And Jennifer?" I asked.

"We stopped hanging out second semester of eighth grade. He was part of the reason. We'd been drifting apart already, but Dylan made things worse."

"How so?" Bishop asked.

"I guess it wasn't his fault exactly. Jenny made her own decisions." She looked behind us as if reliving a memory. "We went to Avalon one weekend. Jenny saw him and she wanted to approach him. I was already over him by then, but I went along with it for her. We followed him around a bit and eventually started talking and stuff. Then we went into the sunglasses place. They each stole a pair of Ray Bans. He got busted, but Jenny and I ran out. We hid by Café Intermezzo and watched security take him away." The side of her lip curled. It was clear she wasn't his biggest fan. "Our friendship died off after that. She hung out with him a lot then. I heard she slept with him, but I don't know if she did."

"Were they a couple?" Bishop asked.

She nodded. "On and off, I mean it looked like it. I don't know if it was official. I kind of kept my eye on her in high school, but definitely from a distance. She was with him a lot. Everyone thought they were together, but he was always screwing someone else." After a pause she said, "I don't know why she put up with that."

We asked her about her other friends both before she changed and after, as well as what she thought caused Jennifer's personality to switch as it had.

"She hung with the stoners, and I really don't remember any of them."

"We have a yearbook from your senior year," Bishop said. "Your friend Julie gave it to us."

"Oh, I'm sure she pointed them out then."

"She did."

"I don't know if it's true," she said, "but Jenny said her father sexually abused her. She really hated him. I think she was looking for a male figure to love her or something." She exhaled. "She picked the wrong one though, for sure."

"Do you know Christina Carter?" I asked.

She glanced to the right. "I don't think so."

"How can we get in touch with you if we have any more questions?" Bishop asked.

She gave him her cell phone.

I handed her my card. "If you remember anything else, don't hesitate to call."

In the car, Bishop said. "Did you see her reaction when you asked about Christina Carter?"

I nodded. "She lied to us."

∼

I almost admired Dylan Harris's record. "This Harris kid looks like a catch."

"Right?" Levy asked.

Bubba finished handing copies of Harris's record to the others. "I thought the same," he said.

Bubba fiddled with his laptop, projecting Dylan's criminal record onto the screen on the far wall.

"Wow," Michels said. "Dude's been busy." He tapped the table, his eyes scanning the first sheet. "Alright, let's start from the top." He looked at me. "Did you try to get his juvie file?"

"Not yet. I'll call Nowak if we determine he's a suspect."

"Got it," he said. "Age eighteen, Harris got booked for misdemeanor shoplifting. Stole a couple of video games from a local store."

Levy nodded. She flipped to the next page then back again. "My mother swore video games would be the death of society."

"Mine said the internet would," Bubba said. "I think she's right."

"It's part of it for sure," I said.

"A month later," Levy added, "petty theft again. This time, it's a bottle of whiskey from a liquor store. Still a misdemeanor, but he's starting to show a pattern."

Bishop pointed at the screen. "Three months after, he's charged for possession of marijuana, less than an ounce. Maybe the alcohol didn't give him enough of a buzz anymore, so he stepped up his criminal behavior."

I leaned forward, eyeing the timeline. "He's definitely escalating."

Michels sighed. "Six months post the weed charge, he got caught with methamphetamine. Looks like his first felony charge, but he got off on a conditional discharge through drug court."

Bubba, breaking his usual silence, chimed in. "Didn't stick though. Records show he was back on meth within the year."

Levy shook her head. "After that, he was arrested for breaking into a car." She glanced at the screen. "He likes his misdemeanors."

"We need a misdemeanor version of the three strikes rule," I said.

"Wouldn't that be great?" Bishop asked. "Crime rates would probably drop."

"Doubtful," Levy said. "They haven't with the felony one."

"Good point," he said.

"He gets worse," Michels added. "Aggravated assault last year. Beat up a guy in a bar fight. Broke three of the guy's ribs. He plea-bargained down to a misdemeanor with a year's probation."

I highlighted three other charges. "He's been involved in multiple bar fights, but all simple battery." I cleared my throat. "He obviously knows about that three-strike rule. He's practically alternating his levels of crime."

Michels flipped a page. "Here's a serious one. Charged with sexual battery. It didn't stick, but it raises red flags."

I took a deep breath. "When was it?"

"Seven months ago."

"And the latest?" Bishop asked.

Michels turned to the final page. "One more. Burglary in the first degree. He broke into a house. Then, armed robbery. Did five months in Atlanta."

I rubbed my temples. "That's a hefty record. Escalating from petty thefts to violent felonies. We'll have a talk with him."

"He's young," Levy said. "He wasn't alive in the 80s."

"Doesn't mean he's not somehow connected to her," Bishop said.

11

Bishop and I shared what we'd learned from Rebecca McVoy and her former roommate. Levy stared at Berman's missing persons photo. "What if her father did it?"

"That would mean he killed Caroline Turner as well," Bishop said.

"Is he the right age?" she asked.

"Looks to be pretty close," I said, "but that's a big jump. We don't even know if he lived here in the 80s."

"As far as I know, he didn't," Bishop said. "At least I've never heard of him."

I held up the Hamby High School yearbook. "Why don't you run home and get yours. We can look for his name."

Michels snorted. "That's brilliant."

"I don't think so," he said. He looked at Bubba. "Can you check on Berman's father? See if he's from here?"

"Already on it." He pounded his keyboard with his fingers. "Nope. Ohio."

"Maybe he's a copycat?" Levy suggested.

"We're planning to talk to him," Bishop said. "We'll look for a connection."

"We'd still like to see your yearbook," I said to Bishop.

"I don't think so."

"Did you have a Flock of Seagulls haircut or something?" I asked. I couldn't hide the smile on my face. "Do you want to run, run so far away right now?"

He smirked but rolled his eyes. "That's it. You busted me."

"That's a song, isn't it?" Bubba asked. "I think my mom listens to it."

Bishop threw his pen at him, and in a surprise move, Bubba caught it.

Michels screamed, "Whoa!"

"Right?" Bubba said. "I should have been a receiver."

"Your technological skills are too valuable to be lost to football," I said.

"We still have to talk to Christina Carter," Bishop said. "What about the lists?" he asked Levy and Michels. "Find anyone we can connect to both victims?"

"Not yet," he said.

"We've gone as far back as great grandparents of the people on our lists but can't find anything."

"Keep looking," Bishop said. "Check the friends again. Ryder and I will interview Dylan Harris while we're out."

Jimmy had walked in a few minutes before. "Keep looking." He looked at Bishop. "Go talk to the Carter woman." He pivoted on his heels and walked out.

The room fell silent. "He's got his undies up in a bunch," Michels said.

I stared at him for a moment, and then burst out laughing.

"Shit," he said, dragging his hand down his face. "I'm spending too much time with Ashley's mom planning the wedding. I'm talking like her now."

Bishop and I swung by Dunkin' for a quick jolt of caffeine on the way to Christina Carter's place in Alpharetta. Idling in the drive-thru, I asked, "Think she'll have any recollection of you?"

He gave a half-hearted glance at the car ahead. "You'll find this hard to swallow, but back in high school, I wasn't exactly the guy people remembered."

My eyes did a quick dance of surprise before I bit down on my cheek, fighting a losing battle with the smirk itching to spread across my face. I dropped my gaze, pretending to be all caught up in the fascinating world of his car's floor mat. "Never would've pegged you for that," I managed, but the effort was a washout. The laughter just rolled out, uncontrollable.

The drive thru attendant handed him our coffees. He thanked her, then handed me mine, saying, "I'm sure you were the prom queen."

"Not even close."

"That was sarcasm, Ryder."

Ouch.

Christina Carter lived in a typical Georgia home. The bricked front and small concrete porch matched the home on its left. "I really don't like these," I said. "They're all the same."

"I live in one, but I don't like them much either."

"At least yours has character."

He pulled into her driveway. "You're saying that because you feel bad for slamming me earlier."

"A little."

Christina Carter's driver's license photo did her no justice. Around five-feet-five-inches, with naturally blond wavy hair, and a wrinkle free, bright complexion, I wouldn't have guessed her to be Bishop's age. I was younger than her and the fine lines around my eyes, as well as the eleven at the bridge of my nose, made it into the room five minutes before the rest of me. She must have had an excellent plastic surgeon.

"I'm not sure why you're here," she said, "but I'm happy to talk. Come on in. What can I do for you?"

"Caroline Turner's remains have been discovered, and we're talking to people who may have known her," Bishop said.

She examined him closely. "You look familiar. Do we know each other?"

"We graduated from high school together."

I bumped his arm quickly with mine.

She tilted her head to the side. Her eyes widened as the figurative light-bulb over her head switched on. "Bobby Bishop? Is that you?"

Bobby?

He cleared his throat. "Yes, Chrissy, but I go by Rob now."

Not anymore.

Her eyes brightened. "You're a detective! That's incredible. I always knew you'd turn out just fine."

Had he not been just fine in high school? I needed more information on that STAT.

"Thank you," he said. He refused to look at me.

I angled my body toward his. "Bishop has the highest close record in the department's history. He's a valuable asset to Hamby." While that was true, I doubted he missed the meaning behind my words.

"That's wonderful," she said. "You were always such a sweet, kind boy, Bobby," her eyes widened. "Oh, I mean Rob." Her cheeks reddened. "Silly me. I remember you started on the football team senior year. Oh my, you were cute as a button."

I threw up a little in my mouth.

She smiled at me. "Bishop was an excellent football player." She squeezed his bicep. "And I bet he still is."

"I work out," he said blushing. "Anyway, we're here about Caroline."

Her voice tinged with a distant nostalgia as she glanced momentarily towards the window, as if lost in the past. "I remember Caroline. We weren't what I would call friends, but we shared some of the same ones, and we did spend some time together." Her voice faltered for a fraction of a second. If I wasn't paying attention, I would have missed it. Her hands, which had been resting calmly on her lap, began to fidget, intertwining nervously. "I didn't always associate with the best people in high school."

"I can't remember," Bishop said. He leaned forward slightly, his demeanor relaxed yet his eyes keenly observant. He tilted his head, giving off an air of casual conversation despite the gravity of the subject. "Were you with her the night she disappeared?"

She shifted slightly in her chair, a subtle grimace crossing her face as the wood beneath her creaked softly. Her eyes darted toward a distant corner of the room before steeling themselves back onto Bishop. "I was looking for her, yes, but we didn't go to the festival together," she said, her voice carrying a hint of defensiveness. "Though we had hung out there most of the night." She drew in a deep breath, her chest rising and falling more noticeably. "I guess what I'm trying to say is we met there, but it wasn't intentional."

"Understood," Bishop nodded. His expression remained neutral yet attentive. Since he had the connection to Christina, I let him do most of the talking. "How long were you there together?"

"It was a few hours. Maybe three?" She tilted her head back. "It was so long ago. It's hard to remember."

"It's important we learn as much as possible about that night," I said. "Anything you remember could help us with the investigation."

"I understand."

"How long had you been separated when you realized she was missing?" Bishop asked.

"That I remember," she said, her eyes sharpened with clarity. "It wasn't long. She'd gone to the portable bathroom and was supposed to meet me back at the tilt o' whirl. I waited there, thinking the bathroom line was probably long, but I got annoyed after thirty minutes, so I went looking for her. There wasn't a line when I got there." Her hands clasped together tightly, knuckles whitening. "I didn't think much of it at first. I figured she'd gone off to get high or something. Caroline had a serious drug problem, and she was always stoned before that." Her lips tightened momentarily, a slight sneer crossing her face, as if she held some contempt or deeper knowledge about Caroline's habits. It would make sense if the two had somehow competed for Steve Copeland's affections.

"What changed your mind?"

"Caroline. She'd told me earlier she had decided to get clean. She missed her family. She said she wanted to be a part of their lives again." Her gaze drifted off, a shadow of worry flickering across her face. "Could she have given in to temptation? Sure. She was an addict, but something didn't feel right about it." She took in another deep breath, her shoulders rising and falling with the weight of her recollections. "I asked a few people in the booths nearby if there had been a line earlier. I went looking for her when they said no."

"Did you elicit help from anyone else?" Bishop asked, his voice steady but probing.

"You know, none of the police asked me anything like this that night.

Maybe if they had, she wouldn't be dead." She paused, a distant look clouding her eyes. After a moment, she continued, "Yes. I asked the group we were with. We checked the entire festival. Of course, back then it wasn't as big as it is now, but it was still large enough that it took us a while. Maybe forty-five minutes or so? As you know, we never found her."

"Is that when you went to the police?" Bishop's tone was gentle, encouraging her to continue.

She nodded, her gaze dropping to her hands, which were now clasped tightly in her lap. "But if I'm being honest, it wasn't because I thought something bad had happened. Not initially that is." Her cheeks flushed a soft pink, the color standing out against her pale complexion. "I feel bad about that now."

"What do you mean?" he prodded gently.

"I thought they'd busted her for getting high. That her desire to get clean had waned." There was a hint of regret in her voice.

"And that's what you asked?" Bishop leaned in slightly, encouraging her to reveal more.

"More or less. I didn't want them to know I'd been with her, so I said her parents were looking for her and were worried she'd gotten in trouble." Her eyes flickered with a memory.

"And this officer was?" Bishop's eyebrows raised.

"That I don't remember, but he's the one I went back to the next day. When I realized something was really off." She looked up, her eyes meeting Bishop's with a newfound intensity.

"Can you explain further?" he encouraged.

"I was worried initially, yes. After we left the festival, a few of us went to hang out together, and we started talking about her. I said I hoped she hadn't gone to get high and gotten in trouble. That's when the others said she told them she was trying to get clean as well."

"Did you think she was genuine?" I chimed in, curious about her perception.

"I might have been naïve, but I did, after they all said she'd told them that too." She looked away, her gaze distant. "As an adult, I'm not sure."

"When did you talk to the police officer?"

"The next day." She smiled sheepishly. "Remember how we used to send one person into the festival and have them come back and get us all in?"

Bishop chuckled as he nodded. "Licking the back of our hands to transfer the stamp."

"That's breaking the law," I kidded.

Christina blushed, that time a crimson red. "I feel awful for that now."

"Kids will be kids," I said. "We did something similar to get into Six Flags."

"Good to know," she said. "But yes, we did that, me, and a friend. I found the same officer and explained the situation."

"And what did he do?" Bishop asked. Though we had the report, her answers could fill some of the missing parts and paint a bigger picture.

"He took down her name, then I guess he talked to someone at the department. He used that radio on his shirt and told us he'd look into it."

"Did you ever follow up with him?"

She shook her head as she sighed. "No. We all thought she'd just left, that she'd changed her mind about wanting to be around her parents and wanting a fresh start. There wasn't much left for her here at the time. She was an adult. She wouldn't have been on a milk carton, and I think we just forgot eventually." She hesitated, then said, "Like I said, we weren't really that close."

"Who went with you to the festival the next day?" I asked.

"Holly Grimes." A shadow passed over her features as she mentioned the name. "She was killed in a car accident two weeks later."

"I remember that," Bishop said. "Sad."

I held my pen ready to take names. "Who else looked for her the night she went missing?"

"Oh, gosh," she said. "It was so long ago. "Maybe Jimmy Wilson. Of course, Steve Copeland. Holly, and I think Sue Waters? It might have been Lisa River." She giggled softly. "They always reminded me of each other, and their last names always messed me up."

Bishop smiled. "They looked a lot alike. The red hair made them almost identical at times."

"It did," she said. I could see she felt relieved for not being the only one to think it.

"Ms. Carter," I said. "Were Steve Copeland and Caroline Turner a couple then?"

"I wouldn't call them a couple." She rolled her eyes. Odd for something that had happened forty years before, and we were talking about a murder victim. "She had a thing for him, but he was never really that into her." She shrugged sheepishly. "I know this makes me a terrible person, but like I said, we weren't exactly friends, just friendly, but I slept with him while they were involved."

"Did Caroline know this?" Bishop asked.

"Oh, of course not. I wasn't a kiss and tell kind of girl, and I'm sure Steve Copeland would say the same about himself."

"He mentioned that you two dated. Is that true?"

"Yes, in high school before he dated Caroline, and then, of course, once he graduated and got his life together."

"You dated after high school?" Bishop asked.

"We spent time together." She smiled. "I guess it wasn't officially dating."

"Do you know Keith and Jeannette Berman?"

She inhaled and shook her head. "I don't think so. Why do you ask?"

"Thank you for your time, Ms. Carter," I said. We turned to leave.

"Of course. If y'all have any more questions, feel free to give me a call." She sighed. "I hope you find whoever it is that murdered Caroline. She didn't deserve to die so brutally."

I turned around. "What do you mean so brutally?"

"Oh," she said, giggling at Bishop. "I'm assuming since you just found her remains that it was a brutal death."

Bishop steered the cruiser with a relaxed, precise grip while I sat beside him forcing myself not to tell him how to drive while mulling over Christina's words.

"I don't trust her." I broke the silence, watching the streetlights flicker past.

"You don't trust anyone." Bishop nodded, keeping his eyes on the road,

"I think she regrets not doing more, especially since she knows Caroline was murdered."

I glanced at him, noticing the thoughtful furrow of his brow. "Most young adults don't have the common sense to do the little she did, I'll give her that, but none of these stories line up. Who did Copeland date, and when? Did the guy just screw every girl in Alpharetta or what?"

He adjusted the rearview mirror slightly. "Like I said before, everyone sees the past through a different lens."

"You didn't say it that way, but I agree." I stared out the window. "But you'd think the stories would line up at least a little."

Our cell phones dinged in unison. We looked at each other. He dug his cell out of his pocket and handed it to me.

I thought you'd be better adversaries. I guess I need to give you a reason.

"The killer's watching us," Bishop said. He checked his rearview mirror. "But I don't see a black, luxury vehicle behind us."

"Maybe they're not watching us at the moment," I said. "Maybe they're annoyed because we haven't made any movement on the investigation."

"They're trying to put us off track," he said.

"Right, and we can't let them win. Let's just keep doing what we're doing. If anything, the killer's getting annoyed, and annoyed killers do stupid things." I glanced back at my notes from our interview with Christina Carter. "Let's move on. I can't dwell on this until we have something that connects the two women. When we get that, the case will take off."

"Agreed," he said.

"Good. Okay. She mentioned they weren't close, but shared friends. And the night Caroline disappeared, they were both at the festival but didn't plan to meet up. It was coincidental." Was that true? I wasn't sure.

"Right," Bishop replied, his voice steady. "She emphasized that point as if making sure we understood they weren't close. I don't know. Maybe she's embarrassed about what she did at twenty?"

I nodded. "Or maybe she's lying? I was already married and working the streets at twenty-two," I said.

He looked at me as a grin formed across his lips. "Working the streets, huh?"

"As a cop, smartass."

Bishop laughed. "You threw me a softball. I had to hit it."

"I deserved it," I said, smiling.

He signaled and turned toward our next interview. I checked my watch. I had hoped to get home early enough to have dinner with Kyle, but I wasn't sure that would happen. I sent him a text to let him know.

Don't sweat it, he replied. *I'm still in Atlanta.*

The car slowed as we approached a red light. Bishop drummed his fingers lightly on the wheel, lost in thought.

"Did you know any of the people she mentioned? Jimmy Wilson, Steve Copeland, Holly Grimes..." I trailed off, flipping through my notes again.

"Knew of them, but that's about it." He sighed. "Holly Grimes. Christina said the car accident was two weeks after Caroline went missing. I can't say for sure, but I was in the academy when mom called about it. It must've been another heavy blow for that group of friends."

"It's a lot for any group of friends to go through. Losing one to disappearance, another to an accident. Even if they weren't that close, they'd feel the losses." I stared out the window and he pulled onto the highway, then I turned to him and asked, "What if they're connected?"

"I was thinking the same thing," he said. "Holly Grimes found out who murdered Caroline and died because of it."

"Tell me about the accident."

"She hit the median on 400. I can't remember where, but this was before 400 went past Holcomb Bridge Road. Her vehicle flipped, went over the median and landed in oncoming traffic. Another vehicle hit her head on. She died instantly."

"She was drunk?"

"I believe so," he said. "I think there might have been drugs involved, too. We can check back at the department."

"If we're right, whoever killed Caroline Turner will kill again if it means keeping their identity secret."

He pulled off the next exit and turned left. Two streets down, we arrived at the extended rental hotel, the home address Dylan Harris's parole officer put on his file.

Three men shared a joint sitting outside a first-floor unit. The smell hit me like a Mack truck. I tolerated a lot of smells, but marijuana wasn't one. It made me want to vomit. Even though my nostrils burned, I smiled at them after exiting the vehicle. Bishop flashed his badge still attached to his hip.

The one with the joint dropped it into his lap, then jumped out of his chair when it singed his leg hair.

"Nice move," I said as we walked past.

"Keep it out of public, boys," Bishop said.

Climbing up the stairs, I said, "We *could* have them arrested." The hotel's location prohibited us from arresting them, but it didn't mean we couldn't call Roswell PD.

"We could probably find warrants for half the residents of this hotel."

"Right? Talk about a paperwork nightmare."

"Why do you think they're still here?"

I laughed. No one in law enforcement wanted to tackle that kind of job. The arrests would take a quarter of the time the paperwork would. Just off the stairwell, I said, "Let's approach this like we don't think he's involved."

"Agree," he said. "A, we don't know if he's involved, and B, given his record, he'll probably try to run if we accuse him of anything."

I sighed. "I'm tired of running after the bad guys."

"I'm faster than I've ever been, but it would be nice if they'd just turn themselves in. Would have saved me from being a punching bag last year."

I didn't want to go there. Seeing Bishop hanging near death from a pole wasn't a memory I liked to relive, and I doubted he did either.

Bishop rapped on Harris's door. It swung open. "Yeah?"

He was leaner than I'd imagined, his hair disheveled, eyes rimmed with red. For a moment, he just stared at us, a flicker of suspicion crossing his face.

"Dylan Harris?" Bishop's tone was casual but authoritative.

"Who's asking?"

We showed our badges with a flair that was almost nonchalant hoping it would ease any paranoia the kid had. "Detectives Ryder and Bishop." I introduced us, keeping it cool and crisp. But before Bishop could even get into the why, Harris tried to play his move, a swift door slam aimed to shut us out. But Bishop was prepared and jammed his foot against the door in the nick of time. "We're here about Jennifer Berman," I said, my voice calm but carrying an undertone that hinted this wasn't a courtesy call.

Harris's mouth dropped open. A look of genuine surprise washed over his face. "Jenny? What about her?" He stepped back, allowing us into the cramped room.

I pointed to a battered armchair. "Have a seat. This isn't an interrogation."

"Not yet," Bishop said.

Harris sat, his surprised look still etched onto his face.

"When was the last time you talked to her?" Bishop asked.

Harris leaned forward, elbows on his knees, his hands fidgeting. "She took off...shit, I don't know, a couple months ago?" His glance darted to a small pile of crumpled beer cans by the door before he continued. "She come back and try to pin something on me or what?"

Bishop exchanged a brief look with me before responding. "Jennifer's dead."

The color drained from Harris's face. His mouth opened slightly, then closed. He sank back into the chair as his hands gripped the armrests. "Dead? Jenny?" He shook his head slowly, disbelief showing in every line of his face. Suddenly, panic hit. He held his arms out straight toward us, showing his palms and shaking them. "I didn't do it, man. I swear. Talk to my parole officer. He can tell you. I'm doing what I'm supposed to. I'm clean, man. It's killing me, but I'm clean."

"We're not accusing you of anything," I said, though it would be a lie to say we didn't suspect his involvement. "We're trying to understand her last days. Can you tell us about your relationship with her?"

He rubbed his face with both hands, then ran them through his grimy hair. "Man, Jenny and I go way back. High school stuff, you know? It was complicated. She had this thing for me, but I never really liked her like that."

"Yet you two were a couple?" I asked.

"Yeah, well, she was convenient, and she liked to do shit for me." He looked to Bishop for support. "You get it man. Girl likes to hang around, maybe put out a little, get you take out. You don't have to call it nothing. Maybe it was a relationship to her? Who was I to say it wasn't?"

Bishop nodded, his voice soft and almost comforting which I thought was an odd approach. He did a fantastic job of keeping his true opinion to himself. "We understand things were a bit tumultuous between you two. Can you tell us more about that?"

Harris shrugged, a half-smirk appearing then fading quickly. "Tumultuous? That means rough, right?"

"Basically," I said.

"Yeah, I guess. We were kids, you know? Did stupid stuff. She was always into the bad boy thing." He chuckled dryly, then stopped abruptly, as if remembering why we were there.

"When was the last time you saw her?" I asked, trying to keep my tone light.

He leaned forward again, his gaze shifting to the worn carpet. "A couple of months ago. Before she disappeared. I figured she got tired dealing with mom and took off."

"Dealing with her mom?" I asked. "How so?"

"Yeah, man. Her mom was always bugging her. You know what it's like. Trying to get her to stop using, you know? Like she wasn't popping pills on the daily herself."

"Did she succeed?" I asked. "Did she convince her to stop using?"

"Nah. Jenny was in too deep. Started shooting up last year."

"Heroin?" Bishop asked.

He nodded. "Yeah, man. I'm an addict, but I won't touch a needle."

Never say never.

Bishop took a small notebook from his pocket and jotted down a few notes. "Did she mention anything unusual the last time you saw her? Maybe she had issues with her supplier?"

"We didn't talk much the last few times I saw her. We liked to get high together, but then I went in, and after that, nothing."

"Was she hooking for her drugs?" I asked.

"Yeah. I didn't like it but it wasn't my call. She couldn't work though, you know? Who's gonna hire someone like that?"

I watched him closely looking for any sign of deceit, but all his body language showed was surprise and a dawning sadness. "Did Jennifer ever talk to you about her past or what led her to use?"

He snorted. "Yeah, man, her family. That was a mess. She hated her dad. He was a dick. And like I said, her mom was always popping pills. She never got into details, but I could tell it messed her up."

Harris claimed he was at work the night Berman disappeared. He gave us his boss's phone number, promising he would verify it.

"Do you know of a woman named Caroline Turner?" I asked.

He blinked. "Who?"

"Caroline Turner. She went missing in 1984," Bishop said.

He laughed. "Dude, I'm twenty-two. I'm not even sure my mom was born that long ago."

Ouch.

"What about anyone with the last name of Turner?" I asked, just in case.

He thought about it for a moment, then shook his head saying, "Nope."

"What do you think?" Bishop asked as we headed toward the hotel parking lot.

A man wearing ripped up jeans and a hoodie sweatshirt with the hood pulled up over his head stood at the edge of the walkway entering the parking lot from the building.

"Hold on," I said. "This might get ugly."

Bishop groaned. "I hate these places."

"Everyone hates these places."

We walked toward the young man. "He's tweaking," Bishop said.

The man stood in front of us scratching his arms which was a clear indicator of meth use. "You got any cash, man?" he asked Bishop.

"No cash, buddy, but I can get someone out here to help you if you'd like," Bishop said.

I watched the guy carefully, ready if things got out of control.

He offered favors neither Bishop nor I accepted.

"Listen," Bishop said, "we're going to get you to the hospital. Looks like you're having a rough time."

His eyes widened. He backed away, then stood at a distance and bounced on his toes, scratching his arms and picking at his face while he panicked. "No, they'll shoot me up with drugs, rot my brain, man."

"I think drugs are your problem, buddy," Bishop said. "Let us get you some help."

The guy flipped around and took off running through the parking lot. He rounded a corner at the edge of the building on the right side and disappeared. We could have chased him, but we knew he'd be back on the streets in a matter of hours anyway.

"We can't save them all," I said as Bishop sulked to his vehicle. Having had a close friend's family member suffer from addiction, he understood the trials of an addict up close and personal. He saw it in a different light than I. I worked hard to follow his example, but sometimes, I failed. Some people considered addiction a disease, which I could understand if the person hadn't made the choice to use that first time. My theory was addiction is a symptom of a disease, and the person had decided to self-medicate whether or not they knew the cause.

He nodded. "It's such a waste." He clicked the lock on his key fob and the lights flashed on and off.

I climbed into the vehicle. "Everyone has their own lessons to learn."

"Right," he said and then changed the subject. "So, what's your take on Harris?"

"You go first."

He exhaled. "He's not our guy."

"I'm not sure the kid is smart enough to do what our killer's done, and he's right. He wasn't around in '84. Not that we didn't go into that talk already knowing that." I leaned my head against the head rest. "I'm exhausted."

"You want dinner?" he asked.

"No, thanks. I want to get home."

12

It hit me the moment I stepped inside our place. The scent of cheese and spice was like a siren call to my stomach. It growled, and I moaned. "Whoa, is that smell what I think it is?"

Kyle smiled. "I got your back, babe."

"Oh, my gosh," I said when I saw that he had practically turned our family room into a makeshift cantina, the wood trunk a buffet of Door-Dashed Mexican delights. "I love you." I tossed my stuff aside, shrugged off the day's burdens along with my belt, and went through the nightly ritual of tending to my sidearm, giving it its rightful place of rest. Hands washed, I slid next to him, ready to dive into the feast. "Have I ever told you how amazing you are?" I snatched a taco from the tray and took a big bite.

"I forgot. Tell me again."

I chewed and nodded as if that would say what I'd thought.

He set a plate of heavenly food in front of me then kissed me. "When you take a breath, I already prepared this for you."

"Sorry," I said with a mouth full of taco. "I've been craving Mexican."

"You're always craving Mexican."

That wasn't an exaggeration.

"I've got news," he said.

I bit into a chip soaked in queso. "Oh, news is always fun."

"I'm going out of town for a few days."

I froze. The last time he'd gone out of town he'd almost died. It was part of his job, and I knew that, but it didn't stop my heart from racing and the panic from swelling in my chest. "Oh, awesome." I tried and failed to act like I wasn't concerned.

"It's not an investigation," he said. "We're deprogramming an agent, and I need to be there."

I exhaled. Depending on the situation, DEA agent deprogramming could take weeks. "Just a few days?"

"I'm only going for the initial interviews. He's one of mine. Been deep for over a year, and I want to see how it's going."

"It's your first," I said.

He nodded. "That's why I want to be there."

I bumped his shoulder with mine. "You're such a good person. Much better than the guy you knocked out of the position."

He laughed. "He who shall not be named."

"Right." I cut into a cheese and bean enchilada and almost drooled as the cheesy mixture steamed from the inside. "When are you leaving?"

"Tomorrow. I'll be in Peachtree City, so not far."

"Got it. You're better off staying there then dealing with the traffic."

"Glad you survived the bank robbery. I hear the guy's got some psychiatric issues."

"His daughter has cancer, and he needs money to pay for her treatment."

"Oh, wow. That's rough."

"I'm not saying he made the right decision, but I feel for the guy. I don't know what I'd do if my kid was sick." I wanted to swallow back my words. A while back I'd had some foreign internal feeling, like my biological clock's alarm had gone off. I toyed with the thought of kids for about thirty seconds, then remembered I made a great aunt, but would have made a terrible mother. Kyle, on the other hand, would win father of the year awards year after year. Thankfully, the subject didn't come up.

"Are you doing double duty with it and the murders now?"

I shook my head. "Jimmy gave it to the sergeant on duty to work with his team. The slick sleeves caught the bone and latched onto it, probably didn't realize it was mostly paperwork."

He smirked. "You know they hate being called that, right?"

"So did I, but it's a rite of passage. Once they've moved up, they'll be called something else."

"How's the investigation going?" he asked.

"Not well. We still haven't found anything that connects the two women."

He dipped a chip in the queso. "Any more communication with the killer?"

I smiled. "You're awfully calm about that."

"Because you are." He grabbed another chip. "Which surprises the hell out of me."

"I'm growing," I said.

He raised an eyebrow. "Is that so?"

"The killer wants me to get emotional. If I do, I let them win. Trust me, it's not always easy."

"I'm impressed," he said.

"Don't be. It's a constant battle. I got emotional with the Anderson situation—"

He interrupted. "Because he abducted Ashley, so understandable."

"I know, but then you were shot, and Bishop almost died."

"And you quit your job."

I felt like an idiot for that. "Don't remind me. I've just had these moments where I've felt almost out of control, and I've been working on reining them in."

"You can still have emotions, Rach."

I laughed. "Trust me, I have emotions. I'm just stuffing them into my dark soul."

"You'll tell me if you need me." It wasn't a question.

"I always need you."

He circled back to the investigation. "What about connecting them to other missing or deceased women from cold cases? Who's doing that?"

He said the two words I despised most about my job. Cold cases. "Bubba's pulled everything he can off of NCIC, but so far, nothing connects."

"That's good news."

"This is going to close soon," I said. "I can feel it. The killer's going to lose patience and do something stupid. I almost feel like hitting the pause button and letting that happen." I topped a bit of my enchilada with jalapenos and took a bite. "Wow, these are hot."

He smiled. "And you think I'm just hot."

"That's not true. You're not just hot. You're incredibly hot." I set down my plate and moved my lips close to his ear. "How about I show you how hot I think you are?"

~

The text came just after three a.m. *Every step you take in the light, I've already taken in the shadows.*

Kyle said, "What's it say?"

I hadn't realized he was awake. "Every step you take in the light I've already taken in the shadows."

He climbed out of bed and got dressed. "Bishop get it?"

"Texting him now."

"I'll check outside." He headed toward the door.

"Kyle?"

He turned around. "I'll be careful."

Bishop called. "I got it."

"Think it's BS?"

"Not sure, but they know where we live, and they ran Michels off the road, so they knew around when he would be going to work."

"He thinks he's smarter than us."

"He?" Bishop asked. "You think the killer's male?"

"I don't know. That's the problem. We're no closer to knowing than we were when the dog found the body."

Kyle returned. "All clear."

"Go back to sleep," Bishop said. "We'll figure out our next step in the morning."

~

I drove past Connie Higgins' horse ranch on the way to work, taking that route to check on the place and grab Dunkin' again for the team. The events surrounding her brother Sean's murder and the motive rocked the area's horse community as well as Hamby itself. Another rancher, Ben Cooper, had graciously taken Connie's animals until she could figure out her next step, but it had been several months, and the ranch looked practically abandoned. Last I'd heard, she'd sold to a developer, but there'd been no movement on the property. I dialed Cooper's number and put him on speaker.

"Well, this is a good way to start my morning," he said. "What can I do for you today, Detective Ryder?"

Cooper was a stand-up guy. I couldn't dislike him if I tried. "Good morning, Ben. I just drove by Connie's ranch. Thought I'd check in and see what's going on."

"She's cleaned out the office and store. I bought everything, but I think you probably knew that. She had a buyer for the property, but the deal fell through. I think she's just walked away. Too many bad memories for her to handle it, I guess."

"Is it in foreclosure?" I asked.

"No. We went through her paperwork, and she owns everything outright. Maybe she's hoping someone will make an offer?"

"Probably," I said. "I hate that everything went down like it did."

"You did the best you could. If I'm ever in a jam, you and Bishop are the first people I'll call."

I had no doubt Cooper could handle himself in most situations, but I appreciated his compliment. "You ever decide to leave the ranch world, you make sure to call me."

He laughed. "I'll keep that in mind. Hey, you ought to know Bertha's been looking for you. She's a little lonely without her cabbage patch girl."

I chuckled. I'd visited Sean and Connie's plus-four-hundred-pound pig at Cooper Creek Ranch multiple times. Cabbage was her favorite treat, and I brought it each time I visited. "I'm working on a case at the moment, but I'll be by soon."

"I heard about it. You'll catch the killers, Ms. Ryder. It's your gift."

I pulled into the Dunkin' drive thru, disconnected the call, then ordered the coffees and two dozen donuts. Bishop would growl at me for it, but like always, he'd take one.

He drove into the department lot behind me and helped me carry everything into the investigation room.

"My lunch plans were canceled for today, so I've got all the time in the world," he said. His words carried a bit of frustration with them. He and Cathy had had lunch once a week since she'd retired.

"Did Cathy find a nine-to-five significant other or something?" I teased.

"According to her, it's a female, but yeah, I've been replaced."

I laughed. "I'm sure you're still her favorite. Cathy's a social person. I don't get why, but I don't like most people. She doesn't know a stranger."

He grumbled something about that annoying him at times, but also that it was one of her best traits.

Jimmy sat at the head of the table in the investigation room. "Update me," he said. He appeared distracted. "I need something to give the mayor."

"You always need something to give the mayor," I mumbled. "Harris is out," I said. "I called his boss on the way from Dunkin', and he can verify where he was when Berman went missing."

"I also called his parole officer," Bishop said. "He feels confident Harris is being truthful with us. Said the guy is trying to clean up his life."

"Didn't see him for this anyway," I said. "Age aside, he didn't strike me as the kind of guy who would kill someone let alone go through the effort of burying them."

Levy grabbed a Boston Crème donut from the box and set it on her paper plate. "You're right. I couldn't see how he'd be connected to Caroline Turner since he wasn't even Daddy's little squirt yet."

The men collectively laughed, and, finally, I did as well. "That's disgusting," I said with a good-humored tone. "But hilarious."

"And accurate," Michels said. He glanced at Jimmy who'd narrowed his eyes at him. "I'm just saying."

Jimmy looked at Bubba. "Anything new?"

"No, sir. I've run over twenty reports, but I can't find anything connecting our victims to other investigations or missing persons."

"That's good news," Jimmy said.

"Unless there are more bodies we haven't discovered," Michels said.

Jimmy exhaled, then said, "We can only work with what we've got."

"And we are," Bishop said.

Jimmy grabbed a chocolate sprinkles donut. "The governor's coming to town tonight," He bit into the donut and continued. "I've assigned Major Naylor and his team to handle the extra security. We've had two threats come in this morning."

"Think it's our killer?" Bishop asked.

He shook his head. "I don't think so, but either way, I want this handled with white gloves." He looked at Michels and Levy. "I want you two assisting him and the governor's team."

"You're pulling us off the investigation?" Michels asked. His tone noted his extreme displeasure. "But we're just getting started."

"It's short term," Jimmy said. "The threats are credible. The mayor is using it as an opportunity to look good. He wants to move up within state government, so let's give him this."

"If we make him look good, he's gone," Bishop said.

"That wouldn't suck," Michels said.

"Watch what you wish for," I added. "Karma's a bitch."

"And God has a sense of humor," Jimmy said. He crooked his finger and motioned for them to follow him out. Michels grabbed another donut and mumbled a few curse words focused on the mayor as he did.

"Well, looks like it's just us," Bishop said. He eyed the donuts. "Can't you bring in an egg wrap or something? Some of us don't want to clog our arteries any more than they already are."

"I'll remember that," I said.

Nikki walked in. "I found some interesting things in the dirt." She handed us each a piece of paper. "It won't change what we know, but it will help the district attorney."

"Spill it," Bishop said.

She grabbed a donut and took a bite before sitting down. "Over time, the soil composition above and around a grave changes. The soil surrounding Caroline Turner has a more settled and compact layer compared to Jennifer Berman's grave." She bit into the donut, took a moment to chew, then continued. "The decomposition process also alters soil chemistry, so the soil above Turner's remains contains different chemical properties."

"What's different about them?" Bishop asked.

"A few things. Berman's soil has higher levels of decomposing organic matter from the body. This includes proteins, fats, and other bodily fluids. In contrast, Turner's grave has no organic matter left. If there were bones, there might have been something, but I couldn't find anything."

"Go on," I said.

"Decomp significantly alters the nutrient content of soil. A newly buried body is in active stages of decomposition. It releases nitrogen, phosphorus, and potassium into the soil, but over the years, the ones left from Caroline Turner's remains have been absorbed by plant roots or leached away."

"Leached?" Bishop asked.

"Literally," she said.

"Gross," I said.

"I think it's cool," she said. "There are other factors, but you can read them. Like I said, it's not going to help with our investigation. It might have when we hadn't identified Caroline Turner, but it can be beneficial to the trial."

"Thanks," I said. "Anything else?"

"Not at the moment, but I'm working on finding something that connects the two."

"Great," Bishop said. "So are we."

After Nikki and the rest of the team left, I dropped my head and gently pounded it on the table. "We have nothing. Not a damn thing. These girls are connected, Bishop, but how?"

"I don't know, but you know what we have to do." He eyed the files in the center of the desk.

I pulled a file toward me "Start from the beginning."

A few minutes later, Bubba had returned and offered to set up two desktop computers in case we needed them. He said the bigger screens would make it easier for us old people to see. While he set them up, Bishop and I organized the files and each took half.

"I need more coffee," he said. "And an egg sandwich since I don't have that lunch date." He stood. "Bubba, you want anything in particular?"

He looked up over a desktop computer. "Dunkin' or Starbucks?"

"Dunkin'."

"Yes." He listed off a drink a mile long.

I laughed.

"Dear God, save that man's kidneys," Bishop said as he walked out.

Bishop returned with our coffees. "I already gave Bubba his drink. I think I'm going into a sugar coma just from smelling that thing." He saw the complete computer set up and smiled. "Some serious stuff's getting ready to happen in here, huh?"

"I didn't want to tell him we didn't need the computers."

"This is his way of helping," Bishop said.

"I know, and I appreciate it."

He sat and situated himself to get started. "Cathy called. She said her lunch date was fun."

"She must love not being bound to the classroom anymore."

"For the most part. She gets a little bored sometimes. She's looking forward to seeing her parents next month."

We spent the next two hours going through the files, looking for something, anything we'd missed. I took detailed notes like I'd do in American history class when I needed to memorize things for a test.

"Nothing," I said. "I can't find a thing that connects Berman to Turner."

"Hold on," Bishop said. He checked a page in a file, then dialed a number on the landline and put it on speaker.

It only rang once. "Keith Berman."

"Mr. Berman, this is Detective Bishop with the Hamby PD. I have Detective Ryder with me and you're on speaker phone. Do you have a minute to talk?"

Papers crumbled in Berman's background. "About that. Have you found who murdered my daughter?"

"We're still investigating, sir. Do you know anyone with the last name of Turner?"

"Turner? Why? Is this the girl you found under mine? You think they're connected?"

It was about time someone from Jennifer Berman's family acknowledged that fact. The poor girl lived and died without feeling any love from her parents.

"As I said, we're investigating."

"You can't tell me you think it's a coincidence they were buried together."

"We do not think that. Now, do you know anyone named Turner?"

"I don't," he said. "And neither does my wife. We have already discussed this."

"What about Copeland?"

"As in Copeland construction?"

"Yes," Bishop said.

"Uh, no, I don't, and I'm sure my wife doesn't either. What's he got to do with this?"

"We're looking at everything, sir. It's part of the process."

Berman's voice lowered to a growl. "Well, if that bastard killed my kid, I'll make him pay."

"Sir," Bishop said, "no one from the Copeland family is a person of interest in either murder."

He breathed heavily into the phone. "Fine. Listen, find the person who killed my kid. When you do, then call me back. But I have a job to do. Funerals aren't cheap." He disconnected the call.

I leaned back in my chair. "Wow," I said. "Just wow."

Jimmy walked in. "Bishop," he said, his eyebrows knitting together in a display of deep concern. A fleeting shadow of frustration crossed his face. "I need you to come with me." He spun around abruptly, his movements stiff and tight with contained emotion, and swiftly left the room.

Bishop eyed me, flickers of confusion in his gaze. He gave a half-hearted shrug, as if to say he was as perplexed as I was. Slowly rising to his feet, and before turning to follow, he said, "Okay, then. I'll be back."

Only Bishop didn't return, but an hour later, Jimmy did. He sat next to me. "How's things going?"

"Nowhere." I turned toward the door, my brows furrowing in confusion. "Where's Bishop? Did he sneak out?"

"That's why I'm here," Jimmy sighed. The weight of his words hung in the air. He exhaled slowly as if bracing himself. "Bishop's been suspended for five days pending a sexual harassment investigation."

I swiveled my chair toward him, my eyes wide. "A what? This is a joke, right?"

"I'm afraid not." He shook his head, a grim expression settling on his face. "Let me just say, I don't believe the accusations are true, but since this person went to the mayor, I don't have a say in it."

I leaned forward, my voice edged with frustration. "Who accused him of this crap?"

"The victim asked to remain anonymous." Jimmy's gaze shifted away momentarily, reflecting his own discomfort with the situation.

"So, you're not even telling Bishop? How can he defend himself if he doesn't know who's lying about him?" That whole *don't get emotionally involved* thing flew right out the window.

"Rachel, I'm upset too. I can't tell him because I don't even know who's accusing him." He paused and rubbed the top of his head. He'd just gotten a haircut, and there was little hair to rub. "The person is only meeting with the mayor." He glanced up, locking eyes with me. "According to him, it's not in association with any case, and it happened within the last six months, but that's all I know."

"Like hell it's not associated with any case. This is our killer, Jimmy. He's leveled up." I breathed in deeply and exhaled. "Did you even suggest that?"

"I did, but the mayor assures me it's not involved with our investigation. My hands are tied."

"Unbelievable." I stood abruptly, my chair scraping back sharply. I began to pace around the other side of the room, my steps quick and agitated. "I can't think of anyone Bishop's ever behaved inappropriately around. Ever." I stopped, pivoting to face him, my eyes fierce with conviction. "It's the killer, Jimmy. I know it is."

Jimmy's voice was low and filled with reluctance. "It gets worse."

"I find that hard to believe." I crossed my arms, bracing myself for more bad news.

"I don't even know if the accuser is female."

I spat out a stream of cuss words sharp enough to cut through the tense air.

"Rachel, the mayor won't even tell me if it's a male or female making the accusations.

"That's BS, Jimmy, and you know it. We can't investigate anything without information."

"He doesn't want us investigating. He's handling it." Jimmy's posture slumped, a sign of him feeling his own helplessness in the matter.

"How? Who's he using?"

"I don't know," he admitted, his voice barely above a whisper.

"He hates Bishop. You know that." My accusation was pointed, my gaze unwavering.

"He said he'll maintain a professional investigation with no bias." Jimmy's words sounded hollow, and from his expression, even to him.

"That's crap, and you know it." I shook my head. My temper quickly escalated. "First the governor gets two credible threats when he's coming to Hamby, and you take Michels and Levy, and now Bishop's off because of some ridiculously false accusations? And you're telling me the mayor doesn't think this has to do with our investigation?" I shook my head. "He's a dumbass."

"Or he's taking out his anger on Bishop by withholding information from us," Jimmy said. "Though that's a bold thing to do, and I'm not sure he would take that risk."

"I need Bishop on this case."

"Five days, Rachel. It's out of my hands for five days." Jimmy's eyes met mine. There was an apology in them, but I knew it wasn't his fault.

I paced back to my seat, my hands clenching and unclenching at my sides. "Five days of Bishop's reputation being dragged through the mud. Five days of him not being able to clear his name." My voice cracked with anger and worry.

Jimmy nodded solemnly. He dropped his gaze to the floor. "I know. It's not fair, but my hands are tied."

I slammed my fist on the table. The vibration caused the screens to flicker momentarily. "It's more than unfair, Jimmy. It's a witch hunt." My voice was a low growl, seething with frustration.

Jimmy sighed, his shoulders slumping further. "I'll keep you updated. Just try to keep a cool head. You've been doing a good job of that with this investigation, Rachel. Don't let this push you over the line. I need you."

I laughed a bitter, completely devoid of any humor, laugh. "My partner is being accused of something he didn't do, and you're asking me to keep a cool head?"

He stood. "Do it for Bishop. Don't make it worse than it already is." He gave me a long, sympathetic look before turning and walking out of the room, leaving me alone with a boiling pot of anger in the pit of my stomach.

I rushed out of the department's back entrance to staff parking and climbed into my Jeep, my heart pounding. I needed privacy for a conversation. I didn't need nosy ears hearing our conversation. I quickly dialed Bishop's number.

"That's some bullshit, isn't it?" Bishop's voice crackled through the speaker as he answered, his tone filled with anger.

"Beyond that. I'm sorry." I leaned back against the seat, my grip tightening on the steering wheel.

"It's not your fault." I heard the tension in his voice. "Where are you?"

"In my vehicle. I didn't want anyone to hear my side of the conversation. You know this is the killer, right?"

"We have to treat it like it is and isn't." He let out a frustrated breath. "The mayor wants me out. He's told me that numerous times. He hates me because of the DUI arrest. He wasn't even mayor when it happened."

"You know he's brought in some internal affairs team from the government side. He won't have the department investigate because we'll find out it's a lie," I said, my voice heavy with frustration. "He's crazy if he thinks we're not going to look into it. I know it's the killer. He's leveling up to get a reaction from us."

"I appreciate that you don't even question the possibility of it being true." There was a softness in his voice now, a hint of gratitude pushing out his bitterness.

"You're my partner. I know you better than I know most people in my life." I let out a laugh, but it was hollow, lacking real humor. "Hell, I know you better than I know Kyle, and I even like you."

He laughed lightly. "I think you're right. The killer is taunting us. I doubt the threats on the governor were credible. It's a distraction, something to take the heat off by getting everyone off the investigation. Which means you're next."

"You nailed it."

He cleared his throat, something he did when mad or uncomfortable. "Listen, I'm on my way home now. Do me a favor, bring your laptop home tonight. I'll come by and get it. I can use your login for NCIC and start going through the missing persons again. Bubba emailed me the files he created. It's not like I've got anything else to do."

"Five days is too long to be gone. We could have our killer by then, but without you, I don't see that happening."

"Hopefully, Levy and Michels will be back on it tomorrow, and then you'll be good to go."

"You're my partner. I need you on this with me."

The smile in his voice was obvious. "Appreciate that. Don't worry. I'll be back."

"You've got muscle, but you're no Arnold."

We both laughed.

"Maybe someone needs to leak this to the news. Mayor deems double murder minor compared to false sexual harassment accusations." I exhaled deeply, my breath fogging up the windshield. "I think it's perfect."

"Don't. We don't need him on me any more than he already is." His voice was firm with a note of caution underlying his words. "Listen, if this is our guy, then he's been watching us for a while. He's done his research. He knows the mayor's kid got a DUI, and he manipulated it to his favor. He also probably knows you react emotionally, so this is a double win for him. Don't give him that."

"I know." I sighed, running a hand through my hair in frustration. "Fine. I'll be by at six. Kyle's gone, so I can look through them with you."

"See you then."

13

Levy, Michels, Bubba, Nikki, and Ashley were all lounging around Bishop's cozy living room, a mix of laughter and casual conversation filling the space when I arrived.

I handed him the small pizza I'd picked up on the way there. My hand cooled when the box left it. "I didn't know y'all would be here."

He chuckled, a mischievous glint in his eye. "I'm going to count every time you say y'all."

"Shut it, Michels," I retorted, though unable to suppress a grin.

Cathy's voice floated out from the kitchen. "We DoorDashed Mondo's. Tonight's special is gnocchi and scallops." Her silhouette moved gracefully between the stove and the counter. She looked comfortable there. Me? I was sure I looked like I felt in a kitchen. Like a woman walking into a filthy porta-potty at a concert. Unprepared, disgusted, and resigned.

With a theatrical sigh, I grabbed the pizza box and tossed it onto Bishop's cluttered kitchen counter. "I guess this is for later." Before I could turn around, Ashley was there, enveloping me in a warm, comforting hug.

"It's been forever," she murmured, her voice muffled against my shoulder.

"It's been a week," I corrected with a soft chuckle, patting her back. "But I'm glad you're here."

"Feels like forever when you don't see someone at work every day," she replied. Stepping back but holding onto my arms, she scanned my face for all the stories a week apart had accumulated. "Justin's right. You're handling this well."

I looked around the place. "You all," I stressed those words, "talk behind my back like this all the time?"

"Yep," Levy said.

"Not gonna lie," Bubba said.

"Only when it's important," Bishop said.

The moment, however, was punctuated by the sudden chime of Bishop's doorbell.

"I've got it," Cathy declared, wiping her hands on a dish towel as she made her way to the front door, her steps light but swift.

None of us were truly surprised to see Jimmy and Savannah step in, though a part of me felt a pang of disappointment at their child-free appearance. "Where are my sweet babies?" I couldn't help but ask; their laughter was what I needed to handle the evening's unforeseeable end.

"With the mother-in-law," Savannah explained in her exhausted tone. "I wanted to be able to help, not sing 'Baby Shark' and chase over-tired, over-stimulated children around."

My gaze shifted to Jimmy. "Why are you here? Won't this get you in trouble?"

He casually hung his jacket on a hook by the door. His posture was relaxed but his eyes were serious. "A captain goes down with his ship."

Savannah's gaze was like steel. "We both believe this is a set up by the killer. Jimmy told me what he's been doing to all of you." Her eyes locked with mine. "You should have told me."

"I was going to after we catch the guy," I murmured, feeling like I'd just been reprimanded.

"Then it's time to cast our rods," she said, determination in her voice.

"Damn straight," Michels echoed, his agreement firm and unwavering.

Cathy rushed back to the kitchen, momentarily flustered by the sudden influx of people, but she quickly regained her composure. Bishop, hearing the familiar voices, emerged from the back of the room. His eyes landed on

Jimmy. "You know I didn't do it." His voice was surprisingly devoid of emotion, though it carried an undercurrent of earnestness.

I found a spot for my bag beneath the hanging TV, the large cabinet serving as a makeshift base of operations. As I pulled out my laptop, ready for the night's endeavors, Jimmy approached Bishop. The rest of the room stilled.

Jimmy's nod was all the affirmation Bishop needed. "Never crossed my mind that you did," he said, his voice steady as he reached out and pulled Bishop into a brief, tight hug. "We've got your back, Rob. Whatever it takes."

"Thanks," Bishop replied, the gratitude evident in his tone.

Bubba pointed at my laptop with a raised eyebrow. "Did everyone bring theirs?" he inquired, scanning the room.

Aside from Jimmy, a collective no followed by sheepish glances and shrugged shoulders filled the space.

"Got my case files," Michels offered, holding up a folder as if it were a shield. "But that's it."

"Not to worry. I've got enough," Bubba said, a hint of pride in his voice. He began setting them up on the dining room table. He logged into NCIC on each one, then helped me do the same with mine, his fingers flying over the keys with practiced ease. Once he finished, he set it on the dining room table as well.

"Levy, Michels, Bubba, and Nikki," Jimmy directed, his voice taking on a leadership tone as he looked around the room, his gaze eventually settling on his wife, Cathy, then Bishop, and finally, me. "Start looking again." After a collective groan, he added, "I know, but it's better than working cold cases."

"What about me?" Ashley asked.

"She can use my laptop," I said.

"Go for it," Jimmy said. He turned to face the rest of us, his expression serious. "We're going to discuss this bullshit accusation."

I sat on Bishop's couch, my gaze fixated on a lone scallop speared on my fork, lost in thought during the conversation. My energy was dwindling, and my mind craved a caffeine kick to keep up. "This isn't an easy task. I need coffee."

"I'll make it," Cathy offered, rising from her chair with a sense of purpose, and heading towards the kitchen.

"If this person is our killer, and I believe it is," Jimmy said, "it's possible Bishop's the common denominator. We need to go through everything, and everyone related to him and see what we can find."

Bubba, flipping through a stack of papers, chimed in enthusiastically. "I pulled all his previous case files and put together a report." He glanced over at Bishop, his face breaking into a grin. "You've got a serious track record, dude. I'm impressed."

"He does," I acknowledged, placing my fork down with a soft clink. "Because half of them were with me."

Bishop, sitting in a recliner across from me, raised his middle finger in appreciation.

Savannah retrieved a spiral notebook from her bag and set it on the coffee table. She rummaged briefly, finding a pen, then settled herself next to Jimmy on the two-seater, poised to document our brainstorming session.

Cathy returned to Bishop and sat on the arm of the chair. Her hand found his. Their closeness in a situation that could have ruined them showed how much they cared for each other.

"We should revisit the break-in series first," Bishop suggested, his voice steady but strained. I knew that case had left its mark on him, a brush with danger that had come too close for comfort.

"I think those women would have been thrilled to have you hit on them. None of them would have complained." The attempt at humor felt out of place, considering the gravity of our conversation and that particular case.

The Blahut investigation—a series of escalating break-ins that unraveled into a complex web of infidelity—was a case that had turned our expectations on their head, and nearly cost Bishop his life.

"No," Bishop responded, dismissive of the light-hearted jab. "And thank God for that. I'm talking about the underwear thefts."

Jimmy leaned in, his fingers drumming a rhythm of contemplation on his knee. "I'd forgotten about those."

"I hated being gone for that one," I admitted, reflecting on the time I'd gone to see Lenny in Chicago and missed the chaos that had unfolded in the Blue Knight subdivision. A women's underwear thief was one of the most bizarre series of break-ins I'd heard about in my career. I was sorry to have missed it.

Bishop nodded, his demeanor focused as he recounted his involvement in the case. "Right, but I interviewed those victims with a team. I was never alone with any of them."

Savannah, looking up from her diligent note-taking, asked, "What about that string of car thefts a while back? The one where you two spent all that time on stakeouts. Could someone have misconstrued something during an interview or something?"

Cathy, her voice gentle yet audible in the hushed room, added, "Didn't one of the victims get a bit emotional when you recovered her car? What was her name?"

"Linda Marshall," I recalled, setting down my fork. "But she was grateful, nothing inappropriate. She even sent a thank you note to the department."

Bishop let out a slow breath, his gaze briefly meeting mine. "Yeah, Linda was just relieved. Nothing more to it."

"I was with him during each interview anyway. He never said anything out of line."

Michels, who had been sifting through case files at the dining table, called out to us. "Look at that string of vandalism at the high school. Lots of interactions with teachers and parents there."

Bishop massaged his temples. He was as tired and frustrated as I. "Rachel and I split those." He paused, then turned to me. "I don't recall anything from then either. Anyone stand out to you?"

I shook my head. "Not off the top of my head."

"The teachers and administration know Bishop and I are a couple. I can't see any of them throwing him to the wolves. The parents and students though? They're another story. Any one of them could lash out without cause."

"Great," I muttered, my sarcasm thinly veiled. "Like the drug murders."

"We'll put a pin in that for now," Jimmy interjected, his voice carrying an authoritative edge. "Let's look at what we can manage first."

"Could it be someone with a petty grudge?" Levy proposed, leaning back in her chair, her hands gesturing broadly. "Maybe someone you arrested for a minor offense?"

Every angle, every lead dissolved into obscurity under our scrutiny. The conversation paused and the room fell silent as we each retreated into our thoughts. The only sounds were the faint clink of cutlery and the rustle of paper as Savannah flipped a page in her notebook. I glanced over at her and saw how focused she was.

"Or someone from a case that didn't make the headlines?" she mused aloud, glancing up. "An old case that didn't go anywhere?"

Bishop reclined slightly, his eyes distant, as if he was scanning the horizon of his memory. "It's possible, but those are a dime a dozen. It could be anyone holding a minor grudge."

I set my fork down on the plate. "I can't see a minor offense or anything close to one causing a killer to come out of retirement just to frame Bishop. And half these people we're talking about aren't the right age for Caroline Turner's murder."

"Can't we narrow it down somehow?" Savannah asked. "By age and severity of the crime maybe?"

"I can, but it'll take some time," Bubba said. "What about the Anderson case? Maybe a parent of one of the victims?"

"I was the one in the hot seat with that," I said. "They'd come after me, not him."

Cathy reassured Bishop. "We'll figure this out. You're not going to lose your job."

Bishop managed a small smile, but his eyes remained clouded with concern. "Thanks, Cath."

Jimmy pushed his plate aside on the coffee table, his posture reflecting a determination that bordered on defiance. "The mayor has a lot of control, but not a lot of friends in City Hall. I can talk to them. Tell them our theory. They might see things differently."

"You'll lose your job for going behind the mayor's back," Bishop warned. "I can't ask you to do that."

"You didn't ask, I'm offering," Jimmy shot back, his determination unwavering.

"You've got kids," Bishop said. "There's got to be another way."

"Oh," Savannah chimed in, her tone suddenly bright. "I'm friends with the wives of two council members. I haven't lunched with them in a while."

"Go get 'em, tiger," I encouraged, recognizing Savannah's unique ability to connect with people and suck information out of them without them knowing.

She glanced at Bishop and then to Jimmy, seeking their tacit approval. Jimmy gave a single nod, then turned to Bishop. "I'll talk to my contacts. They'll give me something. I just have to time and say it right."

"What happens now?" I asked, seeking clarity amid the uncertainty.

"There's a complaint," Jimmy began, his voice grave. "The city's human resources would put the entire city at risk without one, and they know that."

"Can't he go to HR then?" Michels interjected, rising from the table and stretching. His discomfort was apparent in his movements.

"The chairs are fine," Cathy retorted playfully. "You're just getting old."

It was the brief moment of levity we needed.

Michels nodded in agreement, a reluctant admission. "Can't deny that."

"Bishop can go to HR," Jimmy affirmed. "He has the right to an attorney and to fight the charges brought against him."

"I've already contacted my attorney," Bishop announced. "And I told him about the investigation."

"Good," I said. "Then we cross that bridge when we come to it."

"The mayor will do his best to hide what he can," Jimmy added. I believed him. His insight into the political machinations were better than any of ours. "He's probably being manipulated by him as well."

Savannah removed her phone from her purse. "Let me see what I can find out." She tapped out a text message and waited for a response. When it came, she smiled. "It's on. Lunch with the mayor's wife tomorrow."

Jimmy looked as though he wanted to say something, but he did the right thing and kept his mouth shut. No one messed with Savannah when she had a plan. I'd learned that the very first time I met her, and it was one of the reasons I loved her.

"Okay then," I said. "We've spent hours on this investigation and now on Bishop's connection to it, and still found nothing. We're on a roll."

A while later, Cathy went to bed, and Jimmy and Savannah left shortly after, and Nikki offered to drive Ashley home, saying she wanted to pick her brain. Ashley gladly accepted. Bubba followed the others out the door with a promise to find something, somehow.

Bishop, Michels, Levy, and I continued to discuss the murders, hoping for a miracle.

"What about their jobs?" Levy said. She tapped her pen against her notebook with a rhythm that suggested she was onto something. "There's got to still be places open that were in 1984."

"I'm sure there is," I said. "But outside of prostitution, Harris told us Jennifer Berman was too far gone to work."

"Maybe a diner or something?" she suggested. "Someplace where she might have hung out looking for a fix or customer?"

Michels leaned in, and said, "A diner? If they've been around that long, I doubt they've got employees or records from the 80s."

Levy shot him a look. "Maybe the owner's the same and will remember something."

I felt a surge of possibility from her words. "It's worth looking into." I looked to Bishop. "You were here back in the old days," I smirked as I said that. "Any places from then still around?"

"I can think of a few. If necessary, we can get Bubba to check business licenses. See what was around back then and still is."

"What about in Alpharetta?" I asked. "Since Hamby hadn't split off yet."

"I'm sure there's an agreement for this kind of thing."

"I'll text him so he can move on it right away," Levy said.

Bishop's eyes narrowed. "A common thread in a community spot. It's a start."

"Hopefully," I added. My mind raced with potential leads. "They didn't have the same teachers. We've already checked that."

"Or the same administration," Levy said.

"Wait," Bishop said. "That's not exactly true. The custodian Herman is still at Hamby. If anyone knows anything, it's him. He was one of the most popular employees back in the day."

"Herman who?" I asked. "No Herman showed up on the list."

"Maybe Herman wasn't his real name?" Levy asked. Would you want a school full of teenagers knowing your name in that position?" She chuckled. "The janitors in high school angst movies always had ears."

Cathy stepped into the room. "I'm sorry to interrupt, but I was just thinking about Herman and Betty Halliday, and I heard Rob mention him. They're both still there. There's probably a few more, but I'll have to think about it."

"Betty isn't on the list either," Levy said.

"Oh, the staff list? No, they wouldn't be. Not with those names. Herman's real name is Stanley, and Betty's is Elizabeth."

I scrolled down the list from the file and found each name. "Bingo!"

She yawned. "Good night for real this time."

After she went back to bed, Levy asked Bishop, "Herman is Stanley? You'd think he would have picked something cooler than Herman. Or was that popular back in the day?"

She received the same finger of appreciation he'd given me earlier.

Michels laughed. "Herman will help. The janitor always knows what's going on."

"Like I said, they've got ears," Levy said.

"And they're always invisible," I said.

Bishop stood and paced slowly. "We need to map out their lives, see where they overlap, no matter how insignificant it seems. Friends, places, events. Shared experiences could lead us somewhere."

"Levy and Michels have basically already done that," I said.

"And we found nothing," Levy said.

I leaned back and breathed deeply several times, working to combat the hopelessness from taking over. "We need you with us on this, not thrown to the wolves."

Levy closed her notebook. "We'll get him back. The mayor can only do so much."

"I've got some time on my hands. Maybe I'll go have breakfast or lunch tomorrow." He looked at me and winked. "Chat up a few people."

Kyle's vehicle was in the garage when I pulled in. He met me at the door.

"I thought you were going to be gone a few days?"

"Our agent went into rehab."

My shoulders sank. "That's terrible."

"It's a risk we all take when we're deep. They have to know how to play the game but not cross the line."

We talked about it some more as I got ready for bed. "Did you ever get close to that line?"

"Are you asking if I did drugs while undercover?"

"Yes."

"The answer is no, but I'm not the norm."

"Oh, how true that statement is." I brushed my teeth as Kyle stood in the bathroom and continued talking.

"I'm going to take that as a compliment."

"You should," I said with a mouth full of toothpaste. "Were you ever tempted, or I guess I should say pressured?"

"All the time. I was able to fake using most of the time." He studied the scar on his chest from where he'd been shot. "I was lucky. A lot of the agents aren't."

"Some cops aren't, either."

"How's your investigation?"

I told him about Bishop.

His surprise was obvious. "Bishop and sexual harassment are two entirely opposite things."

"We think the killer knows about the DUI he gave the mayor's kid a while back and sent him an anonymous statement."

"Or the mayor knows the accuser and just doesn't want to say."

"That's a possibility, but Bishop got a lawyer, so it'll have to come out. The mayor would have had to realize that."

"Did you look at Bishop's past investigations?"

"We went through them but no one really fit the accusations." I climbed into bed. "We can't find anything to link the women or to link Bishop to one of them."

"Except that he knew the one in high school."

"Knew of her, he said. That's not much."

"Maybe not, but it's a connection."

I set my phone alarm for five hours later. I wanted to get a jump start on the day.

"I can't see how that would work."

"You see it. You just haven't put the pieces together yet. The killer has to be around Bishop's age, right?"

"Give or take."

"Two bodies buried together forty years apart isn't an accident."

"I know, but it could be a serial killer who left town and just came back."

"A serial killer that went to school with Bishop," he said. "Just refocus."

"Look more into the past than the present?"

"I'm not telling you what to do."

"You just said refocus," I said.

He smirked. "That was a suggestion." He kissed me goodnight. "Get some rest. You'll have a busy day tomorrow without a partner."

"You mean today." It was already after midnight.

"Today." He rolled over and fell asleep almost immediately.

14

I checked the growing file we had on Caroline Turner and called Bishop. "Al Castleberry."

"The officer who handled Turner's missing persons report. What about him?"

"Is he still alive?"

"Last I heard he was. I think he lives at an assisted living facility in Roswell. He's got to be in his 80s."

"Do you know the name of the place?" I asked. It was my turn to order in the Dunkin' drive thru. "Large coffee with creamer, please."

"It's Sunset Assisted Living," he said. "Are you getting me a coffee?"

"I can bring you one if you'd like."

"That's okay. I'm going to breakfast. There's a place in Alpharetta that was open when I was in high school, and it's near where the original Hamby high school was, so I thought I'd check it out. I'm meeting my attorney there."

"Keep me posted," I said.

"You too," he said and disconnected the call.

I let the team in on my plan to drop in on Al Castleberry. It should have been on my radar earlier, but Turner's file was a four-page dead end, leading us nowhere, and we wanted to hit the ground running. Turns out we hit the ground, tripped, then fell on our faces. First order of business was to check if Castleberry was still on our side of the grass, which, as it turned out, he was. The drive was going to be a longer haul than I liked, courtesy of the morning gridlock, but that was the hand I was dealt.

"Castleberry," I said out loud. Jokes about Southerners and incest aside, I'd never lived anywhere where five last names dominated the area except Hamby. I'd run into two Pruitts in a previous investigation, and I still can't figure out how they're not related. Large families like that are common in the south. Chicago was a melting pot, and those who were related didn't always want people knowing it.

I first noticed the vehicle on Old Milton Parkway. A black, luxury vehicle with tinted windows, definitely a newer model Mercedes, followed me onto 400. It had lingered a few vehicles behind me for a while, but that wasn't uncommon in rush hour traffic. As the miles stretched on, the car kept a comfortable but obvious distance.

I glanced in the rearview mirror. "Your life must be so boring. Let's see how good of a follower you are." The chase was on.

I moved into the far left lane, passed Haynes Bridge Road, and then just before Mansell, swerved across traffic—to the dismay of everyone around me—and flew off the highway to a dead stop on the ramp leading onto Mansell Road. Finally turning right, with no clear clue how to get to Castleberry's, I feigned a sudden interest in the scenic route, swerving into a side street. I illegally passed two vehicles and laughed as the Mercedes struggled to keep up.

"Hey, whack job. I'm from Chicago. You're not going to win this one."

I zipped onto another street, then looped around in a pattern that made about as much sense as a screen door on a submarine. The idea wasn't to know the streets better than my pursuer but to confuse them enough to make them question their life choices.

"Sorry, buddy, but you signed up for the Rachel special today—unpredictability with a side of chaos."

After a series of what I generously considered 'strategic maneuvers,' involving a few dead ends, a questionable shortcut through a parking lot, and a daring dash across a less-traveled bridge, I dared a glance in the mirror. The Mercedes was gone, lost to the wild goose chase I'd led it on.

My cell phone dinged. "Hey, Siri," I said, "read me my latest text message."

"You have a new message from a blocked number. Would you like me to read it?"

I answered yes.

"You may have won the battle, but the war is far from over. I won't lose." Siri paused and said, "Would you like to reply?"

"No. Hey Siri, send Bubba my location."

"I am sending your location to Bubba."

We couldn't determine the number, but Bubba might be able to work his magic and connect the text to a specific Mercedes in the area, though the chance was slim.

I called Levy and filled her in. "Listen, we shouldn't travel alone right now," she said. "Next time you go for an interview, bring one of us, okay?"

"I'll try," I said and clicked end call.

Ten minutes later, Bubba let me know he couldn't attach the call to any Mercedes in the area. "First of all, there are three hundred within a ten-mile radius of your location, and second, I'm a failure."

"You're not a failure. I knew it was a long shot."

"I guess it's something I'll add to my list."

A cool rush of air-conditioned breeze brushed against my face when I pushed open the heavy glass door into Sunset Assisted Living. It carried with it the faint scents of antiseptic and fresh linen. A dance party in progress in the lounge area caught my immediate attention. Elderly folk with walkers, canes, and even in wheelchairs danced to the electric piano. They did their best to swing dance like it was 1945 all over again. Santa Claus, or maybe his grandfather, noticed me and motioned for me to come dance. I smiled and shook my head. Rhythm wasn't my friend, and dancing wasn't my wheelhouse.

A young woman with a bright, practiced smile standing at the reception counter caught my attention. "Good morning! How can I help you?" she asked, her voice carrying a cheerful lilt. She noticed me looking at the crowd. "Oh, don't mind them. They do this every morning. It's adorable, don't you think?"

I nodded. "I wish I had the flexibility some of them do."

She leaned over the counter and said, "It's the drugs. Half of them aren't feeling a thing right now."

I pretended to laugh. "I'm here to see Al Castleberry." I adjusted the strap of my bag on my shoulder and grabbed my badge from my pocket.

Before I showed it to her, her expression shifted, the smile replaced with suspicion. "Are you family?"

I held up my badge. "No, I'm with the Hamby PD, his former employer. I'm here to ask him about a case from 1984."

Her face reddened. "I didn't mean what I said about the drugs." She turned an even deeper shade of red. "I mean, I did, but the drugs are legal, of course, and we don't give them more than their doctors prescribe."

"I'm just here to see Al Castleberry."

"Right. Just a moment." She stepped around the counter and walked to a small glassed-in office across from me, opened the door, walked in, closed it, and talked to the man inside.

As she walked out, she said, "The manager will be right with you."

I waited impatiently for him, watching the group dance like there was no tomorrow. Hopefully there was for all of them.

"Hello," the manager said as he closed his door behind him. "I'm Brad Jacobs, the manager. You're here to talk to Al?"

"I am."

He eyed me suspiciously. "From the Hamby police?"

"Yes."

"Do you have any ID?"

I showed him my badge. "That good enough?" I asked with a smile.

"Thank you," he said. "Al loves visitors, but you should know, he's in our memory care unit. His dementia has worsened, and his days are a bit unpredictable."

A knot formed in my stomach. "I understand. I just need a few minutes with him."

Two young men walked in and stood behind us. "We're here for the volunteer program through the Fulton County Y."

"Oh," the receptionist said. "Great. We need all the help we can get." She glanced at her boss and quickly added, "I mean, we love our volunteers!"

I'm not psychic, but I saw that girl looking for a new job soon.

After a brief check-in process, Brad Jacobs led me down a softly lit corridor. "His memory comes and goes," he said. "It's unpredictable, so I can't promise he'll be much help, but you're welcome to try. Just be prepared. He might not understand why you're here."

We reached a door at the end of the hall. He knocked gently before pushing it open. The room was small but cozy, filled with the warm glow of sunlight filtering through sheer curtains. The antiseptic smell hadn't disappeared, but the fresh linen had been replaced by something I couldn't name.

Al Castleberry sat by the window with a thin blanket draped over his knees. He had snowy white hair, and his face hadn't seen a razor in days. His hands trembled slightly as they rested on the arms of his chair.

"Al, you have a visitor," Brad Jacobs announced loudly as he stepped aside to let me in. He turned to me. "He has some hearing loss, so you'll need to speak louder than normal."

"Not a problem. Thank you."

The manager quietly excused himself. I took a seat beside Castleberry, noticing the collection of worn books on the table next to him. Was I looking into Lenny's future? He'd made me promise not to put him in an 'old folks home,' and I would honor that promise.

Lenny was my best friend Jenny's father. They lived in the left side of the duplex I grew up in. Lenny was the reason I'd become a cop, and eventually, I reported to him.

Jenny was killed on Lake Shore Drive by a man who'd had enough alcohol in him to kill a horse. I'd never been close to my parents, and Lenny and I had become family. My heart hurt. Was Al a symbol of what came next? I hated to think he was, but it was a possibility.

He looked up at me with cloudy eyes. For a moment, there was a flicker of confusion, then a beaming smile spread across his face. "Tina! You came to read to me again!" he exclaimed, his voice frail but filled with warmth.

A pang of sadness shot through me. He'd mistaken me for someone else. "Mr. Castleberry, it's nice to see you," I said, choosing not to correct him. "How are you feeling today?" I was trying to gauge his lucidity.

"Oh, just dandy, Tina. Just dandy. Did you bring that book we were enjoying? The one about the birds?"

I hesitated. "I forgot it today. But I thought maybe it would be fun to talk about you. Your time with the police department. Do you remember much about that?"

"Oh, sure," he said. "I always love talking about work. What do you want to know?"

"Do you remember anything about a missing person's case? A girl named Caroline Turner?" I showed him a photo of Caroline.

Castleberry's expression clouded over, his brow furrowing in concentration. "Caroline... Caroline..." he murmured, his voice trailing off. He looked out the window, lost in a world of his own. There sat a man who had once been a fountain of knowledge and experience, forever lost in the mists of his own mind. "I knew we wouldn't find her."

"Why did you think that?" I asked.

His eyes cleared for a short while. "Because she was dead," he said. He stared out the window, confusion taking over once again. After a few moments of silence, he turned back to me, his eyes returning to the present. "Would you like some tea, Tina? They make a lovely chamomile here."

Dead?

"No thank you," I said. I tried to bring him back to the conversation and showed him the picture again. "This is Caroline Turner. She went missing in 1984 at a festival in Alpharetta. You handled the report. Do you remember?"

"Oh, that was a tough one. Mayor Copeland was angry. He didn't want his son drawn into it, but you remember that, don't you, Tina?"

"I don't, Mr. Castleberry. Can you tell me about it?"

He chuckled. "You were there, remember? We've talked about this." He smiled. "And I've kept our secret." He handed me a book from the small table next to his chair. "Let's read this one. It's about aliens. They're real, you know."

"What secret?" I asked. "Can you remind me?"

He closed his eyes. "I'm going to rest a bit. Would you tell my wife to wake me for lunch?"

"Sure," I said. I sat there for a while thinking he might wake up, but thirty minutes later, he still hadn't.

I gave the manager two of my business cards on my way out. "If possible, I need to speak to this Tina person who reads to him. Can you ask her to contact me?"

He took the cards. "Tina? I'm afraid there's no Tina who reads to him. Unfortunately, no one reads to him. His daughter visits once in a while, but less and less now that his memory is worse. He doesn't usually remember her."

"He seemed to remember the person I asked him about."

"Possibly," he said. "But he mixes up stories. Different people, different times, different places. It's quite sad, but not unusual. Perhaps he's made her up or is remembering something from his past and mixing it with the present."

"Tina," I said to Bishop. "He's been talking to someone named Tina about Caroline Turner."

"Recently?" Bishop asked.

"I don't know, but he said he's keeping their secret. Whoever she is, he claims she was there."

"Maybe it's a friend or family member?" He must have been emptying his dishwasher. Glasses clinked, and I heard the distinct sound of utensils being dropped into a drawer. "I don't remember anyone named Tina from high school. Sue, Mary, Lisa, Karen. Those, I remember. Not sure if Tina was a popular name back then."

"Maybe she wasn't from back then." A call beeped in. "Hey," I said after checking the caller ID. "It's Jimmy. I need to run."

"Call me back," he said as I clicked over to Jimmy.

"I'm on my way in now," I said.

"Come see me right away." His voice was heavy and clearly frustrated.

My body stiffened. "What's wrong? Is it about Bishop?"

"I'll talk to you when you get here." He ended the call.

I tapped my fingers on my steering wheel as I drove to the station. Had something come to light? If it had, it wasn't good.

Thirty minutes later I'd found out.

I jumped from my seat across from his desk. "You've got to be kidding me. Can he even do that?"

"Not without the approval of city council."

"Does he have it?"

"They're having a meeting in," he checked his watch, "fifteen minutes."

"We're going," I said. "We have to state our case. Did you get a chance to talk to anyone in city council?"

"No. I'm going to the meeting," he said, his tone calm but firm. "You can go if you promise to keep your emotions intact."

I hated making a promise I wasn't sure I could keep, but I did. "What about the others?"

"We'll grab them on our way."

"Does Bishop know?"

"I sent him a text after I called you."

Fifteen minutes later we all sat in the front row of Hamby's City Council waiting for the meeting to start. Tension filled our section of the room. I fidgeted, my hands clammy as the council members muttered among themselves.

The mayor's whiny voice sliced through the charged atmosphere. "We're here today to discuss the employment status of Detective Rob Bishop."

Michels coughed, muttering, "Asshole," under his breath.

Levy knocked her knee into his. "Don't make it worse than it already is."

"Just stating facts."

The mayor, oblivious to the undercurrents, continued addressing the council members from his seat in the middle. "As you are aware, Detective Bishop has been accused of sexual harassment, and after a thorough investigation, it has been determined that the accusation is in fact, true."

He opened his laptop and my stomach turned. He had something. What? What had the killer provided as proof?

His eyes landed on Jimmy. "This is a conversation between the victim and Detective Bishop."

The door to the court-style room opened, and in walked Bishop and a man I assumed was his attorney. The man said, "Mr. Mayor, given this is a meeting to discuss the employment of my client, my client would like to address council."

Bishop's eyes met mine. He mouthed, *what the hell.*

I shrugged, my own eyes mirroring his confusion and fear. We wouldn't let the killer win. Whatever he brought to the table we'd hit with a spray of bullets and rip it to shreds.

"And your name is?" the mayor asked.

"Dexter Lantry, sir."

Levy whispered in my ear. "He better be good."

"I hope so," I said.

The mayor, momentarily taken aback as if he knew the name, regained his composure. "We'll consider your request after this presentation," he said, gesturing to the laptop.

The laptop screen appeared on the white wall behind him. "As I was saying, we've acquired a portion of the conversation between Detective Bishop and our victim."

Bishop sat beside me, but his attorney remained standing in the aisle. "Who is your victim, Mayor?" Lantry asked.

"I am not at liberty to say."

"With all due respect, we will subpoena that information, and request the council hear Detective Bishop's case."

"Feel free," he said. He clicked something on his laptop, and the recorded conversation started quickly.

My stomach twisted as Bishop's supposed voice filled the room. But it wasn't him. It couldn't have been him. I knew my partner, and he wasn't a creep who used his power to intimidate people, unlike our mayor.

'Why don't we have a drink and discuss it?'

'I don't think that's appropriate, Detective.'

'I'm not interested in what's appropriate. I'm interested in being inappropriate with you.'

I clenched my fists, feeling a surge of protectiveness surge through me.

It definitely wasn't Bishop. Something was off. It was close, but it wasn't him. I bit my lip hard, fighting the urge to shout out the truth.

Bishop whispered urgently to Lantry, who nodded, his expression grim. "My client refutes this. It's not him," Lantry declared. "And he is willing to repeat what's on the recording to prove it."

The mayor pressed the pause button and said, "Let it finish." He rewound it back to the beginning.

I was fuming. He'd done that on purpose.

'Detective, please,' the woman continued. *'You're making me uncomfortable.'*

'I can make you feel things you've never felt before,' the male voice said.

We listened to five minutes of someone posing as Bishop offering to tie up the woman, smack her on the ass, and use a leather whip on her.

It lit a fire under me that burned hotter than asphalt. Our killer had decided to up the ante, thinking they were playing high stakes poker with a royal flush. Little did they know, we were about to go all in, pushing the game way beyond their petty cheats. They thought they were climbing the ladder, but we were about to show them the express elevator to justice ran a hell of a lot faster.

Lantry interjected forcefully. "Mayor, we demand a chance to respond."

The mayor conferred with his advisors, which was clearly more of a theatrical display of deliberation than a necessity. "We'll meet again in two weeks. During that time, your client remains suspended without pay."

I couldn't hold back. "Asshole." The word slipped out, louder than intended.

"Detective Ryder?" the mayor's voice dripped with condescension. "I'm aware that insubordination isn't new to you, and it won't be tolerated by the council." He focused his eyes sternly on Jimmy. "Chief Abernathy, I suggest you keep your department in line. I'd hate to have to find replacements for all of you."

Jimmy stood, his stature commanding, but his tone respectful. "Mayor, we need our detectives, Bishop included. We have a double homicide to solve."

The mayor's glance was sharp as a knife. "The suspension stands. Best you keep your other detectives in line, Chief."

"Asshole," I repeated as they left.

"Ryder," Jimmy's tone was a warning. He only used that tone when he was in full chief mode. "Enough."

"That's not Bishop, and you know it. Why didn't you bring up the killer? The text messages or the crap happening to us? It's clearly related."

"We have a strategy," Mr. Lantry said. "I'll get a subpoena for a copy of that file, as well as one for the accuser's identity."

"Good," I said.

"I felt sick hearing that recording," Levy said, "but you can tell it's not him. There's something slightly off. Maybe the way the words are said?"

"It's not me," he said. "I'd never say anything like that."

We all knew that. Bishop could barely look at the S&M room the Blahuts' had hidden in their basement. His face blushed redder than diaper rash.

"I know," Jimmy said. He looked to the attorney for guidance. "Anything specific we should do next?"

"Keep looking for that killer. If it's our accuser like we believe, we won't get an ID on the woman's voice." He said his goodbyes and promised to be in touch with Bishop soon.

"He put it two weeks out on purpose," I said. "He knows we need Bishop, but he doesn't care. Someone needs to let the public know our mayor is more interested in revenge than justice."

"Ryder," Jimmy said, his voice clear and distinct. "Let's not go there. We don't know how far he's willing to take this."

"He can take it straight to hell," I said.

"Rach," Bishop said. He eyed the room as if there might be recording devices hidden somewhere.

I suspected there were.

"We'll figure it out."

Bubba, who had been a silent storm until then, suddenly became the eye of our hurricane. "It's AI. That's how they made it sound like him." He paced, each step like a metronome ticking away in the charged silence of the room. His eyes had that faraway look of a man piecing together a complex puzzle, and we all hung on his next words. "It's definitely AI," he concluded, more to himself than to us.

I hadn't even considered that. AI—artificial intelligence—the digital ghost we'd all heard of but had to the best of our knowledge, never seen. What happened to normal criminals? Ones who weren't tech-savvy? Were we suddenly in a sci-fi movie?

Jimmy pressed on. "Can you prove it?" His voice was steady, but I saw how the gears turned in his head.

Bubba stopped pacing and faced us. "There are programs available that claim they can, but I'll have to try them." His voice sounded more worried than confident which only worried me more.

Bishop sprang into action. He retrieved his cell from his jacket pocket with a suddenness that made me jump. "I'll let my attorney know." He sounded hopeful but also resigned. Hope that Bubba could pull off a miracle, resignation at the nightmare his life had become.

Levy leaned in. "But how accurate is this AI? I've heard it's still got a lot of quirks. Can it really mimic someone perfectly?"

"Not perfectly, which is obvious to us in that recording." Bubba turned to her, the teacher ready to educate. "But it's scary how good they are. They can analyze a person's speech pattern, tone, even their emotional inflections. Just a few recordings of someone's voice, and they can make them say anything."

A collective shiver ran through us as we thought about what that could mean.

Michels whistled low, breaking the eerie silence. "That's some Orwellian crazy right there."

Jimmy rubbed his chin, deep in thought. "We need to move fast. If this AI thing can be debunked, we need to do it yesterday."

Bishop nodded. He was a man clutching at straws. "Whatever it takes."

I agreed. The entire scenario was like walking on a tightrope over an abyss. The idea that someone could be framed so convincingly was terrifying. We didn't have the skillset, or possibly even the technology to combat something so manipulative. It wasn't just Bishop on trial; it was all of us, not to mention truth and justice, bending under the weight of technology.

My cell phone dinged with another text message. I quickly checked the message.

How's your day going, Detective?

15

Tension filled the air at the station as word spread quickly. If it could happen to Bishop, a stand-up guy, everyone thought, it could happen to anyone.

In the investigation room, I said, "How's your day going, Detective?"

"Uh, what?" Michels asked.

I held up my phone. "It's another text. Feels like the killer's trying to stay relevant. The text means nothing."

"Unless it's a passive aggressive warning that something's coming," Levy said.

"I can't wait until we catch this guy," Michels said. "I'm going to beat his ass."

Jimmy said, "Bubba's researching how to resolve Bishop's situation. He and Bishop's attorney have been connected." He looked at Levy, then Michels, then me. "The killer isn't going to stop until we stop him."

"That's the plan," Michels said.

"I understand," Jimmy said, "but we have two homicides to solve, and while I'm just as worried as you are about Rob, we have to do our jobs. The mayor wants us all on a chopping block."

A knock on the door stopped him. I leaned behind me and opened it.

Savannah walked in. "I have information." She flicked her hair back. "And it's good."

Savannah had a way of working a room. She could lighten a tense mood, clear the thickness in the air, and make people forget their problems just by existing. Her arrival was a necessary break and the lift we needed.

"Praise God and thank you, Jesus," Michels said.

I eyed him as I raised my eyebrow.

He blinked. "I meant that." He blushed. "I've been going to church with Ashley to get to know the pastor who's going to marry us."

"No need to blush," I said. It was well known I was a firm believer there wasn't a God, but Kyle had me seeing things through clear eyes, and I couldn't say that any longer.

"Come in," Jimmy said to his wife.

Always a beacon of fashion, she'd chosen what she would call a power outfit: a white, button-down silk blouse, black wide-legged satin pants, red stilettos, and a red and black checkered scarf. I knew when she wore the scarf, she meant business. She sashayed over to his side of the small room and stood behind him, her stilettos not getting her above five feet five inches. "I had brunch with Jenna Matteson." A smile stretched across her face. "That woman could talk the ears off a cornstalk."

Jimmy cleared his throat. "Honey, we're in the middle of something. Can you give us the highlights, please?"

"Of course." She smiled again. "An unknown, completely anonymous woman sent a recording of a conversation she claims to have had with Rob six months ago. She has not filed any official report, nor has she been interviewed. The only reason they know she sent the recording is because the letter she sent with it said it was her in it."

"Wait," I said, "does that mean no one's talked to her?"

"Yes."

"They're basing a man's career, his pension, on a recording alone?" Michels said. "Any half decent lawyer could rip that to shreds, and we now have reasonable doubt that this isn't connected to our double murders."

"Which is why the mayor wouldn't let Bishop state his case today," I said. "Because he knows if we can link it, Bishop's off the hook."

"That's not all. It's absolutely about the DUI Bishop gave the mayor's child nine years ago. Jenna said the mayor is using Bishop as an example to show that crossing him or his family has consequences."

She flipped around, kissed her husband on the cheek, and said, "I'll let you know what else I can find out." She hurried toward the door, making sure to place her hand on my shoulder and squeeze before leaving.

"I'd rule the world if I had half the tact of that woman," Levy said.

I held up my Diet Coke. "I'll drink to that."

Jimmy smirked then quickly shook his head. "Two can play at that game," he said, his smirk growing bigger. "Consider these murders our lifeboat. We fall off, we're done. So, we're all hands-on deck." He looked at me. "Not only do we have to find a killer, we have to be able to prove the anonymous recording is AI and from the killer."

"A woman," I said.

"We can't say that for sure," Jimmy said.

"I wouldn't put it past a killer to fake their gender to put us off track," Levy said.

"I agree," Jimmy said. "Let's continue this without the lean toward a female. If we come to that naturally, then okay." He pointed to me. "Rachel's lead. You need anyone or anything, you've got it." He exhaled, then added, "I've been at this too long to let some scrawny mayor who's only been in office six months walk all over me or my department, killer to blame or not." He nodded once, then charged around the table and out of the room.

"He's pissed," Levy said.

"As he should be," Michels added. He eyed me. "What's next?"

I explained what had happened with Al Castleberry, the detective who'd handled Turner's missing persons case.

"Castleberry?" Levy said. "They're everywhere, aren't they?"

"Pretty much," I said. "This town is too incestual for me."

"It's not just this town," Michels said. "It's the whole area. Any idea who this Tina is? Could she be the killer?"

"I'm not sure, but we're going to find out." I clicked on the landline and dialed dispatch. "This is Detective Ryder. Can you please tell the shift commander we need two officers to help with the homicide investigation, and have them sent to the investigation room STAT, please?"

"Sure thing, Detective," the dispatch woman said.

"What're you doing?" Levy asked. Her smile told me she expected it to be good.

"Staging two volunteers at the assisted living facility to watch for this Tina person."

"How do you plan to do that?" Michels asked.

"There's a volunteer program through the Fulton County YMCA. I'll make a call."

"She could use another name," Levy said. "And a disguise."

"I'll have them take pictures and we'll try to identify her face."

"You think she's our killer?" Michels asked.

"I'm not sure, but I know she's been talking to the detective about the murders, and it might not be a coincidence that a female reported Bishop." I cleared my throat. "If the killer's looking for weakness in the team, using the mayor's feelings for Bishop is a good start. It can go both ways. Use AI for a female voice to put us off track or use a female voice to represent who we're dealing with."

"Because she's cocky and thinks we won't move with it," Michels said.

"I'm hoping that's it, but I texted Bubba and asked him to run whatever it is he's running on Bishop on the female voice as well. If it's not AI, then we have a stronger case for our killer being female."

"And we'll run with it regardless of what Jimmy said," Michels said.

"We're not dropping any options," I said. "We're making sure to cover them all."

I explained the situation to the officers when they arrived and made the call to the Fulton County Y to bring them into what we'd planned. The manager of the program knew Bishop from the Big Brothers program in the county, so he gladly agreed. Since we had no description of Tina, I stressed how important it was for the officers to photograph everyone and watch where they went without being obvious. And most of all, I explained that we didn't want anyone at the facility to know they were law enforcement.

After we sent them off, I assigned Levy and Michels to hit the school and talk to Herman the janitor and Betty Halliday in the cafeteria at Hamby High. They needed to get out of the building and away from the paperwork for a change. I left a message for the night shift commander to call me back.

I was head down into the files in search of something one of us might have missed, frustrated with having to do it again. I repeated out loud what Lenny had told me during my first investigation as a detective. "When in doubt, find another route."

The receptionist called me on the investigation room's speaker. "Detective, there is a Christina Carter here to see you."

"Okay," I said. "I'll be right there." I gathered my things and headed to the reception area. "Mrs. Carter," I said as I closed the door behind me. "What can I do for you?"

"I've been thinking about Caroline. I decided to go through some of my things from my high school years and see if that would help gain any perspective on what might have happened to the poor girl." She glanced behind me. "Is Rob coming?"

"Detective Bishop is on another assignment at the moment."

"Oh, that's too bad. I thought he might enjoy the photos. Is there somewhere we can talk privately?"

"Sure," I said. Hoping she had something worth sharing, I escorted her through security, checked her in, and then walked her to a small conference room. On the way, I asked, "Would you like something to drink?"

"No, thank you. I just had lunch."

I held the door open for her. "Please make yourself as comfortable as possible on our metal chairs."

She giggled. "I'm sure they're lovely."

I sat across from her. "What is it you'd like to tell me?"

"Are you any closer to finding the killer?"

"I can't give you any specifics on our investigation, but yes, we're very close." I'd learned to never say we hadn't a clue even when it was the truth.

"That's fantastic," she said. She removed a photo album from her bag. "I completely forgot about this. It's a photo album from the time shortly before Caroline went missing." She flipped through it and sighed. "I guess we spent more time together than I recalled. I'd just graduated from college and was heading off to graduate school that fall. I ran into Caroline quite often in town." She twirled the album to face me and slid it across the small table. "You know she and Steve Copeland were a hot item for quite some time. Even after they went to juvenile detention. I think I'd forgotten just how long."

"Yes," I said. "We're aware." I studied the photos. "I'm not sure what I'm looking at here. Can you please explain?"

She pointed to the first photo. "That's Caroline, but you obviously know that. The person on her right is me. I had big hair in those days," she said blushing. "And that's Steve on her left."

"Who's next to you?" I asked.

"Oh, that's Billy Jacobs." She sighed. "He passed away shortly after that photo was taken. Overdose."

"I'm sorry."

"It was the 80s. Drugs were different then, yes, but young people still liked to party hard." She took a breath and added, "The woman on the other side of Steve is Holly Grimes, and she's why I'm here."

"Okay?"

"This was a week before the festival. She was gone three weeks later, but she was also at the festival that night, and I don't know how I could have forgotten any of this, but she had a thing for Steve." She rolled her eyes. "Every girl had a thing for him because he was attractive and the bad boy. Like Kevin Bacon in Footloose, but more of a burn out, as we used to call them." She giggled at her comment but then turned solemn. "She tried hard to get in between Steve and Caroline, but it never happened. The night of these photos she told me she'd do whatever was necessary to get Caroline away from him."

I raised an eyebrow. "That sounds pretty intense for a crush."

Christina nodded, a trace of a smirk playing on her lips. "Oh, it was more than a crush. Holly was fixated on Steve. She'd go on about how they were meant to be together, how Caroline was just a temporary obstacle. The night before the festival," she stopped and stared at the wall, "maybe two nights before. I can't be sure. She was almost hysterical. She was adamant about them being together. 'Steve will be mine no matter what Caroline does,' she declared. And when she saw them together at the festival, she looked like she could explode."

Her words painted a picture of a jealousy-ridden young woman, but something about the way Christina relished these details unsettled me.

"Did Holly ever mention any specific plans to hurt Caroline?" I probed for more concrete evidence and to see if she was lying.

Christina pursed her lips. "Not outright plans, no. But she always hinted at it. 'Caroline won't be in the way much longer,' she'd say. And after Caroline disappeared, and Holly still wasn't with Steve, in fact, he'd completely ignored her, she was different. Quieter, but with this undercurrent of, I don't know, guilt, maybe? It's like she got what she wanted, but at a cost."

She sighed, her expression shifting to one of reflective sorrow. "And then Holly died in that crash only two weeks after Caroline went missing. I just realized that maybe she did it? Maybe she killed her out of jealousy, and the guilt got to her. I can't believe this didn't cross my mind before, but looking back now, it all seems like too much of a coincidence."

I nodded, still unsure how much of Christina's story to take at face value. "Did you know Holly well?"

"As well as I could having been at college. We hung out a lot that summer though. After Caroline and the others went to detention in high school, it had become clear that Holly liked Steve. Caroline and I weren't close then, which I think I mentioned, but we did hang around each other some. We just weren't like we'd been before she changed." She glanced at her nails, then smiled. "Would you like to keep any of the photos?"

"I would," I said.

"I'd like them back, of course."

"Of course," I said. "Thanks, Christina. This gives us a new angle to consider." Her story had the pull of a well-crafted mystery, detailed and engaging, yet something in my gut whispered that there was more beneath the surface. More that Christina, despite her apparent openness, kept carefully under wraps.

Christina's story hadn't jibed with Copeland's, so after texting the others, I left to talk with him again.

"Oh, Mr. Copeland is at a work site," his receptionist said. "He won't be back in the office today."

"Do you know which site?" I asked.

"Yes, ma'am, he's at the Resurgeons site on Ronald Reagan in Cumming. Are you planning to stop there?"

"I am."

She smiled. "I drive past it on my way home every night. You can't miss it, but you'll need a hardhat."

"I've got one." I smiled. "Thanks for the help."

"Sure thing."

It wasn't a long drive to the construction site, but traffic on Bethelview added an additional ten minutes. I parked my Jeep on the side of the road in front of the site, grabbed my hard hat from the back, and headed to the trailer.

A stout man, his frame enveloped in a neon reflective vest that clung to his broad shoulders, leaned heavily against a makeshift counter in the cramped construction site trailer office. Dust and the scent of fresh timber and the faint aroma of stale coffee filled the air. It reminded me of the coffee at the department.

The man was engrossed in the site drawing spread before him, tracing lines and measurements with a calloused finger. The fluorescent lights buzzed overhead highlighting the creases of concentration on his forehead. As I stepped in, the sound of gravel crunching underfoot must have reached him. He jerked his head up, his eyes narrowing slightly as they shifted from the blueprint to meet mine. "Help you?"

"I'm looking for Steve Copeland." I showed him my badge. "Can you tell me where I can find him?"

He eyed my badge. "We're not breaking any laws here, ma'am."

"I'm not here about the site."

"Thank God. We had someone complain about us last week. Cops were here for five hours. Put us back a day, and we're already running late on the project."

That wasn't uncommon in Chicago, but in Cumming, Georgia, it seemed highly unusual. "What for?"

"Someone said there was a body buried here. Gave some cryptic message about its location. Cops had dogs on the site sniffing everything, but they never found anything."

"Who filed the complaint?" I asked.

He shrugged. "Said it was anonymous."

Someone calls in an anonymous buried body call right before someone accuses Rob of sexual harassment and multiple texts and followings? Didn't seem like a coincidence to me. "I'm not here looking for bodies," I said, "but if I happen to find one, you're the first person I'll tell." I smiled.

He laughed. "Don't come to me. Find Copeland." As I slipped on my hard hat, he added, "Hold on. You can't wear a yellow hat." He tossed me a gray one. "This is for visitors. Keep it. It's new."

"Thanks. Know where I can find him?"

He pointed behind him and to the left. "Toward the back. But he's a mover, so you may be on the chase a while."

"Not my first time," I said and headed out of the trailer.

Steve Copeland, decked out in his neon-orange vest and a hard hat as white as a Hollywood smile, stood like a lighthouse of order in the middle of the construction site's bedlam. The moment his eyes caught mine, his head dipped in a kind of *here we go again* nod, and then he was on the move. He marched over, each step with his steel-toed boots hitting the gravel like a drummer keeping beat, a clear sign he was coming full throttle. "Detective Ryder, correct?" he called out over the din of machinery. "What can I do for you?" His voice was almost drowned out by the sounds of jackhammers and the distant, rhythmic thudding of heavy equipment.

"I've got some follow up questions regarding the days surrounding Caroline Turner's disappearance," I said, raising my voice to be heard.

Workers in similar bright vests moved like ants on towering steel frames. He surveyed the area. "I'm a little busy at the moment. Can this wait?"

I met his gaze squarely, my voice firm against the backdrop of shouting workers and the distant whine of a circular saw. "How would you feel if your child was dead, and someone didn't want to answer questions?"

He exhaled. "Got it. Follow me." We moved to a quieter corner of the site, the sounds of construction finally a dull rumble in the background. Once in the area, he asked what I needed to know, though his tone dripped with annoyance.

"We've interviewed several people associated with you and Caroline, and the information they've provided conflicts with yours. I'd like to go over your relationship with her around the time she disappeared."

He chuckled at this, but it was a hollow sound, devoid of real amusement. "Conflicting information? I'm sure that's because it was almost forty years ago." He chuckled, but it didn't sound genuine. "I can barely remember last week let alone back then."

"We've been told that you and Caroline were, in fact, still in a relationship at that time, and that it was hot and heavy. Perhaps you confused the night she went missing with another time?"

He glanced behind me, where workers were unloading tools and materials from a truck, before focusing back on me. "Yes, I might have made light of my relationship with Caroline. It wasn't a good time in my life," he said. "I'd begun straightening up after high school, which I think I told you before."

"You did."

"But I couldn't drop Caroline." He fished out a small plastic tube from his pocket, popped it open with a click, and offered me a mint. I declined, so he took one for himself, the mint's sharp scent briefly cutting through the dusty air.

"I'd stopped doing drugs like we did in high school, but did I still get high? Yeah. Mostly pot, a little speed every now and then, but nothing other than that. I knew I needed to get myself together, and I was trying."

"Was Caroline into heavier drugs?"

He nodded, his gaze softening with a hint of sorrow. "We'd fought about it multiple times, but she couldn't stop. She was in deep."

"And you stayed with her?"

His eyes softened. "I loved her. I thought I could save her."

"Tell me about Holly Grimes."

He blinked. "Holly? I haven't heard that name in forever. What do you want to know?"

"Did you have a relationship with her?"

"I wouldn't call it a relationship. We had sex a few times, but that was it."

I pressed my lips together then asked, "Were you dating Caroline at the time?"

"I wasn't a good guy back then, Detective. I also wasn't picky, no matter how I felt about Caroline."

"Did Caroline know?"

"About Holly?" He nodded. "But she understood. She forgave me. She and Holly hung out together sometimes after that too. I don't think it was a big deal."

"Did Holly ever mention having feelings for you?"

"I mean, sure, in high school mostly, but I don't think it came up after we graduated." His brows furrowed, leaving a deep wrinkle on the bridge of his nose. "Holly died around the time Caroline disappeared. Car accident." His eyes widened. "Wait a minute. You don't think Holly had something to do with Caroline's murder, do you?"

No, but I couldn't tell him that, and I had to rule out everything in the event we did make an arrest. I didn't want some defense attorney blowing the case. "We're looking into every angle," I said. "Do you think it?"

As we delved deeper, Copeland's expression became increasingly troubled, his brows knitting together in concern. "Holly wasn't the type. She was nice. Too nice, really." He shook his head. "Who's telling you she could have killed Caroline?"

"I didn't say anyone told me that. Do you recall Caroline doing any drugs the evening she disappeared?" I asked.

"She didn't. That much, I know. She knew I was struggling with staying with her while trying to improve my life, and she promised to stop. She'd been clean for a few days. I think she was truly trying, though I can't say it would have lasted."

"Why didn't you tell me any of this before?" I asked.

"Detective, I have a large business that does most of the commercial construction in the metro area. I have a reputation, and I don't want to damage it. The more I distance myself from this, the better." He cleared his throat. "I've already said too much." He scanned the area. "I've got to get back to work." He turned to walk back to where I'd found him.

"One more thing, Mr. Copeland."

He turned around but didn't say anything, so I asked, "Did you murder Caroline Turner?"

"If you want to speak with me again, you can do so with my attorney present."

Officer Gregory called as I walked back to my vehicle. "Detective, we've had three women come into the assisted living, but none have gone to see Detective Castleberry."

"Did you get pictures?" I asked.

"Yes, ma'am, but they're not great."

"I'm sure you did the best you could. Please send them to me."

"I will," he said.

I stopped a few feet from my vehicle, the gas smell hitting me hard. "What the ever-loving—" I swiped my phone open again and called Levy. "My Jeep is trashed. I'm at Copeland's construction site. I've been here for no more than 45 minutes, but my car's toast. Every window is busted, my tires are all slashed, and," I opened the hood, "they poured gas all over my engine." I dropped a paragraph full of cuss words. "I need a ride."

"Call the Forsyth County Sheriff and file a report," she said. "We're finishing up at the school and will be on our way."

"Thanks," I said. I disconnected the call and contacted Forsyth County. They said they'd have someone to me within the half hour. As I hung back waiting for them to arrive, my eyes did a quick sweep of the scene—standard issue nothingness. Had our friend the killer shadowed me again? I'd thrown looks over my shoulder enough times on the route to make a paranoid twitch, but saw nothing. Either I was batting a big fat zero in the tail-catching game, or this killer was playing chess while I was stuck on checkers.

I examined the exterior of my vehicle noting several new scratches, then checked inside through the broken windows. A piece of copy paper folded in half sat on my seat. I opened the door and carefully removed it with the tips of my fingers. It had one word written on it.

Boom.

The moment was surreal, like a bad scene from a B-movie I wouldn't even watch on Netflix. One second, I was standing there, the next, my skin crawled with the kind of realization you didn't get in a fortune cookie.

My heart didn't just beat; it beat like a Phil Collins drum solo. Adrenaline wasn't just a word in a medical dictionary anymore. It was my reality. I spun around and booked it away from my Jeep with the grace of a gazelle on a caffeine high.

Boom!

In a flash of light and smoke, the world turned into a Tom Cruise movie. I leapt towards a ditch across the street. The ground shuddered like it was auditioning for a dance competition, and I hit the dirt, hard.

Curled up and madder than hell, I felt the heat roll over me. I peeked out to see my Jeep putting on a fire show. "Well, that's just great," I muttered. Flames were making a meal out of my ride, sending up smoke signals that could be seen from the moon.

Anger bubbled up inside me, not your everyday frustration, but the kind of anger that could make a nun swear. My Jeep, the one Tommy had purchased just days before his murder, had turned to burnt toast. My case, my whole day—blown to smithereens. It was no accident. It was a hello note written in fire and brimstone.

One the killer would regret.

Brushing off the dirt, I stood up and coughed. The air tasted like a rubber and gasoline cocktail. A few onlookers from the construction site did their best statue impressions, watching the firework display like children.

Staring at the remains of my Jeep, I felt something click. This wasn't just a warning call; it was a full-on rock band in my living room. The killer wasn't playing games anymore. I must have been onto something he or she didn't like. If this was a last man standing thing, I was all in, and I wouldn't let the bad guys win.

They thought they could scare me, but they just cranked up the volume on my determination. I turned from the barbecue that used to be my Jeep, my mind already leaping ahead. Deputies were already on their way, but we needed more. It was time to roll out the red carpet for the Forsyth County bomb squad and forensics.

The air was a smorgasbord of burnt offerings—a metal and rubber entrée with a side of vengeance. I coughed so much my lungs hurt. There I stood, a detective turned avenger, eyeing the remains of my former Jeep, ready for the infinity war.

It was showtime.

Forsyth County Sheriff's deputies and firefighters worked in unison to stop the flames, keep traffic from passing, and interview the construction workers from Copeland's site. I just watched, furious, my mind racing, my heart ready to mimic the explosion.

Levy and Michels pulled their vehicle to the edge of the scene, climbed out and showed their badge to the attending deputy. He turned and pointed at me. They jogged over, their eyes wide with unspoken questions.

Levy placed her hand on my shoulder. "Are you okay?" she asked, her voice barely rising above the commotion.

I stood across the street, watching the action, trying to stitch together the why and how, with Detectives Levy and Michels as my less-than-enthusiastic choir. "Physically, yes. Mentally? Not even close."

"It was Tommy's, wasn't it?" she asked.

I nodded. "And now it's gone." A charred remnant of memories of Tommy. I clenched my fists, feeling the anger boiling inside me.

"Whoever did it didn't want you dead," she said.

"No, but they wanted to make a point."

Michels offered to listen in as the deputies asked questions of Copeland's employees.

"It's not one of them," I said. "This wasn't about the site."

"I know," Levy said. "You think you were followed?"

"I checked, but not well enough, I guess." I held the crumpled note in my hand. "This is ruined." I showed them the note.

A deputy approached with a look of seriousness etched on his face. "Detective Ryder. Can you share what happened?"

I recounted the events leading up to the explosion, my words laced with a venom I didn't know I possessed. I left out the fact that I believed the murderer of our investigation was the likely suspect.

The deputy nodded as he scribbled notes. "Anything else?"

"Yes," I said. "I'd like copies of the camera files for the area." I pointed to the two lights on each side of the street a few blocks away. "When can I have them?"

"I'll have to check with my supervisor," he said. "I believe this is our investigation."

"I'll have my chief call the sheriff," I said.

"Yes, ma'am." He excused himself to coordinate with the fire team.

"Michels, can you call Steve Copeland's office and request any surveillance video from the site?"

"Got it," he said.

Levy's eyes narrowed, her detective instincts kicking in. "Is it a coincidence this happened in front of Copeland's site?"

"Nope," I said.

Boom!

16

The world turned upside down again when another deafening blast cut through the air, a sound no human being should ever have to hear, and that I'd heard twice in less than two hours. From the corner of my eye, I watched as a fireball erupted from the construction site. The ground beneath us shook.

"Holy—" Instinct kicked in. I bolted toward the explosion, my legs moving faster than my brain. Behind me, Levy and Michels were close on my heels, their protests lost in the chaos.

A portion of Copeland's eight-story apartment building had become an inferno. Flames devoured the half-built skeleton, hungrily clawing at the sky. Heat hit my face like a physical slap, the air hard to breathe, heavy with the stench of burning plastic and scorched dreams.

"Ryder, wait up!" Levy barked. But caution was a train that had left the station.

The trailer. My mind fixated on it. I had been in there, talking to the man, but it had become ground zero for a firestorm. I tasted ash on my tongue, bitter and invasive, as I scanned the pandemonium.

Paramedics rushed by. The shrill sound of sirens merged with the crackling roar of the fire and created a melody of despair. Firefighters battled the blaze, like David against Goliath, but made of flame and smoke.

I coughed from the thick and hostile air and wiped my eyes. If blowing up my Jeep was about the investigation, then blowing up the construction site was as well. Which meant it was about Copeland.

I watched as a section of scaffolding groaned and then gave way, showering sparks like some twisted Fourth of July fireworks. The heat was relentless, an uninvited dance partner pressing too close, but I kept going.

"Lady, back off!" a firefighter shouted. He grabbed my arm. His grip was firm and insistent. I knew he was right, but damn it, it was my battle to fight.

For a moment, I stood there, the chaos swirling around me. Someone had turned my life into a blockbuster action movie, but I hadn't auditioned for the role. I looked back at Levy and Michels. They seemed just as determined as I felt.

"Two dead," a firefighter called out.

I channeled my high school track runner and raced to the firefighter. "In the trailer?"

"Ma'am?"

I showed him my badge. "Were there men in the trailer?"

"One was. The other was just outside it."

"This is Steve Copeland's site," I said. "He's here today. Find him."

17

I sat on my couch with a bag of ice on my forehead.

Savannah stared into my eyes. "Are you sure you're alright? Your pupils are dilated." She turned around and hollered toward my kitchen. "Babe, can a bomb cause brain damage?"

"I don't have brain damage. I have a headache."

"Lauren showed me photos of your Jeep."

"My previous Jeep."

She sighed. "It's toast."

"I know," I said. "And so is Copeland's apartment building." I thought about the man I'd talked to in the trailer. Was he the one they'd found deceased? Prior to leaving the scene, we'd heard five men had died, but identities hadn't been determined.

Kyle handed me a glass of water.

Jimmy had been on the phone with Barron. He walked from my garage back into the living area. "Copeland wasn't one of the deceased."

I never wished death upon someone, but I couldn't help but wonder if that had been the goal. Murder Copeland. Was the whole thing about Copeland in the first place? If that was the case, then we had to rethink him as a possible suspect. Of course, there was always the chance he'd set it up to look like someone wanted him dead to throw us off his scent or even for insurance purposes. I let that sit and stir in my aching brain for a while. "That's good."

After a moment of silence, Kyle said, "I ordered Rosati's. They're delivering here."

I blinked. "From Cumming? Aren't we a little out of their delivery zone?"

"I called in a favor," he said. He winked. "Connections."

"I appreciate it, but I'm not very hungry."

"We are," Bishop said, "and we need the nutrition to figure out what to do next."

"Nutrition?" Savannah asked. "Why pizza then?"

She had a point, but I loved Rosati's and would have at least a piece regardless of my lack of hunger. "I have a plan. We find the bastard who killed Turner and Berman and take him down."

"Good plan," Jimmy said. "But we need to flesh it out."

"Are you sure it's the same person?" Cathy asked.

"Yes." I sipped the water Kyle gave me, giving myself a moment to think it through. "Because nothing happened before the dog found Jennifer Berman. Bishop and I are primary on the investigation. I was followed when I went to see Al Castleberry, Bishop was accused of sexual assault by an unknown accuser, Michels gets run off the road, and now my Jeep becomes Wonder Bread?" My eyes widened. "Jimmy, whoever did this knows I went to see Castleberry. The night shift commander never returned my call." I jumped from the couch. "We need to check on him."

The pizza arrived. Levy grabbed it and distributed it out on paper plates from our cabinet.

"I've got it," Jimmy said. He contacted the Roswell Police Department and explained the situation. He asked their shift commander to make a courtesy call to check on Al Castleberry and requested a man on his room until we could get someone there. After disconnecting, he said, "They're on their way."

"What about Bubba?" Levy asked. "Did he figure out if the voices were real or AI?"

"I'll text him," Bishop said.

Five minutes later, Bubba was on his way to my place.

"Does he have it?" Levy asked.

"He said he's got news, but that was it," Bishop said.

Cathy whispered into Bishop's ear. He responded with a nod. "Cathy has plans, and it's too late to cancel."

"I'm sorry," she said. "I really want to help."

"Don't be sorry," I said.

"This is police business anyway," Jimmy said. "We'll be discussing confidential information." He made eye contact with Savannah. "Babe, I hate to—"

"Don't sweat it, sweetheart. I'll grab the kids and head home." She hugged me and then Bishop. "See y'all soon." She and Cathy walked out together.

"Guys," Levy said, "Something happened to me the other day, but I didn't think much of it until now."

"To you?" I asked.

She nodded. "I've been going through some things I've had in boxes since I moved to town. They're spread out in my garage, and I haven't been able to park in it for over a week now. Two mornings after the bodies were discovered, I walked out to my car, and the driver's side window was shattered."

"Why didn't you say anything?" I asked.

"Did you file a report?" Jimmy asked.

She shook her head. "It didn't seem like a big deal. It's low-level vandalism, not following someone or running them off the road, and Bishop's accusations hadn't happened yet. I figured it was a teenager, so, I called the window repair company, and they came out right away and fixed it. This kind of thing happened in Pennsylvania all the time. I just let it go."

"Any time something happens, report it," Jimmy said frustrated. "You know the rules."

"Yes, sir," she said.

"You have cameras, right?" Michels asked.

"Of course."

Kyle walked to the dining room and retrieved his laptop. "Let's look."

She signed into her security site. "There," she said. She paused the video, allowing us each a chance to study the image.

"It's hard to tell," I said, "but the build looks masculine."

"I agree," Bishop said.

"So, there's something," Michels said. "If we can link everything together, we know we're dealing with a male killer."

"Except we can't link everything together yet," Bishop said. "But we've got a female meeting with Castleberry which could turn out to be nothing, and a woman accusing me of sexual harassment. I could be wrong, but that looks like we're dealing with a female."

"The evidence will come if it's the same person," Jimmy said.

"I asked for the videos from Copeland's site and Forsyth County's traffic lights," I said to Jimmy. "Can you light a fire under someone to get the FoCo ones?" I coughed. It hurt my lungs. "I'll contact Copeland."

"I'll make another call," Jimmy said.

I had swiped a business card from Copeland's office the other day. I dug through my bag for it, and then called the emergency number on the back.

"Copeland Construction," a woman said. "This is an answering service. If this is an emergency, please call 911 and call us back."

"The emergency's already happened," I said. I gave her my information and asked to have Steve Copeland return my call immediately.

The call came less than two minutes later. "This is Steve Copeland. Were you injured?"

"My Jeep is history, but I'm fine," I said. "How about you?"

"In shock. We lost five men. Do you have any idea who did this?"

"We're looking into it. What about the man in the trailer? The stout one with a bald head. Is he okay?"

"He had gone to see the fire outside the property," he said. "He's fine."

"May we have copies of your security videos from the site?"

"I can't give you copies tonight, but I can give you temporary access. You can download them on your own."

"That would be great."

He provided us with a temporary, limited password giving us access to his videos.

"Detective," he said, "Five of my men are dead. Find the person who murdered them." He disconnected the call.

Levy sat beside me. "Maybe he's innocent?"

"Or he's a sociopath that just murdered five of his employees to make himself look innocent," I said.

"My gut says it's a woman," Bishop said.

"There is that."

I opened a laptop and accessed the videos. "There! The Mercedes. That's the vehicle that followed me the other day." I watched as it pulled into the construction entrance of the site. I took a screenshot and then downloaded the video and continued on to the next one.

"Where's the car?" Levy asked.

"I can't find it." I scanned through the rest of the videos and only found the Mercedes leaving the site the same way it had arrived. "Either we're not getting all the videos, or part of the site isn't covered."

"Maybe someone broke the cameras," Michels suggested.

"It's possible," Jimmy said. "I've got the FoCo videos. Look at this." He brought the laptop to the coffee table. "There's your Mercedes."

Michels cringed. "That's bold."

The Mercedes had pulled up next to my Jeep. A person dressed in all black with a black cap on climbed out of the driver's side, placed the explosive device under my vehicle, and then returned to the Mercedes.

"Wait," Levy said. "That's a woman."

"Holy hell," Bishop said. "It is."

I leaned back into the couch. "Women don't mess around. This is going to get worse."

Bubba arrived. "It's AI," he said right as he walked in. "I tried several different programs to check, and they all say the same thing."

"For both voices?" I asked.

"Just Bishop's. I did run a program to see if the other voice had been edited, and it has been."

"Can you determine who made the recording?" Bishop asked.

"I can do a lot, but technology hasn't caught up with AI enough just yet."

Levy looked at Jimmy. "At least we've got confirmation the complaint against Bishop is BS."

"We knew that the minute a woman bombed my Jeep."

"I'll contact City Council first thing in the morning."

"The mayor's going to be livid," Levy said.

"Let him be," Jimmy said. "He got duped. He should have looked into it before flying off the handle like he did."

"Wait," Bubba said. "The Jeep is gone?"

"Someone bombed it and then a Copeland construction site in Cumming," I said.

"Oh, man. That's terrible."

Bishop said, "Copeland's the key to this. We need to figure out how he's connected to Jennifer Berman."

"This isn't about now," I said. "This is about 1984. He did something bad enough to drive a young woman to murder."

"I can get behind that, but Bishop's right. What about Jennifer Berman?" Levy said. "What's her connection to Copeland?"

"That's what we need to find out," Jimmy said.

"What about Herman and the cafeteria woman?" I asked.

Jimmy's cell phone rang. "Chief Abernathy." He paused and listened. "Thank you." He turned to us. "Al Castleberry is dead."

I collapsed back onto the couch.

"Please tell me he died of natural causes," Bishop said.

"They don't know anything yet," Jimmy said. "They found him in bed."

"Maybe he died in his sleep," Levy said.

"Or maybe our girl killed him," I said. I dragged my hands down my face. "How is Copeland connected to this?"

"Bring him back in tomorrow," Jimmy said.

"He'll lawyer up," I said.

"Let him."

18

Jimmy had my department issued vehicle ready and waiting on my driveway. I hurried to work and straight to his office. "Any news?"

"I've requested a meeting with the mayor and council for nine."

Levy, Michels, and the rest of the team stood at the door.

"Yes?" he asked.

"We're ready," I said.

"You're not going," he said. "Any of you."

I laughed. "You're kidding, right?"

"Nope. Lantry asked for a closed meeting."

I couldn't put up a fight when it was done by the attorney. "Any word on what happened to Castleberry?"

"Barron was there last night. He's doing the autopsy today as a favor. You know it wouldn't happen otherwise."

I knew that. I also knew he was murdered, and Barron would verify. Officer Gregory stepped into Jimmy's doorframe. "Sir? May I have a moment with Detective Ryder?"

He stood. "You can have all the moments." He gathered a pile of papers. "I've got a council meeting."

I asked everyone to meet me in the investigation room. I locked eyes with Gregory. "Where are the photos?"

He shuffled uneasily, the tension evident on his face. "I tried texting them to you four times," Gregory explained, avoiding my gaze as he handed me a file. "But they kept bouncing back. I printed them out instead and forwarded them to your email."

"Thanks. I appreciate it."

Clutching the file, I headed toward the investigation room, my steps quick with anticipation. The photos inside were blurry—a challenge, but not insurmountable. Absentmindedly, I sent a text to Bubba, hoping for a miracle on the image clarity, and then I called Barron on speaker phone.

He answered on the first ring. "Dr. Barron."

"It's Rachel Ryder. Got a minute?"

"You're calling about Mr. Castleberry? I haven't begun the autopsy yet."

"Do you have any thoughts on what happened?" My question hung in the air, weighted with unspoken urgency though he'd probably noticed it in my rushed tone.

He sighed. "My thought is he died of natural causes, but I'm doing your chief a favor."

"I appreciate it," I said. "Could you let me know if you find something?"

"I plan to."

"Thanks." I ended the call.

"What's next?" Levy asked.

"Update me on Herman and Betty."

"Herman wasn't there," Michels said. "He's there today, so we're heading back once we hear about Bishop's meeting."

"Betty was, but she's a dead end. Doesn't remember either of the girls. She says she sees hundreds of kids daily and has for almost fifty years. She doesn't know who's who, nor does she care. She just does her job and goes home."

"She was a waste," Michels said. His cell phone rang. He checked the caller ID but didn't answer. "So, we know the Mercedes driver is a woman."

"Which means our killer is a woman," I said. "And if the killer is one of the women in one of those photos, then we're close."

Bubba walked in as Michels' cell rang again. He muttered, "I need to take this," and excused himself with a brisk nod before stepping outside, the door clicking shut behind him.

"Can you clean up the photos?" I asked Bubba.

"That's why I'm here. I'll give it a try."

Michels reentered moments later, his face a mask of barely contained fury "She canceled the wedding."

My eyes widened. "What? No way."

"Ashley canceled the wedding?" Levy asked. "That's impossible."

"Not Ashley," he said. He held up his cell phone. "Our killer. She canceled my damn wedding."

"Are you sure it's canceled?" I asked.

"Hold on." He contacted the wedding venue and put the call on speaker. "This is Justin Michels," he said after they answered. "I need to know what's happened with my wedding."

The manager got on the phone and explained the situation. "We're working with the couple who scheduled your time to see if they can reschedule."

"Listen," Michels said, "we did not cancel our wedding. My fiancé has explained this to you. Someone did this as a prank or to cause problems. We need our date back. The wedding is in a month. You can't possibly have someone who's capable of putting a wedding together in a month."

"Get the couple's name," I whispered.

"Can you tell me who the couple is?"

"I'm not comfortable giving that information," she said.

I whispered again. "Ask if it's a Tina."

"Is the woman named Tina?" he asked.

"Actually, yes," she said. "How did you know that?"

"Ma'am," he said, "As you are aware, I'm a detective with the Hamby Police Department, and we are currently involved in a serious investigation. This hoax of a cancelation may very well be connected. I'd like the full names and addresses of the couple, please."

We didn't recognize the name, but she gave him the address.

"I'll call them and say there was a mistake," she said.

I shook my head.

"Hold off on that, please. I'm leaving now." He ended the call and looked at us. "What the hell?"

"Here," Bubba said. He printed out new versions of the photos and handed them to Michels. "Find out if Tina is one of these women."

"I'll be back," Michels said and hurried out.

"I'll go back to Hamby High School," Levy said. "Want to come?"

"No," I said. "I'm going to talk to Copeland again." I asked Bubba for copies of the photos, glanced at them quickly, then shoved them into a file and headed over to the City Council room.

I texted Bishop. "How's it going?"

He didn't reply, but I could hear an argument inside. The door flew open, and Jimmy rushed out. "Lantry is one hell of an attorney."

Bishop walked out smiling. "I'm back. Where are we?"

"We're going to see Copeland. Tell me about it on the way."

"I'll drive."

Bishop secured his seatbelt and started the ignition. "Lantry methodically presented my defense. He went right into the dangers of advanced AI and voice alteration technologies. Bubba sent him a recording last night. He'd recorded me at your place."

"Really? I hadn't noticed."

"Neither had I, but he piecemealed together a sample of me saying words similar to the ones in the recording, and that and Lantry's speech were enough to sway council in my favor."

"I think I love that guy."

"He's good," he said. "His argument was clear. He said that in an era where digital evidence could be fabricated, establishing truth required more rigorous scrutiny, and the mayor hadn't done that. Then he went into process of investigation, and the mayor's argument fell apart." He drove north on Birmingham Highway. "You should have seen how mad he was. I thought he was going to have a heart attack."

I asked Bishop to stop at his place and grab his high school yearbook.

"You're kidding, right?"

"Nope."

"I'm not sure I'll be able to find it."

"I'll call Cathy and ask if she knows where it is."

"She's not going to know, either."

Yet, she had. After picking it up I filled him in on Michels's situation, and for the grand finale, added, "I think we're right. Our killer is a woman."

"Who just canceled Ashley's wedding. Does she know what she's up against?"

"Bridezilla from hell."

He laughed. "Damn straight."

Walking into Copeland's HQ was like hitting a dive bar at closing time—chaos with a side of despair. Women in the lobby shed tears like they were going out of style, while the men argued as if it was their last chance at being heard. It was an eyesore of human emotion spilling over in all the wrong ways.

"I feel for them," I said. "They lost five employees."

"May I help you?" the receptionist asked.

"Steve Copeland," I said as we showed our badges.

"He's in a meeting. Can I set an appointment for you?"

"Ma'am," Bishop said. "Your company lost five employees to a bombing yesterday, and two police detectives just showed you their badges. Interrupt the meeting."

Go Bishop.

A man escorted us to Copeland's office.

"What have you found out?" Copeland asked.

"Tell us about your connection to the Berman family," I said.

"I already told you I don't know them."

"Okay then," I said. I placed the yearbook on his conference table. "Tell us who you dated, who liked you, who you slept with, who you looked at and winked at."

"What?" He stared at the yearbook. "You think this is about me?"

I nodded. "And we believe it's a woman."

He blinked. "What? A woman bombed my construction site?"

"And murdered two, possibly three people," I said.

He opened the yearbook. "This isn't going to work. It's been a long time, and I think I already mentioned I was a little on the wild side."

"Give it a shot," Bishop said.

"How would this be connected to me?" he asked. "I don't understand."

"That's what we're trying to figure out," Bishop said.

"So, you're grasping at straws." He closed the yearbook. "With all due respect, I lost five men yesterday, and I've got a shitshow to deal with here. Can we do this another time?"

I swiped through the yearbook then removed the photos from the file and showed them to Copeland. "Do any of these women look familiar?"

He scanned the photos, then froze at the last one. "This is Chrissy."

Bishop and I made eye contact. "Chrissy Carter?"

"I'm not sure of her last name now. I can't remember it, but it's her." He swiveled the photo our direction. "The hair's darker, and she did something to her lips and nose, but the eyes are the same." He pointed to her left arm. "And that tattoo. I can't be sure, but it looks like an angel."

"Does Christina have an angel tattoo?" I asked. I'd only seen her wearing long sleeves.

"I'm pretty sure she does," Copeland said. "I saw it when I ran into her. I could be wrong, but I don't think so."

Bishop and I examined the picture.

"Why would Chrissy have something against me? We dated, but she knew it wasn't going to last."

"But you ran into her a few weeks ago, correct?" I asked. "Was this before Jennifer Berman went missing?"

"I'm sorry to say I don't know when she disappeared, but I was meeting my attorney for lunch." He checked his calendar.

He gave us the date. It matched the day Jennifer disappeared.

"Tell us what you talked about," Bishop said.

"The usual stuff. What we'd been up to, our family, the regular things people talk about when they haven't seen each other in nearly forty years. She told me she'd recently been married, and she had a daughter from her first marriage."

"A daughter?"

He nodded. "Said she just got married, and the wedding was stunning." He exhaled. "Come to think of it, she acted like it was a pretty big deal. Said they had it at a winery where the girl goes to school. Dahlonega, maybe?"

"Rebecca McVoy," I said.

Bishop quickly pushed himself from the chair. "Thank you, Steve. We'll be in touch."

Copeland looked confused as he stood. "Did I say something troubling?"

I was already halfway to the door. "We'll be in touch," I said as we hurried out.

I dialed Bubba as Bishop drove toward 400. "Hey," I said on speaker. "What are the odds of the system missing a name for Carter?"

"It's possible," he said, "but I've got other options I can try. Want me to?"

"Yes, please."

"Sure thing," he said. His fingers tapped on his keyboard loud enough for me to hear.

A few seconds later he said, "Looks like she went by one more, but I don't think it was for long. She doesn't have any credit cards and only one address in that name. I can't guarantee it's right. Sometimes identities are mixed up. I'd have to dig deeper to make sure."

"What's the name?" I asked.

"Hahn. Wait. Isn't that Rebecca McVoy's maiden name?"

Bishop and I made eye contact. "It is. She's Christina Canfield's daughter."

"What's that mean?" Bubba asked.

"We're still working through that. Thanks."

"Will do." He hung up his landline.

"You think Christina is—holy hell, Ryder. Christina. Tina. It's her." He dropped a sentence full of cuss words, then added. "Are we that stupid?"

"Yes," I said as I dialed Rebecca McVoy's number. It went straight to voicemail. "Rebecca, this is Detective Rachel Ryder. I need you to return my call right away, please." I gave her my number, but I didn't explain the reason for the call. I flipped around and checked for the black Mercedes. "If she's tailing us, she's well-hidden." I texted Bubba and asked for any vehicle titles, loans, or rentals in any of Christina's names, including Tina.

He called me. "Rentals can take a while, but I'll run the others ASAP."

"Are Levy and Michels back yet?"

"Not yet."

"Okay, I'll get in touch with them. When they return, they'll contact the rental companies. Can you get everything they'll need ready for them?"

"Sure thing. I'll call you back as soon as I have what you need."

"Thanks. After disconnecting, I called both Levy and Michels on their cells and merged the call.

"It was one of the women in the photos," Michels said.

"Which one?" I asked.

"Hold on. I'm sending it to you all now."

The photo that came through was the one of Christina Carter. "That's Christina Carter, who happens to also be Rebecca McVoy's mother."

"McVoy's the one that knew Jennifer Berman, right?" Levy asked.

"Yes."

"Damn," she and Michels said in unison.

"Are you bringing her in?" Levy asked.

"We're on our way to her place now."

"Need an assist?" Michels asked.

"The vehicle stuff can wait," Bishop said.

"Yes," I said and gave them the address.

19

Bishop pulled up behind Michels on the side of the road into Christina Carter's community. Levy arrived shortly after and immediately hugged Bishop after exiting her vehicle.

"Congratulations," both Levy and Michels said to Bishop.

Michels hugged him and said, "Glad you're back."

"Glad to be back," he said. "Okay," Bishop's voice cut through the hum of traffic just outside the subdivision. "Let's make this as simple as possible." He glanced at me. "And don't break procedure."

"Why does everyone always say that?" I asked, only partially kidding.

"Seriously?" Michels said, laughing.

"This is serious," Bishop said. "Carter's been toying with us long enough. The last thing we want is to screw up and get the case thrown out of court on a technicality."

"Got it. We bring her in smooth and by the book. No surprises," Levy said. "We'll take the back. Make sure she doesn't slip out if she spots us coming."

Michels added, "I kept an eye out for a tail on the way here, but I didn't see one."

"Neither did we," I said.

Levy confirmed she hadn't either. "If we're lucky, she'll be home. If not, we'll need to get an assist to watch for her."

I asked Michels, "Did you get the wedding issue fixed?"

Bishop raised an eyebrow.

"Yes, thank God. Ashley was a wreck. I had twenty-two text messages from her before I got to the venue."

"Fill me in later," Bishop said.

Michels and Levy returned to their vehicles and drove deeper into the community to park a street over from Carter's home. Bishop pulled into her driveway five minutes later, giving Michels and Levy enough time to park and hit the backyard. I removed my spare Glock from my bag to the back waist of my jeans. Bishop added one to his as well. Neither of us spoke, both having been down that road multiple times. He left the vehicle running and the doors locked as we exited.

"All clear in the back," Michels whispered over our radio.

"We're going up now," I said.

We approached the front door, our steps measured, our senses heightened to any sign of movement inside.

I knocked, a part of me hoping she would simply answer, ending the investigation with quiet compliance though I knew that was about as sure a thing as hell freezing over.

The door swung open to reveal a man, his surprise at seeing two detectives on his doorstep evident in his wide eyes and the quick step back he took. "Uh, yes?"

I introduced us as we showed him our badges. "We're looking for Christina Carter," I said, my voice steady despite the adrenaline coursing through me.

"She hasn't lived here in eighteen months," the man replied, his confusion turning to agitation. "I'm Darren Carter, her ex-husband."

"Ex-husband?" Bishop asked.

"Yes. Divorced a year ago. Worst decision I've ever made was marrying that nut case. Best decision I've ever made was divorcing her." He looked Bishop in the eye. "Is she dead?"

"No, sir." Bishop and I exchanged a look, the puzzle pieces not fitting as they should. "When did she move out?" Bishop asked.

"About a year and a half ago." He narrowed his eyes. "Why?"

"We were just here interviewing her the other day," I said. "Does she still have a key?"

Darren's agitation spiked, his voice rising. "No. Damn it." He ran his hand over the top of his head. "I thought I'd gotten that under control."

"Sir?" I asked.

"She's done this before. I changed the locks myself. She must be getting in through a basement window. I was out of town for a week. I should have known she'd try something."

I leaned my head to the side. "Do you have cameras?"

He nodded. "And neighborhood watch said they'd come by."

"Did you check the cameras?" Bishop asked.

"No." He exhaled. "I'm an idiot."

"Can you check them now?" he asked.

"With you here?" He moved to the side. "Come on in. If she's on them, I want to press charges for breaking and entering."

"We have two officers out back," I said. "May we call them in?"

"Go for it," he said.

I made the call on my radio.

"On our way," Michels responded.

I surveyed the home while we walked into the kitchen. Had I paid closer attention the first time, I would have noticed there were no pictures of Christina or anyone for that matter. Women filled their homes with photos, especially of the people they loved. Men might put one or two up, but rarely more than that.

Michels and Levy knocked on the door. Carter answered and after a brief introduction, had them sit at the table as well.

"Have a seat," he said. "Can I get you anything?"

"Water would be great," I said.

"Yes, water," Bishop replied.

Levy and Michels responded with yes as well.

He retrieved four bottled waters from the refrigerator and handed them to us. After we thanked him, he said, "I got the system because of her, but honestly, I didn't think she'd come around again. Last time I walked in and she was here, I called the cops. They came out, talked to her, but I didn't press charges. I had a feeling she'd done it a few times before that, but I couldn't prove it, and I didn't think anything would come of it anyway."

As he located the files on the internet, I asked, "May I ask why you got divorced?"

"Because she's a psycho, that's why."

There was definitely no love lost with the guy.

"Psycho in what way?" Bishop asked.

"It was little things at first. I couldn't do anything right. The world was against her. That kind of thing. But it got worse." He clicked his mouse multiple times. "Then she got physical. Threw things at me. Smashed lamps on the floor."

"Did you report her?" Levy asked.

He shook his head. "I thought about it when she threatened to kill me, but I filed for divorce instead."

"How did she take that?" I asked.

"Not well. She said I was another person who deserted her." He looked up at us. "She has this skewed vision of what life's supposed to be. Everyone's got to cater to her. To lavish her with love. I should have run when I found out her own daughter disowned her."

"Rebecca?" Bishop asked.

"Yes. She kicked her out of her life a year before we met. Tina gave me this sob story, claiming Becca was selfish and entitled, and wrote her off when she couldn't help her pay for college."

"You call her Tina?" Michels asked.

He glanced up at him. "Yes. Most everyone does."

"Did Becca confirm any of this with you?" Levy asked.

"I've never met her, but one of Tina's friends says she's a good kid. I figure she got that from her father."

"Where is he?" Bishop asked.

"He died in a car accident when Becca was six. Got drunk and hit a median on 400, but she considers her stepdad her father. She even took his last name."

The four of us exchanged looks.

"Did Rebecca ever say her father had a drug problem?"

He blinked. "Drugs? Not that I know of."

"Do you know if Tina," my voice came out through gritted teeth, "went to Becca's wedding?"

"If she did, she got by a security team. According to one of Tina's friends, Becca's husband's parents paid for a security team to make sure she didn't crash it. She's been harassing her daughter for years."

I rubbed my eyes. Un-freaking-believable. She was there, the entire time, taunting us. Basic detective 101 stuff, and none of us saw it. "Do you know if she's ever threatened Becca?"

"I heard her multiple times, but again, didn't take it seriously." He smiled. "Here they are." His smile changed to a frown. He dropped an F-bomb and turned the laptop toward us. "She just broke the camera. Full daylight too."

"So much for your neighborhood watch," Bishop said.

"Which camera?" Levy asked.

"The one on the left side of the basement door."

"How do I get to the basement?" Levy asked.

He pointed to a door just across from the kitchen. "Right there."

Once she went downstairs, Carter added, "All right, I wasn't going to ask, but it's clear you weren't here just to interview my ex-wife. What's going on?"

Bishop looked at me. I nodded. "Christina Carter is a suspect in a double, possibly triple, murder investigation."

His eyes widened. "Do I need a security system?"

"We recommend them to anyone," I said, "but I would consider her threats seriously."

"She hasn't threatened me in a while. In fact, when I caught her here, she was calm. At first, I thought it was an act, but then I thought maybe she was trying to change."

"People don't usually change," Michels said. "Not ones like Christina Carter."

Bishop's and my cell phones dinged with text message notifications. The timing wasn't lost on us. The blocked caller was expected.

Despite my warnings, you persisted, detectives. Your refusal to heed my

obvious desires to stay out of my business has consequences. Another life extin-
guished—courtesy of your relentless pursuit. Consider this blood on your hands.

I spoke to Darren Carter. "Where does she live now?"

"I don't know," he said. "I didn't want anything to do with her." He blinked. "Should I leave? Do you think I'm in danger?"

"It would be wise to find someplace to stay until we find her." I glanced at Bishop. He steeled his eyes on me for a moment, then handed his phone to Michels, who read the message, and then gave the phone to Levy as she headed toward the table.

"Looks like she jimmied a window open," Levy said.

"You mentioned being in contact with a friend of Christina's," I said. "What's her name and phone number?"

"Wait," he said. "I didn't tell you everything."

"Okay," I said.

"I'm in a relationship with a woman. Liz Scott. Tina doesn't know it."

"Are you sure?" I asked. "Call her."

He grabbed his cell phone from the kitchen counter, and asked Siri to call Liz. His hand shook as he held the phone. The call went straight to voicemail. He looked at us with fear in his eyes. "You don't think she'll go after Liz, do you?"

"Do you have a photo of Liz anywhere in the house?" I asked.

"There's one of us from Valentine's Day on my nightstand. Why?"

"She's seen it," I said.

"She probably went through the entire house when she broke in," Levy said.

He tried his girlfriend again and left a message for her to call him.

"What's her last name and address?" I asked.

"Scott." He gave us the address but added, "She's at work," and provided her work information as well.

"Do you have a number for her work?" Bishop asked.

"I've got it," I said. I'd immediately located the number online.

I stepped into the hallway and called, listening as Bishop asked Carter, "When was the last time you talked to Liz?"

"We texted this morning before work. She...she was fine."

I returned to the kitchen. "Liz didn't show up for work yesterday or today. Texted her boss and said she had the flu. When did you see her last?"

"Before my trip. I was gone a week. Just got home last night."

"And you talked to her when?" Bishop asked. "Not text. Talk."

"Yesterday morning." His hands shook. "What's happening?"

Liz lived in the community next to the Publix grocery store just before downtown Hamby, close to the station. Bishop got on his radio and asked dispatch to send a team out.

"Mr. Carter," I said, "Do you have a recent phone number for Tina?"

He shook his head while dialing Liz again. "Liz, it's me. Call me." He looked back at me. "Does Tina have her?"

"We're going to try to find out, but we have more questions. It's important that you answer these the best that you can, okay?"

He nodded.

"Do you have any idea where Tina is living? I know you said you don't, but it's possible she's mentioned something, and you forgot."

He shook his head again. "She wouldn't tell me anyway. She said I wasn't a part of her life anymore and I didn't deserve to know anything about her. She changed her cell number too." He chewed on his fingernail. "Our dentist is a friend of mine. She was having dental work done around the time we went to court for the divorce. Maybe he knows where she is."

"Please call him. Tell him you're with the police and that they need to talk to him about her whereabouts. Then hand me the phone. Do you understand?"

"Yes."

While he dialed, Bishop told Levy and Michaels to get back with Barron about Castleberry's autopsy and follow up with Bubba about the vehicle.

Carter handed me the phone. I explained the situation to the dentist, and he gave me the information he had on Christina Carter with the caveat that he hadn't seen her in nine months and wasn't sure if it was recent. I repeated it to Bishop, and he contacted dispatch with the address.

"She's in Hamby?" Carter asked. "She hates that town. She said she would never live in that area again."

"Did she say why?" I asked.

"I'm sure she did, but I can't remember." He grabbed his keys from a key box over the kitchen's built-in desk. "I need to find Liz."

Bishop moved to block him. "You can't do that."

"But she could be in trouble because of me."

"Not because of you," I said. "But we need to get someone out here to keep an eye on you."

"I don't need to be babysat," he said defiantly.

"Not babysat. Protected." I called the Alpharetta PD and explained the situation. He said he'd send two officers out and offered additional assistance if needed. "They'll be here in five minutes," I said to Carter. "We'll let you know when we find Liz."

"You're leaving now?" he asked.

"We're preparing," I said. "Stay inside, please."

Bishop and I jogged to his vehicle. He clicked the key fob and the trunk popped open. We each grabbed our Kevlar vests and put them on over our shirts. Levy and Michels followed us out.

"Castleberry was suffocated," Michels said. "Jimmy's on it with Roswell, and he's sent Nikki there to gather evidence."

"Good," I said. "It was her. It has to be." Castleberry didn't deserve to die, nor did he deserve to have his mind betray him. A man who spent his life helping people deserved a long, happy, and healthy life with a peaceful ending.

"Tina Canfield rented a 2024 Mercedes E-Class a week ago in Roswell," Levy said.

"So, she's got other IDs," Bishop said.

Levy nodded. "Bubba's sending us a copy of the license."

I checked my extra magazines to make sure they were full. I knew they were, but it was procedure, though I would have done it anyway. "He found out quicker than he thought."

"He enlisted the help of a few newbies," she said.

"Good move."

"I also called Dahlonega and asked for a wellness check on Rebecca McVoy," she said.

"Thank you," Bishop said.

"What do you need us to do?" Michels asked.

"We're going to Liz's place first. Remember the address?"

They each nodded. "We'll see you there," he said.

The officers sent over to Liz Scott's reported that a vehicle registered in her name was present at the condo, but no one answered the door. We told them to stay put until we arrived.

I drummed my fingers on my leg while Bishop turned into Liz Scott's community. "She's not going to be there."

"Scott or Carter?" Bishop asked.

"Yes. She had to assume we'd come here once we figured out Liz was missing. She's been one step ahead of us from the start, Bishop. We're thinking like detectives here. We need to think like a sociopath murderer."

He pulled onto Liz Scott's street and parked in front of her driveway. Michels and Levy followed suit.

The two officers stated they had checked the home's windows and saw nothing out of order but also no signs of life. Given the situation, we went straight to using a battering ram to open the door.

"Ready?" I whispered, my voice barely cutting through the tense air. A series of curt nods was my answer. I stood to the side of the door and said, "This is the Hamby Police. If someone's inside, please make yourself known."

The home remained silent.

On my signal, Michels and Bishop advanced. The ram's heavy thud against the door was a shockwave echoing through the area. Once, twice, and on the third strike, the door gave way with a splintering crash.

We moved quickly, the initial burst through the door carrying us inside. Bishop and Michels headed for the stairs while the two officers moved toward the back of the home. Levy and I took the front and basement. I noted signs of someone leaving in a hurry. A half-empty cup of coffee sat on a table next to a partially eaten donut in the living room. A magazine lay open, as if just set aside. The TV remote was on the floor.

"Purse is on the counter," Levy said. "Keys inside, but the cellphone is missing."

"She's got her." I immediately contacted dispatch and requested an APB on Christina Carter and each of her aliases.

Bishop's cell phone dinged with a text message. He ignored it.

"Check it," I said when mine dinged right after.

Mine read, *look at your partner*.

Bishop's face turned red. "She's got Cathy."

I grabbed his phone and read the message.

I've had lovely lunches with Cathy. In fact, we're together right now.

20

"Cathy's new friend," I said. "Do you have Cathy's location on your phone?"

"Yes, but it's showing unavailable. Wait." He swiped up his phone screen saying, "Cathy's fob has a GPS tracker on it. We put it on after I got my ass kicked." He held up his keys. "I've got one too."

"Liz Scott's purse was left in the house. It's unlikely Cathy has hers."

"Cathy keeps her fob in her pocket. She hates carrying a purse and leaves it in the car all the time. Drives me crazy, but I won't complain about it ever again."

"She's in Dahlonega," he said. He showed me his phone. "At the nursing resource center."

"Let's go." I pointed to Levy. "Call Jimmy. We're going to need a task force out there."

I called Rebecca McVoy again, but the call went straight to voicemail. Bishop, Levy, and Michels put their cherries on the top of their vehicles, and within a few minutes, we were joined by seven other department vehicles and three additional squads.

I called Julie Hansen, Rebecca's former roommate.

"No," she said. "I talked to her yesterday. She seemed fine."

"Did you know about the situation with her mother?"

"That they didn't talk? Yeah, but it wasn't that big of a deal. She said it had been going on forever and that her mom is psycho."

"She lied about knowing her mother," I said. "Any idea why she would do that?"

"No, she didn't lie. She told me about it yesterday. She said no one calls her mom Christina. She's always been Tina to people. And she had no idea her mother had gotten married. She seriously had nothing to do with her." She paused and asked, "Is something going on?"

"What exactly did Rebecca say to you yesterday?"

"Just that she realized you were asking about her mom, and she was going to call you, but she couldn't find your card."

"Did she say what made her realize this?" I asked.

"No. I'm sorry. She was kind of vague about it, but she didn't sound nervous or anything."

"Did you give her my number?"

"No. I think I threw the card away. I'm sorry. Is Becca okay?"

"Do you have her husband's number?"

"Yeah. Hold on." She rattled off the number. "I don't know if this makes any difference, but she told me her mother always hated Jenny because of Dylan Harris."

"I thought she hadn't spoken to her mom in years?"

"She hasn't, but I guess her mom still tried to get in her business. Becca said her mother said she was trying to protect her, but Becca didn't see it that way."

"How did she see it?"

"I don't know. She hasn't said a lot about her mom, but I guess she knew Becca liked Dylan, and caused some problems or something." She exhaled. "Like I said, I don't really know much about her mom."

"Did Rebecca like Dylan when Jennifer was with him?"

"I don't know, but she was upset when they hooked up. I think she was jealous, you know? Do you think her mom is involved in Jenny's murder?"

"Thank you," I said, ignoring her question. "Keep my number on your cell. If you hear from Rebecca, please let me know."

I contacted Rebecca's husband Drew but got his voicemail and asked him to return my call ASAP. After disconnecting, I told Bishop,

"Christina Carter hated Jennifer Berman because of her kid and Dylan Harris."

"And she hated Caroline Turner because of Steve Copeland."

"That's motive."

He gripped the steering wheel.

"She's not dead," I said.

"You don't know that, but if she is, Carter's not going to survive it."

"Cathy's her ace, Bishop. Think about it. She knows we're coming for her. She's got to have a bargaining tool."

"You think a person like her wants to live? She'd rather die than go to prison. If they're not dead yet, they will be, and so will she."

I didn't know how to respond because he was probably right. "Hold on." I dialed Copeland's number.

He answered on the second ring. "Any news?"

"Tell me about your relationship with Christina Carter in high school."

"We didn't have a relationship. We went out a few times, but that was it. I was still involved with Caroline. Chrissy was just for fun." He cleared his throat. "I'm really not that guy anymore, Detective."

"I'm not worried about that. Did you ever have to tell Carter it was over?"

"I think we had a conversation, yes. I'm going off a forty-year-old memory, here, so I might not be completely accurate."

"Understood," I said. "Just tell me what you can."

"She wanted to get together again, but I'm pretty sure I told her that Caroline and I were a thing at the time."

"Was she angry? Did she say anything that would make you think she wanted to hurt Caroline?"

"Chrissy had a temper back then, so, yes, but no one ever took her seriously. She was this tiny thing. Caroline probably had twenty pounds on her. Even when her drug use got bad."

"Anger outweighs size more than you think."

"Are you saying you think Chrissy is involved in Caroline's murder?"

"That, the bombs, and Jennifer Berman's murder."

"What? That's unbelievable. Why would she bomb my site?"

"That's what we're trying to figure out."

"Chrissy liked me, sure, but I don't think it was anything serious."

"It might have been to her."

"I apologize, Detective. I should have been honest about my relationship with Caroline from the start. Is there anything I can do to help?"

"Just keep answering my questions."

"Go ahead."

"I need to know if you recall any discord between Caroline and Christina. She claimed they were sort of friends, but then talked as if they were not. Could they have had issues because of you?"

He was silent for a moment and said, "You know, now that you mention it, Caroline did tell me they'd argued about me a few times, but again, I don't recall it being a big deal."

"How long after telling you that did Caroline disappear?" I asked.

"The first time was in high school. The second time was probably a few weeks before the festival." He exhaled. "Dear God, you think I'm the reason this is happening, don't you?"

"No. We think Christina Carter's warped sense of reality is the reason this is happening."

Dahlonega PD had already cleared the building and the two near it through a text messaging system designed for students and staff. The circular drive in front of the health and science building was choked with police vehicles, their blue and red lights painting the scene like a crime drama on TV. A barricade of yellow tape fluttered in the breeze, cordoning off the area from the growing crowd of onlookers and media that had gathered at a safe distance.

Bishop parked at the yellow tape, flashed his badge at the officer, and we jogged to where he said their chief was. We quickly introduced ourselves, Levy and Michels included, and provided a quick but detailed explanation of the events leading up to then.

"We have six sharp shooters," he pointed to each location, "ready and able to move quickly. Do we have any idea where the hostages are inside?"

"No," Bishop said. "We believe there are three hostages." He gave their names. "But we don't know if they're alive."

Jimmy arrived with Bubba. He discussed the situation and a plan of attack with Dahlonega's Chief Williams. Bubba never came to scenes. He wore a Kevlar vest and carried a laptop.

"I've never been to a scene," he said.

"I know," I said. "Why are you here?"

He held up the laptop. "To locate Carter."

"Set up on the table there," Chief Williams said to him.

"The building's too big for a foot search," Chief Williams said. "We can lock down sections if necessary but not until we know where the hostages are."

I watched Bishop carefully. His stoic face and unemotional demeanor gave me nothing, but I knew it was the calm before the storm.

"How's Bishop?" Bubba asked.

"He's a bomb waiting to explode." I glanced back at him in discussions with the two chiefs. "Can you find Carter?"

"Yes," he said without question. "I'm accessing the layout and security system right now."

Bubba was our link to the inside, his fingers flying over the keyboard as he navigated through the school's architectural and security plans. Every now and then, he would pause, zooming in on a section, his brow furrowing in concentration searching for any clue that might reveal the location of Carter.

He called the team over. With them came Chief Williams and his team.

"There are three places she could access without exterior view," he said. "Two are easily accessible, but the third will be rough."

The officers and I leaned in closer, our collective focus narrowing to the glow of the laptop screen. Bubba pointed to the first location, a small room labeled as storage on the digital blueprint.

"It's centrally located, but there's no direct line of sight from any windows. It's accessible through the main corridor, but there's also a less obvious service entrance from the back."

"How many ways are there to access it from the interior?" Chief Williams asked.

"Well, several, depending on how long you want to take," he said. "But for quick access, there are two direct routes." He clicked a spot and opened a section of the drawings. "The fastest route is here, off the freight elevator."

Williams got on his radio and alerted the sharp shooters to the possible location.

Bubba pulled up the second route and explained it as well.

After Williams notified the shooters, Bubba swiftly moved to the second point, a section marked janitorial. "This area has a series of closets and a small office. The closets wouldn't work, but the small office is perfect for hiding. It's at the end of the west wing, with a secondary exit that leads to the parking lot. The exit is usually alarmed, but if the school can't silence it in time, I can."

"Access?" Jimmy asked.

He clicked on three sections which all popped up at the same time. "Here," he said tracing the route with his finger. "Here, and here."

"Any windows on any of those routes?" Chief Williams asked.

"Several," he said. "There's one more place they could be though."

"Where?" Williams asked.

"The basement utility room," he said. "Anywhere in the basement really, but I'm assuming it's all locked up outside of the utility room."

He pulled up the map of the basement. "Here," he said. "It's not an ideal spot for a prolonged stay, but it's off the grid in terms of regular foot traffic. Access is through a door by the north staircase, heavily used, but there's a blind spot in the camera coverage there."

He pulled up the building's security cameras. "There are two other entrances to the basement, but again, those should be locked."

"We can't guarantee that though?" Williams asked.

"I can't, but you can check with the university."

"We don't have time for that," Williams said. "Locked or not, we'll need people on them."

"Right," Bubba said. "The problem is, I can't find her anywhere," he said as he scanned through the sections. "But I can't access the closets in the rooms either." He exhaled. "So, if they're unlocked, there is a slight possibility she's in a closet."

"They could be in any room with a closet then?" Bishop asked.

I held the side of his arm.

"How the hell can we find them if they're in a closet?"

"I don't think they are," Bubba said. "At least not on the main floors. They'd be too crowded." He tapped on his laptop. "Look." He showed the size of the closets in the building. "They're all the same size, and too small for two, let alone four people. Anyone with any intelligence would know that." He sat back, a brief moment of silence enveloping us as we absorbed the information. "Based on the evacuation patterns, my bet is on the janitorial section or the basement. They offer the best balance of concealment and access to exits and each have larger closets or what I would call storage rooms."

The team behind us stirred, the tactical gears turning in their minds as they began to discuss the approach. Bubba's insights had given us what we needed to hunt down Carter. I hoped it wasn't too late.

"Teams Alpha and Bravo," Chief Williams said. "You'll take the west wing. Focus on silent entry, we don't want to spook her. Gamma, you're with me in the storage room. Hamby's team will take the basement. Let's keep communications open, updates every five. Remember, Carter is desperate, but we have the advantage now. Let's use it and end this safely."

My cell phone dinged. "Wait." I checked the screen and saw it said blocked. "Bubba, it's her."

"Oh, perfect," he said. "I've been manipulating burner programs to see if I can hack their locations, and I think I've figured it out."

I read the text out loud. *The clock is ticking. Make your next move a good one.*

Bishop swore under his breath.

"You can hack into a burner phone when it's a text message?" Williams asked Bubba.

"He's a savant," Jimmy said.

"I can sometimes," he said. "Although tracking a burner phone can be challenging, really almost impossible without the provider's assistance, I've figured out how to trace the signal and triangulate a phone's location when it's used to text. I might be able to pinpoint her location in the building."

"When did you figure this out?" I asked.

"Last night." He yawned, then stood and stretched. "Don't remind me."

His fingers raced across the keys. On his screen, lines of code scrolled past faster than I could follow, a blur of commands and responses that read like an alien language to me but were as familiar to Bubba as his own reflection.

"Can we get a drone here?" he asked.

"Already have one," Chief Williams said. "Where do you want it?"

I watched, fascinated, as Bubba opened multiple windows, each with its own stream of data and analysis tools. He cross-referenced signal strength maps, digital blueprints of the health education building, and real-time data feeds. He was the maestro conducting his alphabetic orchestra, each movement deliberate and essential to the creation of the symphony.

Suddenly, he paused, his eyes narrowing as he zeroed in on a section of the code. "There," he muttered, almost to himself. He began typing a new sequence of commands, his concentration obvious as he chewed his bottom lip. I found myself holding my breath.

The map of the building reappeared on his screen, this time with a blinking dot indicating a signal source. "Gotcha," he whispered. The dot was located in the basement, not near the janitor's space or the storage room, as we had initially suspected.

"I can't say conclusively if it's the basement. It could be the first floor, but they'd be out in the open, and we'd be able to see them through the windows, so I'm ninety-nine percent sure it's the basement. We need a drone with thermal to make sure she's not anywhere else in the building."

"Carter isn't stupid," I said. "She's been one step ahead of us since we found Berman's remains. It's possible she's already ditched the phone."

"But she just texted you," Williams said.

"I'm just saying we need to cover all bases."

"The drone will do it," Bubba said. "Like I said, if it's got thermal imaging. It just won't work in the basement."

"Bryson," Williams yelled. "Get the drone ready."

The drone was up and searching within three minutes. Five minutes later, it had cleared the multiple floors of the building.

"They're in the basement," I said. "It's underground and insulated. She knows we'll struggle to find her there."

"It's twenty against one," Williams said. "We won't lose." He looked at

Jimmy. "We'll come in from different entrances." He turned to Bubba. "Can you shut down the alarms?"

"Yes, sir," he said. He finished in less than two minutes. "Done."

"I'll get men at every exit."

"Don't forget the emergency exits," Bubba said.

Williams narrowed his eyes at him.

Bubba cringed. "You probably already know to do that. My bad."

"Our men will take lead on the basement," Jimmy said. "This is our case. We need to finish it."

"Understood," Williams said. "We'll follow your direction."

"Bishop," Jimmy said. "You stay with me."

Bishop's chest heaved. "I'm going, Jimmy. Don't try to stop me."

I didn't think he should go, not with the mayor out to get him, but given my history, I understood, and wasn't about to try to stop him. "I've got him," I said to Jimmy. "He needs to do this."

He closed his eyes then nodded at Bishop. "Don't give the mayor reason to fire you."

"Let's go."

21

We glided through the shadows, a dance we'd perfected over countless investigations. Bishop was all business, his focus cutting through the air like a laser, but the tightness around his mouth betrayed his tempest raging within.

"We'll get Cathy," I said.

"She has to be alive," he said.

The basement door loomed before us, a barrier to Bishop's future happiness, something I understood well. Carter could be anywhere, her madness a wild card in a deadly game. Bishop's grip on his weapon tightened, the subtle change speaking volumes of the war within him—caught between hope and dread for what we might find beyond the door.

My fingers brushed the cold metal of the door handle, pausing just long enough to exchange a look with my team. Nods all around, and we breached the threshold.

The basement was a surprise, vast and unnervingly sterile, the kind of place that made your skin crawl for reasons you couldn't quite name. Our steps echoed off the concrete, too loud in the stillness, a beacon for anyone —or anything—lurking in the shadows.

Room by room, we moved with a precision that felt almost like breathing. Each locked door a question, each open space a potential trap. Carter was a ghost, felt but unseen, her presence hanging over us like a shroud. She was everywhere and nowhere.

"Bubba," I whispered into my mic. "Any movement on the main floor?"

"No. No one's used the basement exits either."

Bishop's pace had a new urgency, a silent scream against the quiet. The line between the man and the mission blurred with every step. We followed a blood trail to a door, anticipation tightening like a noose around my neck. Bishop was in another world, his focus so intense I could almost touch it.

We stepped into a scene straight out of a horror movie. The women, bound and beaten, fear etched into their faces. My heart skipped, then roared to life. Cathy's eyes caught mine, a silent signal to be careful. A young man, Drew McVoy, I assumed, or what was left of him, lay in a blood-soaked heap.

Then Christina moved into view, dragging her daughter along with her, all Carter madness and maternal instinct twisted into a sick parody. She had Rebecca in a chokehold, the gun pressed tight against her temple. "Put down your guns and don't come any closer."

We stood our ground.

She laughed. "You can't think I'm joking. Come on, you should know better than that." She pressed the gun harder against her daughter's temple. "I will kill her."

We set our weapons on the ground. The ones in our hands. The weapons stuffed into the backs of our pants stayed put.

Carter's arm was firm around Rebecca's neck, the gun pressed so tight to her head you'd think she wanted it to become a part of her.

Bishop inched forward, each step measured, a tightrope walker seeking balance.

"Stop!" Carter said. She clamped her arm harder around Rebecca's neck. "One more move, and I'll kill her."

Our radios were on for the entire team, and we needed to let them know what was going on, to keep her talking until we could figure out what to do.

"Tina," Bishop said, his arms above his head to show he meant no harm, even though he wanted her dead. "Let her go. We can sort this out."

"Sort this out?" Her voice cracked like a whip. "Like she sorted things out by forcing me out of her life? Like everyone always does?" The gun stayed deadly still, her hold on Rebecca unyielding. "She doesn't deserve to live, not for what she's done to me."

Rebecca sobbed under her mother's grip. I made eye contact hoping she'd stay calm.

"Just shoot her," she screamed.

So much for calm.

"Shut up," Carter hissed. She whipped her daughter's body back and forth like a cloth doll. "I will drop you in a second. You mean nothing to me."

"No, you won't," I said. "Or you would have already. Your beef isn't with her, is it, Tina? It's with her husband, isn't it? And he's already dead, so let her go."

"Shut up!"

"Think about what you're doing," I said. "Don't do something else you're going to regret." I moved slightly to the side, one tiny millimeter at a time. I needed to block her view of Levy behind me. It was the only way to get a clean shot.

"Regret?" she laughed, the sound sharp and cold. "My life's a string of them. But this? This will be my curtain call."

"Let the women go, Tina," Bishop said, "or this isn't going to end well for you."

We were on a razor's edge, Carter's pain a live wire between us, her finger twitching on the trigger, a heartbeat away from a decision none of us could walk back from.

She narrowed her eyes at Bishop and me. "You had to keep pushing, didn't you?" she spat, her voice laced with venom. "I threw you off, again and again, yet here you are." Her words were a twisted mix of accusation and warped justification, and the barrel of the gun a punctuation mark to her bitter tirade. "Don't you get it? I've already won." She jerked her daughter again. "I'm the one in charge."

I moved again, inching forward and to the side barely enough for her to notice. "Let her go."

Carter's eyes flashed dangerously, her tone chillingly composed. "You think you've cornered me, but I'm the one holding all the cards. This finale?

It's going to be explosive." She casually glanced around the room, her arm tightening around her daughter. "I've planned a departure that'll ensure we're all closely connected—right to the very end."

The slight shift of her arm around Rebecca's neck abruptly painted a terrifying picture.

In that split second, everything shifted. I felt it, a surge deep in my gut, a now-or-never kind of moment. Without a second thought, I threw myself at Carter, adrenaline pumping, heart hammering against my chest like a drum.

My arm swung out, wide and sure, connecting with the gun in Carter's grip. It flew from her hand and skidded across the concrete with a clatter that might as well have been a church bell tolling. It was more than just metal on stone; it was the sound of the endgame.

Carter's hold on Rebecca slackened, and Rebecca bolted toward her husband's body.

I tackled Carter like a linebacker. We hit the ground hard, the impact knocking the wind out of her. For a moment, the world reduced to just the two of us, locked in a struggle on the cold basement floor. She scratched and clawed at me, swiping her long nails across my face. The pain was sharp and quick, and it pissed me off. I yanked her arm to the side, then up and behind her head. "It's over, Carter!"

"Don't move," Bishop said.

Carter's eyes widened at the sight of three guns pointing at her head.

"She's got a bomb in here somewhere," I said. I cuffed her hands together while Levy cuffed her ankles. "Where's the bomb, Carter?"

She laughed.

She smiled, again, a wicked, unstable smile. "I told you I would win."

Boom!

A deafening roar swallowed everything, a blast of force that lifted me off the ground and slammed me back down, the concrete floor suddenly as soft as air and as hard as iron all at once. My ears rang, a high-pitched whine drowning out everything else. I opened my eyes and saw the room had gone white. Dust settled around me like snow in hell, a fine, choking layer that covered everything. I blinked, trying to clear the grit from my eyes, my body a map of aches but somehow, miraculously, intact.

Bishop was already moving, a shadow through the haze, heading straight for Cathy. "I've got them," he said. His voice sounded like a whisper behind the ringing.

Rebecca was a crumpled form beside her dead husband, her body shaking with sobs that cut through the ringing silence.

"I'm good," Levy shouted.

"I'm good," Michels said.

Men stormed the room.

I looked for Carter and found her dragging herself away from the chaos she'd created, her movements desperate but weak. I shook off the disorientation, my anger and adrenaline cutting through the fog. My body protested as I moved, crawling at first, then gaining my feet in a stagger.

I reached her just as she reached the door behind the screen, grabbing her by the ankles and pulling her back with all the strength I had left. She screamed, a sound muffled by the persistent ringing in my ears.

"We won, Carter." My voice sounded distant, even to me. "You've got nowhere to go."

She kicked out, but I held on, dragging her back into the center of the room. Three men grabbed her, and one, a man the size of the Hulk, lifted her with one arm, then hung her over his shoulder like a bag of garbage, which she was, and carried her out of the room.

I coughed, the smoke from the explosion making it hard to breathe. Bishop had freed both Cathy and Liz Scott, and along with Michels, got them to safety. Thankfully, the explosion was minor. Carter must have used it as a means to escape, but for the life of me, I couldn't figure out how she'd set it off. A remote in the hand of the arm wrapped around her daughter's neck was my best guess.

Levy and I rushed to Rebecca who clung to her husband's body. Two paramedics tried to detach her, calmly asking if she was okay.

"The blood belongs to her husband," I said. "We'll take her outside." I crouched down and carefully touched her back. "Come on. There's nothing you can do for him now. Let's get you out of here."

I helped her stand. Her clothing was a canvas of her worst nightmare, painted in blood that belonged to her husband, and it got all over me when she collapsed into me and sobbed, but I didn't care.

~

The world outside the building was a deceptive kind of calm, a stark contrast to the maelstrom we'd just left behind. Neon lights flickered, but sirens had been silenced. I escorted Rebecca to an ambulance with her arm looped through mine for support, and her body shaking from shock. The paramedics looked like angels geared up for a war zone.

"It's not her blood," I said, catching the eye of a paramedic. "But she's in shock. Do me a favor, please. If you decide to take her to the hospital, come find me, got it?"

"Yes, ma'am," one of them said.

I pivoted on my heel, ready to be updated on our process for escorting Tina Carter to jail. She was waiting in a Dahlonega cruiser, her face plastered to the window, watching everything with a sick smile on her face. It wasn't a look I'd come to recognize in my line of work. Not one that said she was braced for the worst but still praying for a miracle, but instead said, *bring it.*

A chill slithered down my spine, the kind you get when you know the universe is about to tilt on its axis as I walked toward the vehicle.

And tilt it did. Darren Carter emerged from the shadows with a gun aimed straight at the face in the window. Time, traitorous and cruel, slowed to a crawl, stretching each moment into an eternity. I saw the determination etched into Darren's face, the way his hand didn't tremble, all signs of the resolve of a man who had suffered at the hands of his ex-wife for too long and believed there was no turning back.

Muscle memory kicked in before my brain could catch up. My hand went to the back of my pants, gripping the cold reality of my weapon.

Bubba's voice shattered the eerie silence, a desperate, gut-wrenching, "No!" He launched himself toward Darren. A shot rang out, a thunderclap that silenced everyone, a sound so final it all but erases everything else.

Bubba was in the air, a tragic ballet of humanity caught in the crossfire. His arms were thrown wide, as if embracing his fate or perhaps reaching out for salvation that would never come. Then he hit the ground with a loud thud.

Another shot rang out immediately after, and I watched as Darren

Carter's neck flicked back, and he immediately fell to the ground. I turned around and saw Levy, her gun still aimed where Carter had last stood.

A collective scream echoed from my team. "Bubba!"

Levy and I hit the asphalt running, the world reduced to the sharp, desperate beat of our shoes against the ground. Jimmy got to him first, dropping to the concrete with the precision of a soldier, his hands hovering like he was afraid to confirm the worst.

I skidded to a stop as he ripped off the vest. Levy kneeled on Bubba's other side and checked his pulse. "No pulse!" She then checked his breathing, and added, "He's not breathing!"

Jimmy began pumping his chest with the palms of his hands.

Bishop, Cathy, Michels, and I loomed over them, only to be shoved to the side by the swarm of paramedics. They worked on Bubba like a well-oiled machine of life-saving precision. One took charge, hands pressing down on Bubba's chest with the rhythm of survival as another breathed into his mouth.

She checked his pulse. "We got a heartbeat!"

Jimmy's jaw was set, his eyes hard, but he relaxed. Michels, standing next to him, wrapped his arm around him. It took a moment, but Jimmy pointed to Levy, and said, "You need to wait in my vehicle."

"Yes, sir," she said and headed to his cruiser.

"Chief," I said.

He didn't let me finish. "Check on the shooter."

I took off running as Bishop said, "That's Carter's ex-husband."

Dahlonega would process Christina Carter, then graciously hand her over to us to transport to Hamby. Since the crimes were related, we would take lead. Dahlonega would be there if needed.

They took the lead on Darren Carter, though we agreed to assist with information if necessary. They had him for aggravated assault, a felony in Georgia, but it was possible the charges would be dropped to simple assault through a plea deal and the stress he was under. I felt bad for the guy. I knew the emotional intensity one felt when someone they loved was in danger. He nearly lost his fiancé to a woman who he'd once called his wife. He'd probably felt responsible, and he believed killing Christina was his only option to stop her.

I couldn't fault him for wanting to do what he did, but legally, there were consequences, and he'd have to take them.

Bishop rode to the hospital with Cathy. The paramedics with Rebecca let me know they were leaving with her. She'd asked me to call her father. After contacting him, I sat beside her in the ambulance. "Your mother's going to pay for what she did, Rebecca. I promise you that."

"It doesn't matter," she said. "Drew is gone. Nothing matters."

"Tell your dad to call me later. I'll come by and talk to you tomorrow, okay?"

She nodded, unable to speak as the tears flowed from her eyes.

22

Jimmy and Levy went to the hospital, leaving me and Michels to interrogate Christina Carter. The best way to get information from a narcissistic sociopath was to let them sit in their failure, and that's what we did. It was glorifying for us, knowing she'd be devising a plan that was guaranteed to fail.

And I needed to wash the explosion off. I took my time in the shower at the station.

Shortly after I finished getting dressed, Kyle knocked on the women's locker room door. "All clear in there?"

"Clear," I said. "Come on in."

He closed the door behind him and handed me a Dunkin' coffee.

"You're a saint."

"I know." He smiled but his tone turned serious. "Rough night, huh?"

"Savannah tell you about Bubba?" I knew Jimmy would have let her know.

He sat on the bench beside me while I stuck my weapon into one of my Doc Martens and laced them up. "They're keeping him for observation for a few days."

"I know. Thank God for the vest." I sat with my hands on my knees. "We lost him for a few seconds."

"I know. He took the shot in the heart. Savannah said the doctor said his light weight caused the impact to cause more damage than it would be for someone like me."

"He's a rail," I said. "Are his parents at the hospital too?" I asked.

"Yes."

"Good. What about Cathy?"

"She's okay. She took a blow to the stomach. They can't find any internal bleeding, but they're keeping her for observation as well."

"Poor Bishop. I know he feels responsible for this."

"We can't vet every person in our loved one's lives."

"That's irrelevant when someone we love is hurt because of our job."

"I know," he said. "I'd like to watch the interrogation if you're okay with it?"

"Sure," I said. I checked my watch. It was getting late. Michels would be knocking on the door any minute ready to get started. "Let's do this."

Christina Carter sat in the small room facing the one-way mirror. Kyle, Michels and I studied her carefully.

"She's insane," Michels said.

"I know," I said.

"She's the worst kind of killer," Kyle said. "For the most part she looks normal, but her eyes tell a different story."

"And her smile," I said. Her chillingly confident smile was unsettling. It was a calculated display of arrogance and superiority marked by a slight, knowing smirk that didn't reach her eyes. Instead, her eyes betrayed a cold, calculating nature.

Jimmy, Levy, and Bishop walked in.

Bishop and I made eye contact immediately. "How's Cathy?"

"She's okay," he said. "She kicked me out. Said I had more important things to do than watch her sleep."

I looked at Jimmy. "Can he interrogate Carter with us?"

"We've discussed it," he said, "and he can as long as he keeps his cool."

I eyed Bishop. He just shrugged.

"She's done something to all of us," I said. "I'm not sure any of us can keep our cool."

"That's why Levy's taking lead," Jimmy said.

"Me?" Levy asked, surprised. "Seriously?"

"Yes. Her personal attack on you was minimal."

"I think Rachel should have lead," she said. "She's done multiple deep dives into all the notes. She knows the case far better than any of us."

He looked at me.

"She's right," I said.

"Fine. You've got lead. If it gets out of hand, Levy's on top. Got it?"

"Yep," I said.

We all walked into the interrogation room. Michels had flipped on the heat prior to her being brought in, and the room felt like Chicago in August. Hot and humid enough to make the back of your knees sweat.

Levy and Michels stood against the wall. Levy by the door, and Michels on the side wall. Bishop and I sat in front of Carter.

"Christina," I said, "or should we call you Tina?"

She smirked. "My attorney will be here any minute."

Zach Christopher, Fulton County's assistant district attorney, stepped into the room. "Have I missed the party?"

"We're just getting started," I said. "But Ms. Carter wants to wait for her attorney."

"Mr. Davis will be in in a moment," he said. He removed his blazer. "It's a bit warm in here today." He glanced at me. "AC broken again?"

I nodded. "Yes, sir."

He took a seat at the end of the small, metal table just as Carter's attorney arrived.

"Chuck," she said as if she'd known him forever. "Thank God you're here." Tears streamed down her face. "They're trying to intimidate me into answering questions without you here. Isn't that illegal or something?"

Okay, so she'd chosen to play the dumb victim card. I knew how to work with that one. I smiled at her then pointed to the two cameras in the corners of the ceiling. In a sweetly sarcastic tone, I said, "Yes, and the video will prove that's not what we were doing."

"I'd like a moment with my client," he said.

We all piled out of the room one by one.

"Why does he even bother?" Michels said. "We've got a solid case against her."

"For the most part," I said, "but we're missing some key information."

"I've got some of that," Nikki said as she walked toward us holding a file. "Our girl here likes to wear disguises. She's just not smart enough to know she should still avoid cameras." She handed Christopher the file. "Clear view of her looking right at the camera as she walked into Al Castleberry's room."

"She's not stupid," I said. "She's mocking us. She doesn't care that we know she murdered him."

"We're talking sociopath," Bishop said to Christopher. "She's not going to give us anything."

"That's not entirely true," I said. "She wants us to know what she's done. She's made a point of involving us in it from the beginning."

Davis opened the door. "We're ready." Once we were all back in the room, he added, "My client would like to strike a deal."

I busted out laughing. "And the Easter Bunny is real." My tone turned serious. "Your client has been charged with multiple homicides, three bombings, three counts of aggravated assault on a peace officer." I smiled at him. "And several other felonies I'd be happy to list for you."

"I have them," he said. "However, my client is willing to provide information regarding certain deaths you might not be aware of." He was the one smiling. "But only if the death penalty and life in prison are taken off the table."

Christina Carter had just effectively screwed us.

"No way," I said, pacing the floor outside of the interrogation room. I stopped and pointed my finger at Christopher. "Don't even think about it."

"The DA will want what she's got," he said. "What can you tell me? I need ammunition or we're going to have to sit on this until I can speak to the DA."

"Call him now," I said.

Bishop didn't give me an opportunity to continue. "Ben Pyott, Holly Grimes, and Carter's first husband, but we don't have a name."

"We don't even know how many husbands she's had," Bishop said.

"We know it's at least three," I said.

"I'll get it," Levy said and hurried away.

We explained how each of them had died in similar ways, two more similar than the others, but all from drunk driving incidents.

"She couldn't force them to drink," I said, "but it's possible Holly Grimes had drugs in her system. If so, we need to know which ones."

"They'd test for that," Michels said. "It should be in the report."

"It depends," Bishop said. "Forty years ago, if drugs weren't suspected, they wouldn't."

"And if they smelled alcohol on the deceased or found open bottles in the vehicle," Christopher said, "they might not have either."

"It's worth a shot to check," I said. "Michels, can you be Bubba on this? Check on Ben Pyott as well, then pray it's the same drug."

"Absolutely," he said.

"Get with Levy to check on the first husband too."

"Got it," he said and left as fast as Levy.

"Let me handle this for now, okay?" Christopher asked.

I liked the guy. He was overconfident and even a bit stuck up, but he was good at his job. "You got it," I said.

Bishop agreed.

Twenty minutes later, after having stayed in the hall waiting for Levy and Michels to return, we had our information, and something that could easily sway a jury in our favor. Christopher instructed Levy and Michels to wait three minutes and then walk into the interrogation room together, whisper something to him, and then let him take it from there.

I gave Christopher my seat and took the one at the side of the table. Bishop sat next to the ADA.

"We suspect we'll need more than what your client is willing to give," Christopher said. "However, we would be willing to consider a deal, but only after we're told what your client wants us to know."

I studied Christina carefully. If she was worried, she didn't show it.

Davis conferred with his client, their soft whispers and her psychotic smile were meant to intimidate, but they only gave me more determination.

"I'm afraid that's not an option," he said.

Levy and Michels walked in.

"Detectives," he said, "glad you're back." He stared straight into Christina Carter's eyes as first Michels, then Levy whispered in his ear. "Thank you, detectives." He closed his file and pushed it to the side. "Well, Mr. Davis, what's it going to be?"

Carter and her attorney whispered to each other again. After a few head nods, Davis said, "I'm afraid it's a no. I believe this interview is over."

"As you wish," Christopher said. "I just have one additional thing to say. It appears your client has lost their opportunity to bargain."

Davis raised a brow, but the best part was when Carter squirmed in her seat. She leaned into her attorney and said something under her breath. He nodded. "My client would like to know what you're getting at."

"Diazepam," Christopher said.

Carter's jaw dropped.

"Ben Pyott, Holly Grimes, and your first husband, the father of your daughter, Rebecca McVoy, Ryan Pellini."

"I don't know what you're talking about," Christina said.

I couldn't have wiped the smile off my face if I'd tried. "May I?" I asked Christopher.

"Go for it."

"Three people, three similar drunk driving accidents, all with diazepam in their system."

Davis's face reddened. "How is this related to my client?"

"None of the victims had prescriptions for the drug," I said, "but your client takes it, and with a warrant, we could get her medical records from high school and the time of Caroline Turner's death."

"What makes you think my client was taking valium?" he asked. She leaned into him and whispered in his ear. After a moment, he added, "We're done here. When can we expect my client to see the judge for bail?"

"Bail?" Christopher laughed. "In your dreams," he said. He stood and walked out.

Everyone followed but Bishop. I stood in the doorway while he set his hands on the table and glared into Carter's eyes. "Consider yourself lucky. There are more painful ways to die than lethal injection." He stood up straight, turned around, and walked out.

"You okay?" I asked.

"Better than ever."

23

Savannah, Levy, and I hit the precinct at the crack of dawn, two days after Carter's arrest. She was cooling her heels in Fulton County, rubbing elbows with crooks who were probably choirgirls compared to her. She'd sit there a while, all queued up for a trial that was light-years away.

A couple of hours in, and it was showtime for Nikki and Bubba, marking his grand re-entry. We jazzed up the joint for a little welcome back shindig. Bubba's hero badge wasn't for playing savior to a serial psycho but for making sure she faced the music. We were all grateful.

Savannah, turning into a chipmunk courtesy of a helium balloon, was betting on Bubba getting a kick out of our setup.

I lost it, snagging the balloon for a hit of that squeaky voice magic, agreeing between hoots, "He's going to eat it up."

Levy, rolled her eyes but snagged the balloon with a cutthroat mom line, "Give me that thing before you lose more braincells."

My comeback, helium-voiced and cheeky, "Too late," I said laughing.

Wrapping up our circus act, Savannah dropped back to earth tone, and Levy, with a helium twist, sounded more bovine than badass, sending me into another laughing fit.

"Why are you laughing at me?" she asked with a smile and then burst into laughter herself.

Bishop stood leaning against the doorframe with his eyebrow cocked at my meltdown. "What's going on in here?"

"Helium," I said through my laughter.

He rolled his eyes. "Get it together, the eagle has landed. They'll be here any minute."

"Oh, I'll get everyone in here then," Levy said. She tapped out a text on her phone.

Cathy walked in showing no signs of the beating she'd taken a few days before. She was a trooper, and Bishop was lucky to have her.

"How are you feeling?" Levy asked her.

"I'm fine, thank you, but I'm looking forward to Carter's trial."

"You're planning to testify?"

"Most definitely. Carter needs to pay for her crimes."

"She will," I said.

Jimmy and Michels walked in.

"Where's the guest of honor?" Michels asked.

"Right here," Nikki's voice, laced with a hint of mischief, floated from just outside the door. The room erupted into cheers and claps as Bubba stepped into the limelight—or, more accurately, the fluorescents of the squad room. His smile, sheepish yet triumphant, spread across his face as if he'd just won an award for most dramatic entrance. "Please, guys," he joked, his voice dripping with the kind of sarcasm only a man who'd stared down a bullet could muster, "clap louder."

We obliged with laughter, the sound bouncing off the walls, carrying with it the relief of his recovery. Bishop patted him on the back with a grin that betrayed his usual reserve. "Welcome back, Bubba."

"It's good to be back," Bubba replied, sinking into a chair with the grace of a newborn giraffe. I handed him the sweetest, most diabetes-inducing concoction Dunkin' could muster, microwaved to a temperature that could melt steel but topped with fresh whipped cream courtesy of Savannah's culinary adventures. "It's reheated, but it's your favorite."

"Thank you," he said. "You think the coffee here is bad, you should try the stuff they give you at the hospital." His nose wrinkled in disgust.

"That's not coffee," Bishop interjected. "It's water and dirt."

"That's what I told my mom," Bubba chuckled. He grew somber for a moment, his gaze sweeping across each of us. "I shouldn't have jumped in front of that bullet. I'm sorry I put you all through that."

"Bubba," Jimmy said, stepping forward, his voice imbued with the kind of gravitas one usually reserved for award ceremonies or interventions. "You put your life on the line to make sure a serial killer is brought to justice. You deserve a heck of a lot more than donuts and coffee."

"Right," I said.

"Thank you for being there for me. You all are family, and I appreciate it." He plucked a donut from the box. "What's going on with the case?"

We filled him in, explaining how Michels had done his best imitation of Bubba's tech genius and that we had cause to connect Carter to the additional deaths.

"What about your Jeep?" he asked me.

"Still toast. I'm using a department vehicle for the time being."

He looked at Michels. "And the wedding's still on, right?"

"You kidding? You think Ashley would let me live if it wasn't?"

The receptionist spoke over the phone's speaker. "Chief, the ADA is here to see you."

He eyed me. "Send him to the investigation room, please."

"Something's happened," Bishop said.

"She's alive," I said. "Christopher put her on suicide watch just in case."

Christopher walked in. "Bubba," he said when he saw him. "Glad to see you back." He noticed the decorations in the room as he slid his laptop toward him. "I hate to break up the party, but I've got something you're going to want to see."

"All of us?" I asked.

He glanced at Cathy and Savannah. "Just personnel." He shrugged. "Sorry ladies."

"Don't be," Cathy said.

Savannah snatched a donut from the box. "I best be heading home anyway. My mother-in-law has a hair appointment at ten. Free babysitting comes with restrictions."

Bubba connected the laptop to the large flatscreen Jimmy had installed the day before.

"You all might want to sit for this," Christopher said.

We sat.

Christina Carter appeared, wearing the orange jumpsuit Fulton County used for inmates. Her hair hung like greasy French fries from her head. Dark circles framed her eyes, one swollen shut, and her bottom lip was split and swollen as well.

"She's been through the ringer, and it's only been two days," Bishop said.

"She deserves it," I said.

"Here it comes," Christopher said.

"My name is Christina Carter," she said. Her hands trembled as she spoke. "I am confessing to the murders of Ben Pyott, Caroline Turner, Holly Grimes, my ex-husband, Ryan Pellini, and Jennifer Berman, however, I did not intend to kill anyone. I have been abusing prescription drugs for many years, and—"

Bishop slammed his fist on the table. "Are you kidding me?"

Bubba quickly paused the video.

"It's a strategy," Christopher said. "It won't hold up in court."

"It better not," Jimmy said.

"Bubba, please continue the video," Christopher said.

"I acted under the influence, and because of that, in a way I would never behave if not on drugs. I am officially pleading guilty, but by reason of insanity and ask to be moved to the psychiatric treatment ward of Fulton County Jail. Given the severity of my crimes, I am afraid for my safety in the general population. I am asking the court to commit me to a psychiatric facility to receive treatment for my addiction and mental disorder over a prison term or something worse."

"That's too bad," I said. "I'm sure the people she murdered were afraid for their safety when she killed them."

"We're moving her," Christopher said.

"What?" Bishop asked. "Are you going to offer her a plea bargain?"

"It's not up to me," he said. "The DA is waiting for an offer, but he's assured me he won't go easy on her."

Bishop exhaled. "She's been charged with multiple felonies. How can he deal?"

Christopher pointed to the screen. Bubba hit play again.

"In exchange for such a deal, I can offer information that will lead to the resolution of two other murders, ones I will not discuss until a deal has been made. This is my offer. Thank you."

"The nerve of that woman," Levy said. "She acts like she has control of this."

"She might," Christopher said. "Do we have any additional murders we can link to her?"

"Over the past forty years?" Jimmy asked. "You want us to guess?"

"No, I want you to check."

"There's nothing," Bubba said. "I've gone through NCIC multiple times, run several reports, and couldn't find anything."

I exhaled. "They don't have to be in the system. We might not even know about them yet."

"Whatever happens, she's going to be locked up for the rest of her life," Christopher said. "Unfortunately, the death penalty is off the table. That much I know."

"When will we know the DA's decision?" Jimmy asked.

"I'll tell you as soon as he tells me." He stood. "You all did an excellent job. She's going down. It just might not be as we expected."

"Way to ruin our celebration," I said.

"Sorry about that." He gave us a nod and left.

Whatever it was, whatever information Christina Carter had wouldn't be enough to let her walk. She had to know that. "I need to see Rebecca McVoy," I said.

"I'll go with you," Bishop said.

"I think it's better I go alone."

Rebecca sat on the couch in her stepfather's Alpharetta home. Her eyes, swollen and red, teared as we talked.

"I'm okay," she said. She pulled her legs up, knees to chest, and curled her arms across them. "I mean, I'm not okay, but my mother's in jail, so that makes it a little better."

I chose not to tell her about the video. "I'm so sorry for your loss." No one should have been subjected to the trauma Rebecca had.

"I watched her shoot Drew. I watched him die."

"I know."

"No one understands how that feels."

"I do," I said. "Someone murdered my husband in front of me. I understand. There are no words to describe how that feels, Rebecca, and it's going to hurt forever. Maybe less later, but the hurt will always be there."

"But you look okay now. Will I be too?"

"I'm not okay," I said with a slight laugh. "But I'm living on. It's what my husband would have wanted, and it's what Drew would want for you as well. They're gone, but we're still here. Don't let his death kill you slowly. Live to honor his life."

"I don't know if I can do that."

"You can. It will just take time. I don't know why it has to be this way, but I can promise you at some point, you'll be able to breathe again. The physical pain you feel? Your heart breaking? It will lessen, and you'll be happy again. It will just be a different kind of happy."

"Is that what happened to you?"

I leaned back and smiled. "Yes."

FOUL PLAY
Rachel Ryder Book 10

Find my killer.

Rachel Ryder's world is catapulted into chaos with the discovery of a dire note on her front door begging her to solve the murder of former MLB star, Ryan Hicks. Ryan Hicks, who is very much alive. Initially written off as a dark twist on a promotional campaign for his new charter school, the grim reality hits home when Rachel and partner, Rob Bishop, find Hicks's lifeless body in his lavish home, turning a dismissed warning into a desperate plea for justice.

As Rachel and Rob dive into the investigation, they quickly realize their understanding of the former MLB star turned public figure was merely surface-level. Their initial suspicions point to Hicks's ex-wife, leading them down a dark path marked by financial instability, clandestine opioid connections, and the remnants of a bitter divorce. With each complexity unearthed, the duo inches closer to a truth that is as unsettling as it is dangerous, uncovering a network of deceit that binds the town's most celebrated figures to its most criminal.

As the investigation deepens and the body count escalates, Rachel and Rob must race against time to unearth a betrayal so profound it threatens to unravel everything they hold dear. With stakes higher than ever, they must sift through lies and danger to bring a killer to justice before another victim falls.

Get your copy today at
severnriverbooks.com

ACKNOWLEDGMENTS

Behind every great book is a backstage crew, buzzing with the unsung heroes who truly make the magic happen. So, let's roll out the red carpet for the wizards at Severn River Publishing—my very own ensemble cast. They've been the directors, the producers, and occasionally the crisis managers, teaching me the art of book-making, one page at a time. Their wisdom? Invaluable. Their patience? Saintly.

In the shadowy corners of my narratives, where crime and justice tangle in an intricate dance, stand the guardians of reality – the criminal justice mavens. Among these champions, one stands taller, his thoughts spreading far and wide across my pages. Ara, my beacon in the murky waters of criminal psychology, lends an authenticity to Rachel and Rob that would be lost without his eagle eye. Here's to you, Ara, for the sleepless nights your insights have gifted me. May our readers be as deliciously haunted as I am.

Let's not forget the real-life muse who dared to lend her name to a character living in a world of fiction. Chrissy Carter, the antithesis of her literary counterpart, proves that reality is indeed stranger (and kinder) than fiction. Twelve years of friendship, and here we are, sharing a byline in a way neither of us could have imagined.

And then there's the heartbeat of my world. Jack, the man who's braved the tempest of my imagination, enduring nights filled with whispered plots of murder and mayhem. His is the support that turns the dreamer's gaze towards the stars, ensuring that my stories find their course. Jack, for every word of encouragement, every cup of coffee, every moment of unwavering belief – I am eternally blessed.

ABOUT CAROLYN RIDDER ASPENSON

USA Today Bestselling author Carolyn Ridder Aspenson writes cozy mysteries, thrillers, and paranormal women's fiction featuring strong female leads. Her stories shine through her dialogue, which readers have praised for being realistic and compelling.

Her first novel, *Unfinished Business,* was a Reader's Favorite and reached the top 100 books sold on Amazon.

In 2021 she introduced readers to detective Rachel Ryder in *Damaging Secrets. Overkill*, the third book in the Rachel Ryder series was one of Thrillerfix's best thrillers of 2021.

Prior to publishing, she worked as a journalist in the suburbs of Atlanta where her work appeared in multiple newspapers and magazines.

Writing is only one of Carolyn's passions. She is an avid dog lover and currently babies two pit bull boxer mixes. She lives in the mountains of North Georgia as an empty nester with her husband, a cantankerous cat, and those two spoiled dogs.

You can chat with Carolyn on Facebook at Carolyn Ridder Aspenson Books.

Sign up for Carolyn's reader list at
severnriverbooks.com